"What are you running from, Gabby?"

Austin demanded. "Did you rob a bank? Skip bail? A twenty-six-year-old woman doesn't hop trains with nothing more than the clothes on her back without a damn good reason."

"I . . ." She wanted to tell him! Clenching her fists, she told herself not to mistake the desire he'd stirred for anything but what it was. She couldn't start to trust him, couldn't let down her guard because of a kiss.

"I have my reasons," she said huskily. "Let's just leave it at that."

He wanted to shake her, to kiss her senseless. But if he touched her now . . .

"I've got one more question. Just how experienced are you?"

It was the last question she'd been expecting, the only one he could have asked that could be answered without words.

A fiery blush singed her cheeks, telling him everything he wanted to know.

Dear Reader:

The year is almost over, but the good things go on in Silhouette Intimate Moments. For instance, this month we begin a special two-book series by one of your very favorite authors, Nora Roberts. *Time Was* is an exciting—and romantic—story of a love so special that even time itself can't stop it. Liberty Stone is a twentieth-century woman, while pilot Caleb Hornblower is a twenty-*third*-century man. Fate literally seems to be against them ever even meeting, much less finding a way to spend their lives together, but, as the saying goes, love conquers all. Next month look for *Times Change* and find out that adventure—and romance—seem to run in the family!

Think of the rest of this month's books as a bit of a Christmas present, because we have new novels from favorites Paula Detmer Riggs, whose *Tender Offer* will make you shed a tear or two through your smiles, and Linda Turner, who will introduce you to a very different—and very special—couple in *Flirting with Danger*. New author Joanna Marks rounds out the month with *Love is a Long Shot*, a book that once again demonstrates Silhouette Intimate Moments' knack for picking the winners.

Enjoy them all—and come back next year for more great reading.

Leslie J. Wainger
Senior Editor
Silhouette Books

Flirting
with Danger
LINDA TURNER

Silhouette Intimate Moments

Published by Silhouette Books New York

America's Publisher of Contemporary Romance

Special thanks to Blanche Sitzer and Juanita Syre for the information they collected for me on Weiner, Arkansas, and its annual Rice Festival.

To Reed and Tisha Westerman for their help and friendship. Without them, I wouldn't have gotten the tractor started or the rice in.

And to Dr. John Covert, who came to my rescue with ten pages to go. Next time I need to knock off somebody's grandmother, I'll know who to call.

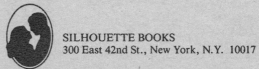

SILHOUETTE BOOKS
300 East 42nd St., New York, N.Y. 10017

ISBN: 0-373-07316-X

First Silhouette Books printing December 1989

Printed in the U.S.A.

Books by Linda Turner

Silhouette Desire

A Glimpse of Heaven #220

Silhouette Special Edition

Shadows in the Night #350

Silhouette Intimate Moments

The Echo of Thunder #238
Crosscurrents #263
An Unsuspecting Heart #298
Flirting with Danger #316

LINDA TURNER

began reading romances in high school and began writing them one night when she had nothing else to read. She's been writing ever since. Single and living in Texas, she travels every chance she gets, scouting locales for her books.

Chapter 1

The house was quiet, dark but for the moonlight that spilled in through the paned windows. Wide-awake, Gabriella Winters stared at the luminous hands of the clock on the nightstand. One-thirty. From down the hall, the deep, steady rhythm of her stepfather's gentle snoring shook the walls. During all the years of her childhood, the sound of his snoring had never failed to reassure her whenever she'd chanced to wake during the night. But she was no longer a child, and Baxter Hawthorne was no longer a man she trusted.

He, or someone else in the house, was playing nasty little games with her mind, deliberately and cold-bloodedly pushing her to the edge, testing the very boundaries of her sanity.

Even now, she wanted to deny the truth and accept the excuses her family had been giving her for months. "You're reading those Gothic novels again.... No one's trying to hurt you, sweetheart. We love you."

How easily Baxter and her half-sister, Sarah, had explained away her fears. And how easily she had let them. From the time she was five and diagnosed with epilepsy, she'd been taught to trust, to give in gracefully, to accept the judgment of those who loved her best over her own. And the habits of a lifetime were hard to break. How she'd clung to their logic. Since her mother's death ten years ago, they were the only family she had left, and she had desperately wanted, *needed*, to believe them. So she'd let herself believe that the misplaced books, the medicine and keys that never seemed to be where she'd left them, were nothing more than signs of absentmindedness.

Then the little "accidents" started haunting her.

She shivered, pulling the covers tighter around her as she recalled all too vividly the loose board in her balcony railing that could have resulted in a long fall to the patio below her bedroom, the near hit-and-run "accident" while she was shopping, the horrifying dream of being smothered with her own pillow that had been so real she'd regained consciousness gasping and screaming. Only Craig, Sarah's husband, had been inclined to believe her and had insisted on calling in the police. But they had found nothing—no forced entry, not a clue that anyone had set foot in her bedroom.

It had been so easy then to think that she really was going out of her mind.

Then, this morning, she'd found a penicillin tablet mixed in with her regular medication. There had been no attempt to hide it—someone had placed it right on top of her other pills so that she couldn't mistake it for anything but what it was. A threat. She was deathly allergic to penicillin.

At first, she'd only felt relief. It wasn't her imagination! She had tangible evidence that someone was playing vicious tricks on her. She'd been all set to go to Baxter with her proof when she'd realized that only someone very close to her would have the opportunity to doctor her medicine. That's when the terror had started to build. It had to be someone she loved, someone she trusted.

Coldness seeped into her blood, chilling her all the way to the bone, but she couldn't afford the luxury of running from the truth. At the age of three, she'd inherited from her father a cosmetic company worth millions, interests in oil and gas refineries, the Thoroughbred horse farm that had been the Winters' family home for fifty years. Baxter, a financial wizard who had been one of her father's most trusted advisers, had been managing things for her since he'd married her mother when Gabriella was five.

It was an arrangement that had, through the years, been mutually satisfying. She'd been free to pursue her education, eventually earning a master's degree in English, while Baxter had run her companies as he saw fit. He'd made it a point to always discuss any major decisions with her, though it was really only a formality. She'd always bowed to his judgment. Until three months ago, when he'd urged her to take Winters Cosmetics public and use the money from the sale of stock to expand into the European market. It was a risk she hadn't been willing to take, not with the company her father and grandfather had loved and worked hard to establish. For the first time in her life, she'd held her ground against Baxter's gentle persuasion. At first, her stubbornness had stunned him, then angered him, then infuriated him. He'd had no choice but to accept her decision, but he'd made no attempt to hide his resentment from her.

How desperately did he want the European market? How far would he go to gain complete control of her and her money? He was the only father she remembered, and she loved him dearly, but lately they had become strangers. She knew he could be ruthless in his business dealings, but could he be ruthless with her? Was he trying to drive her over the edge of reason and have himself declared her guardian?

She shuddered, fear rising in her throat to choke her. If only she knew whom to trust, whom to fear! She knew the attacks wouldn't stop with the penicillin. There would be another and another—subtle, deadly assaults against her sanity that were so clever there was never any proof to take to the police. Even the penicillin could be shrugged off as a pharmaceutical mistake. She couldn't stay there, waiting for the terror to slowly drive her out of her mind.

Throwing off the covers, she eased from her bed without a sound, reaching for the clothes she'd hidden under her pillow: a threadbare flannel shirt discarded by the gardener and a pair of faded jeans that were tattered at the knees. They were too big for her, but it didn't matter. Nothing mattered but getting away. Now, while she still could.

She dressed in the dark, her heart jumping into her throat as the rasp of the jeans' zipper seemed to bounce off the walls of her room. She froze, her palms growing damp. From down the hall, Baxter's snoring continued, undisturbed. Relief nearly melted her knees. Releasing the breath she hadn't realized she'd been holding, she turned to her dresser and soundlessly pulled open the top drawer. Her fingers trembled as they closed around the scissors concealed under her lingerie.

No. Don't!

From somewhere deep inside her, a voice screamed at her in protest, but she ignored it. Her mind carefully empty of thought, she stared at her image reflected in the mirror and picked up a dark strand of her waist-length hair. With two slashes of the scissors, she cut it free just inches from her scalp and let it fall with no more than a whisper of sound to her feet. A heartbeat later, she reached for another handful of hair. And then another.

When she was finished, a fallen cloud of sable lay at her feet. Only then did she allow herself to survey what she had done. Pain clutched at her heart. The woman watching her from the shadowy depths of the mirror was a stranger and not really a woman at all. A shorn lamb with a pixie face, a waif too young to be let out at night alone. She was twenty-six, but with her cropped hair a jagged cap around her head and her five-foot-two frame shrouded in baggy clothes, she could have easily passed for an adolescent. The innocence and despair darkening the big brown eyes that were too large for her triangular face only added to the illusion of youth.

Hesitantly, she touched the short curls, refusing to regret the loss of her one claim to beauty. It was for the best. Baxter would send a hired bloodhound after her once he realized she'd bolted—his reputation as a doting father wouldn't allow him to do anything else. But she was taking no chances that he'd find her. Not until she'd had a chance to get away from the fear long enough to think clearly again. While he turned the countryside upside down looking for Gabriella Win-

ters, the sheltered and pampered heiress, she would
be...Gabby, one of the countless homeless who
slipped through the cracks in society, roaming the
country unnoticed. She wouldn't be found until she
was ready.

Taking a pillowcase from the bed, she stuffed it with
the cutting from her hair, carefully removing every
tendril from the carpet so there would be no clues as
to how she had altered her appearance. After that,
there was nothing left to do but slip the scissors and
her medication into her purse and grab the worn corduroy jacket she'd found in the garage. Moving to the
door, she dragged in a bracing breath and carefully let
herself out into the hallway.

Five minutes later, she stepped out into the night.
Wood smoke lingered on the cool autumn air, along
with the fresh, sweet scent of hay. On the distant horizon, the lights of Louisville set the dark sky aglow.
Cutting across the yard, she headed toward the train
station that lay two miles to the north through the
woods. Behind her, the neat pastures of the Thoroughbred horse farm blended into the Kentucky
countryside. She and her father had been born in the
grand old manor that was now fading into the shadows. Everything she held dear was there, but when she
stepped into the woods, she never looked back.

The train station was deserted, the ticket office
closed, but Gabby had already decided she wasn't
buying a ticket. She wasn't foolish enough to leave a
trail for Baxter to follow. Quickly burying the pillowcase of hair under the trees that lined the tracks, she
stood in the deep, concealing shadows, her throat as
dry as the gravel that spilled out from between rails of

track. Whatever confidence she'd had in her decision vanished as her eyes rested on the huge freight train before her. She'd never ridden on a train before, let alone tried to illegally hop a ride. What if she was caught?

She'd be returned to Baxter, and everyone who knew her would have one more reason to think that poor Gabriella had finally lost her marbles.

Her eyes flared at the thought, determination stiffening her spine. Then she'd just have to make sure she didn't get caught.

Down the track, the steady idling of the train's engine slowly increased in tempo until it set the night air humming and seemed to match the pounding of her heart. Instinct warned Gabby it would be leaving any second. Doubts forgotten, her eyes shot up and down the track, but there wasn't a soul in sight. Quickly jerking the shoulder strap of her purse over her head so she wouldn't have to worry about losing it, she darted from the woods.

There was only one empty boxcar, its sliding doors pushed wide open to reveal an interior that was as black as the night. Sprinting toward it at a dead run, Gabby felt as if she were confronting a giant. It was huge, dirty, as silent as a tomb. Repressing a shiver, she ignored the dark interior and grabbed on to the door frame to pull herself inside. She wasn't even halfway in when the train began to move.

"Oh, God, no!" Crying out in dismay, she clutched wildly at the door frame, but her legs and feet were hanging in midair, dragging her down. Horrified, she felt her fingers losing their grip, and she started to slide. "No!"

The hand that came out of the cavelike interior of the car to grab the seat of her pants was thin and long-fingered and as tough as leather. It was also as strong as a vice. It unceremoniously hauled her inside as if she weighed no more than a baby.

Gabby landed in a heap on the boxcar's dirty floor, gasping for breath, images of the train's wheels rolling over her legs flashing before her tightly squeezed eyes. Too close, she thought numbly. That was too close for comfort.

"You all right?"

She nodded, forcing back hysteria, and somehow found the strength to push herself to her feet. "Every bone in my body feels like it's turned to jelly," she said huskily as she turned to her unseen rescuer. "Thanks—"

The rest of her words died in her throat as the box-car passed the well-lit station. The light only lasted a second before darkness once again shrouded the boxcar, but it was enough for her to get a good look at the man who had saved her life. He was a hobo, a tramp. Thin as a rail, he was dressed in dingy khaki work clothes that were stained and tattered and probably hadn't seen a washing machine in months. Stringy brown hair and a dirty beard concealed most of his features, but it was his hot blue eyes that provoked Gabby to back away from him. He was looking at her as if he'd just found her under his Christmas tree.

"Well, well, well," he purred, almost smacking his lips in satisfaction. "Looky what we got here. We don't get many young gals like you hopping old dirty face. What's your name, sweetheart?"

She took another step back, never taking her eyes from the dark shadow of the man before her, the taste of terror bitter on her tongue as she realized there was no place to run. She swallowed. " 'Old dirty face'?"

His low laughter slid down her spine like hot oil. "You are a babe in the woods, aren't you? The freight train, sweetheart. Seems like you got a lot to learn, and old Joe'll be happy to teach it to you."

"No." Her voice was hardly more than a whisper, infuriating her. "No!" she repeated, this time stronger as her fingers fumbled for her purse. "That's not necessary." Stay calm, Gabby, she told herself sternly. Stress and fear were her two biggest enemies, and she couldn't afford to let this man scare her into a seizure. If she could just get to the scissors in her purse...

"Now don't be that way," he scolded, reaching for her. "It's going to be a long, cold night, and we ain't going anywhere until the train stops—"

Over the gathering rumble of the train wheels, the click of a switchblade sliding into place was soft, deadly. "The kid's not going anywhere, but you are," said a voice as smooth and sinister as the night.

Gabby's palms went damp at the sight of the man who suddenly materialized from out of the darkness. Bathed in shadows, he was like an inhabitant of one of her dreams—dark, towering, the shape and form of him blending in with the night so that all she knew of him was the power that seemed to radiate from him in waves. It was the type of power that had nothing to do with physical strength and everything to do with the confidence that he wore like a cloak. A woman could be seduced by such confidence before she caught the scent of danger.

Gabby felt her heart begin to pound and made an instinctive move to step back. His eyes, as sharp and silvery as the knife he held in his hand, shot to hers for just a moment, but it was long enough to trap her where she stood. She froze.

With his knife blade glinting in the darkness, the man motioned for the hobo to move back to the open door. White teeth flashed mockingly. "I think you need a walk outside to cool off that hot blood of yours."

"'A walk'?" the tramp sputtered incredulously, glancing over his shoulder at the sleeping countryside that was whizzing by with increasing speed. "Are you crazy? We must be going twenty or thirty miles an hour!"

"Maybe," the man with the knife agreed. "But in another few minutes, we'll be going twice that speed. If I were you, I'd jump now. It won't hurt as much."

His tone was as casual as if he were commenting on the weather, but the hobo wasn't stupid enough to take him lightly. Staring at the knife, he only dragged his eyes away long enough to shoot Gabby a blistering look, then prepared to jump. Seconds later, he landed with a thud on a grassy knoll, his angry cursing lost in the roar of the quickly disappearing train.

Danger. The scent of it was in the air, flirting with her senses as the man beside her turned, and Gabby knew it had nothing to do with the shiny weapon he held in his hand. This was a danger that was much more than physical, a danger that was as old as man and woman, as hot as the brush of skin against skin. He'd saved her from a possible rape, but all Gabby could think of was how big he was, how close, how alone they were in the night, with nowhere to run. The thunder of fear echoing in her ears, her blindly searching fingers tightened convulsively on her scissors. "S-stay away from m-me!" she ordered hoarsely, cursing her shaky voice as she clutched the scissors before her like a gun. "I mean it! I'll gut you like a fish if you so much as touch me."

Austin LePort stared down incredulously at the scissors jabbing him in the stomach before jerking his eyes back up to the girl's. The moon passed from behind the clouds, illuminating a pale, wide-eyed runaway dressed up in her daddy's castoffs. She couldn't have been a day over eighteen, if she was that old, and she was looking at him as if she expected him to jump her bones any minute. "Well, hell," he muttered in disgust. So much for doing his good deed for the day.

Swearing under his breath, he jerked the switchblade up until it was directly in front of her face and snapped it shut. "Sorry to disappoint you, sweetheart," he drawled, "but I don't get my kicks with snotty-nosed kids. If you're looking for a fight, you might try those guys," he suggested, glancing past her shoulder to the darkness behind her. "They look interested. I'm not." And without another word, he turned and strode off to the opposite end of the boxcar.

Her heart hammering wildly, Gabby whirled, stumbling to keep her balance in the swaying car, her eyes frantically searching the blackness. There, in the corner, glistening eyes watched her every move.

She didn't wait to see more before she hurried after the man with the knife. Better the devil she knew than the ones she didn't, she reasoned. And she didn't doubt for a minute that he was a devil. Sitting on the floor, his head resting back against the side of the boxcar, he didn't even open his eyes when she stopped three feet away from him and tried to apologize. "I'm sorry if I misjudged you—"

He only snorted and slouched farther on his spine.

If she'd have had the luxury of giving her emotions free rein, she would have told him then exactly what she thought of his rudeness. Instead, she struggled to remain calm, ignoring the irritation that curled into her stomach. "I'm trying to apologize, Mr...."

"The name's Austin," he retorted, his eyes snapping open to glare at her. "Not that it's any of your business. And if that's an apology, you're doing a damn poor job of it. Where I come from, apologies don't start with *if*."

"And where I come from, only a boor would have the gall to criticize someone when they're trying to say they're sorry!"

Even in the very poor light of the boxcar, Austin could see the regal set of her chin, the contempt in her large eyes. She might be just a kid, but he knew her kind. She could twist a man in knots with nothing more than the lift of her brow. His mouth curled mockingly. "You know, little girl, for someone who's hopping trains, you've sure got a highfalutin opinion of yourself. If you don't like the company, you're always welcome to run back to Daddy. What'd he do? Cut off your allowance?"

Gabby felt a flush fire her cheeks and thanked God for the concealing darkness. "I'm *not* a little girl!"

"Yeah, yeah, and you're not running from anything, right? You're taking a midnight ride on a freight train just for the hell of it." When she only stared at him mutely, he snorted in disgust. "Yeah, and my name's Pollyanna."

Gabby winced. Once, she wouldn't have thought twice about trusting a man who had come to her rescue, but those days were behind her forever. She couldn't trust him or anyone else with her reasons for hopping the train. If it somehow got back to Baxter where she was . . . Wrapping her arms around herself, she asked stiffly, "Do you know where this train is going?"

He lifted a brow. "Does it matter?"

"No. . . . I—I guess not."

Sliding down to the floor, she circled her drawn-up knees with her arms and blinked back sudden tears. The train raced on through the night, taking her farther and farther from home, while the man next to her stretched out to catch some sleep. Across the length of the boxcar, the other two occupants had lost interest in her and were already snoring. She'd never felt so alone in her life.

Austin came awake with a start, the stillness of the night ringing in his ears like an alarm. The train had stopped. How long? he wondered. A minute? Ten? Swearing at his carelessness, he jumped to his feet. He'd been riding the rails since the middle of July, and he knew better than to take more than a catnap on a moving train. Especially in the South. The brakemen always checked for riders whenever it stopped, and if he was caught, he could be spending the next twenty days in jail. The tramps who had occupied the other end of the car no doubt knew the dangers. They were long gone and hadn't bothered to wake him.

Muttering an expletive, he started to move toward the open door but stopped when he saw her. The kid. He'd completely forgotten about her. Curled up on her side, with her knees brought up to her chest, she was sound asleep.

Leave her!

The voice echoing in his head urged him toward the door, giving him all the reasons why she was none of his concern. He was an anthropologist, an author, not a baby-sitter. The research he was doing on hoboes was nearly completed, and he was on his way home. In another two weeks, he could be in his cabin blocking out the book he'd already signed a contract for—*if* he didn't run into any problems. And something told him the girl at his feet could give a new definition to the word *problem*.

He stared down at her, scowling. A girl her age had no business traveling cross-country by herself, let alone hopping freight trains. Next time, her feeble attempts to defend herself with a pair of scissors might backfire in her face. What the hell was she doing out here, anyway? She might be dressed like a bum, but she was obviously educated and belonged to someone somewhere. And that someone, if he had any sense, was going to come looking for her.

Austin told himself a man would have to be a fool to take on that kind of trouble. But even as the thought registered in his brain, he was nudging her awake. "Come on, kid, wake up. If you don't want to find yourself in the hands of the juvenile authorities in the next town, you'd better haul your little butt out of here."

Her mind muddled and heavy with sleep, Gabby heard little more than the word "authorities." Panic streaked through her like a ricocheting bullet. If she was caught, they'd send her back to Baxter.

"No!" Her breath escaping in a sob, she bolted toward the open door of the boxcar and the freedom that lay beyond.

"What the hell!" Cursing under his breath, Austin jumped after her and caught her before she could fall headlong to the ground. "What the devil do you think you'd doing?" he growled furiously as he jerked her away from the doorway. "You want to fall and break your neck? Or worse yet, get caught?"

"Don't touch me!" she cried, pushing frantically at the restraining arm hooked around her waist. "Let me go!"

He frowned at the terror he heard in her voice, but he couldn't release her until he knew she wouldn't make a break for it and possibly give both of them away. Grunting, he blocked the kick aimed at his shin, sustaining a punch in the gut, instead. His patience snapped.

Clamping his fingers around her upper arms, he gave her a rough shake. "Listen, you little brat, I'm only trying to help you."

"Let go of me!"

"When you promise to calm down. You go stumbling out of here half-cocked and you're liable to run right into the arms of a brakeman."

Gabby strained away from him, desperately trying to close her mind to the memory of other hands holding her, offering to protect her. At the same time one family member was trying to drive her crazy. Terror, dark and insidious, crept out of the corners of her mind to confront her, and at that moment, she would have promised anything just to be free of her rescuer's touch.

"I promise," she said huskily. "I'm all right now." But she wasn't. Not until he released her and she stepped back. Only then was she able to draw a steady breath again and will away the tension that stretched her nerves taut.

Austin watched her struggle for self-control and knew something wasn't quite right. But there was no time for questions. Moving to the open door of the boxcar, he peered out and swore silently at the sight of a brakeman making his way toward them, the flashlight in his hand swinging in time with his steps. They only had seconds before they would be discovered.

"Come on," he murmured, and hurried over to the other side of the car. A quick glance satisfied him that it was clear. "Let's go."

He would have helped her down, but she avoided his touch and awkwardly climbed to the ground unaided. Her face pale and ghostly in the darkness, she didn't wait for him but sprinted into the nearby woods as if the hounds of hell were after her. Seconds later he, too, ran for the concealing shadows of the trees. They'd hardly caught their breath before the locomotive engines revved up again and the train chugged off into the darkness.

Long after the last car had disappeared from sight, they could still hear the distant singing of the iron wheels on the rails. With every passing moment, it grew fainter until, finally, there was nothing left but the empty silence of the night.

The lack of sound went through Gabby like a cold north wind. Shivering, she wrapped her arms around her chest and tried to convince herself that the thick woods surrounding her were no more threatening than those that surrounded her farm. But when the man at her side turned and started crashing through the underbrush, moving deeper into the shrubs, her heart jerked in alarm. She hurried after him. "Hey...wait! Where are you going?"

He never slowed his pace. "To find someplace out of the wind to sleep."

"Do you know where we are?"

"Kentucky."

Did he think she was an idiot? Impatiently pushing aside a low branch that had almost tripped her, she scowled at his back and struggled to catch up with his long strides. "I know what state we're in," she huffed, "but what's the closest town?"

"I haven't the foggiest."

"Then how do you know where you're going? Shouldn't we wait near the tracks for the next train? Could you slow down, please? My legs aren't as long as yours."

Biting back an oath, Austin stopped abruptly and whirled to face her. Damn it, he knew he should have left her sleeping on the train! She was trailing after him like a puppy, and the last thing he needed was to be saddled with a teenage girl. "Look, kid," he growled, "I'm not a tour guide. If you wanted to keep track of the towns, you should have taken the bus. Now why don't you do us both a favor and go home like a good little girl before you get in any more trouble?"

This was the second time he'd called her a little girl in that patronizing tone of his, and Gabby didn't like it any more now than she had the first time. She would never again have the blind faith of a child who trusted the voice of authority. Stopping directly in front of him, she shot him a look that should have dropped him in his tracks. It didn't, and that only irritated her more. Struggling to hold on to her control, she said coldly, "I'm not a 'little girl,' and I'm not going

home. What I do is none of your business. Now if
you'll excuse me, I won't bother you with my company anymore.''

He told himself later he never would have touched
her if she hadn't tried to push past him with her nose
in the air. Little snot! He'd damn near had to fight a
man because of her, and now she was telling him what
she did was none of his business. Like hell!

Snatching her back in front of him, he jerked her up
on her toes before she could do anything but gasp in
protest. "Now you listen to me, *Miss Astor!* In case
you hadn't noticed, you're out of your league. You
keep hopping trains and some tramp is going to mistake you for his favorite dessert and eat you right up.
He isn't going to give a damn if you're still as innocent as the day you were born. Do you understand?"
he demanded, dragging her closer until they were
practically nose-to-nose. "Because if you don't, I can
certainly spell it out in more graphic terms!"

Her toes barely touching the ground, Gabby hung
between his hands like a rag doll and could only stare
into the dark, smoldering depths of his gray eyes.
Something stirred in her, something that had nothing
to do with fear, and suddenly all she could manage was
a hoarse, "Please—"

Through his anger and frustration, unwanted
impressions bombarded Austin from all sides. The
fragility of her bones under his hands. The flare of
confusion in her impossibly large eyes. The innocence that stuck out all over her. The attraction that
seemed to slip out of the darkness, tugging at him.

It was the last thing he expected, the last thing he
wanted. He swore and released her as quickly as he'd
grabbed her. He was thirty-three years old, for God's

sake, and she was just a teenager! "Go home," he ordered coldly, and turned back into the woods.

Stunned, Gabby stared after his retreating back, waiting for the starch to return to her ridiculously weak knees. At that moment, she would have given anything to be able to do as he said and go running home. But even if she'd known which direction to go, that was no longer an option. And she wasn't spending the rest of the night by herself in the woods. Straightening her weary shoulders, she started after the dark, shadowy form of her rescuer.

The trees eventually gave way to pastureland. Austin sighed in relief when he spotted the tin roof of a hay shed in the distance. It had no walls, but the roof was steeply pitched and came down far enough over the stacked bales of hay to block out the wind. Climbing the bales like a pyramid, he made his way to the top, then stretched out on his stomach in the sweet-smelling darkness, his eyes closing before his head had even hit his folded arms.

His heartbeat hadn't settled into the slow, steady rhythm of sleep, however, when he heard the soft, whispered movements of someone else climbing the hay. Seconds later, a soft sigh floated on the night air as a feminine body collapsed on the hay in exhaustion less than fifteen feet from him. He didn't have to open his eyes to know who it was. Trouble.

Chapter 2

Hours later, dawn silently crept under the shed's pitched roof, diffusing the darkness with a hazy light. His senses coming awake slowly, Austin lay unmoving, his eyes closed, the scents and sounds of the morning washing over him: the sweet hay; the cool, crisp air searing his lungs; the crowing of a rooster in the distance; the inviting softness of the woman snuggled against his back.

Woman!

His eyes flew open, the events of the night flooding back to him in a rush. The kid! She was so close, he could feel her breath on the back of his neck, warming, *heating* his skin. Swearing under his breath, he jerked away from her as if scalded. From six feet away, he sat staring at her, his frown growing darker as he got his first good look at her.

Curled on her side fast asleep, her cheek cradled against her palm, she looked like a princess who had stumbled upon hard times. She might be dressed in clothes fit for the rag barrel, but she couldn't hide what she was. Educated, refined, rich. It stuck out all over her. Hands as smooth and well tended as hers had never known hard work; her baby-soft skin had no doubt known nothing but the most expensive creams and lotions since birth. Her bones were as delicate as a Dresden figurine, her flawless features the result of generations of excellent breeding.

Innocence. It wrapped around her as surely as the soft, grainy light that was only just now reaching the high rafters of the shed. Austin felt the tug of it, the lure, and knew it had nothing to do with age. At thirty, fifty, even eighty, this woman would have a purity, a guilelessness that could pull protectiveness from a man, tie him in knots and hang him out to dry. Austin had decided long ago that no woman was going to do that to him. He liked his life just fine the way it was, answering to no one but his editor when a deadline rolled around. If the princess here was looking for a knight, she'd just have to look elsewhere.

He rose to his feet, intending to leave, but before he could even take a step, she stirred, stopping him in his tracks. More asleep than awake, she stretched sensuously, her soft sigh floating on the morning air like the call of a lover. A muscle ticked along Austin's jaw in response, yet he couldn't look away. Even as he watched, she rubbed her cheek against the hay as if it were the finest silk, her dark hair a mass of tumbled curls. Slowly, languorously, she opened her eyes.

The sleep thickening Gabby's brain vanished at the sight of the man glowering at her from six feet away. The man with the knife! What was his name? she thought with a frown, then relaxed as it came to her.

Austin. She hadn't been able to see him clearly last night, but she would have recognized him anywhere. In spite of the ragged jeans and Levi's jacket he wore, strength, power, impatience pulsed from him with every breath he took. Tall and lean, his black shaggy hair badly in need of a trim, he had the hard, unapproachable look of a man who belonged to the night, the shadows. There was no softness in his chiseled face, no warmth in the bottomless depths of his intense gray eyes. Several days' growth of beard darkened an angled jaw and square chin that could only be described as unyielding.

How had she gathered the nerve to approach him last night when he'd made it clear he wanted nothing more to do with her? Gabby wondered wildly. And worse still, could she have really turned to him to warm her during the cold, black hours of the night? She had no memory of consciously seeking him out, but somewhere in the back of her mind, the image of her pressed against his back burned like a flame. Oh, God, how could she!

Mortified, her cheeks bathed with color, she pushed herself to her feet; the control that was usually at her fingertips was now as shaky as her smile. "Good m-morning."

A man could grow old waking to that husky greeting and never become tired of it, Austin thought angrily. Innocence and sex. Was there ever a more potent combination? "Who are you?" he demanded. "You never hopped a train in your life before last night. What are you doing out here in the boonies by yourself?"

Stunned by the attack, Gabby stepped back. "I . . . my name is . . . Gabby—"

"And?"

He pinned her before him with a hard look that seemed to penetrate clear through to her soul. Fighting the urge to squirm, she grabbed the first lie that popped into her head. "I—I'm on my way to California. My grandmother's . . . sick," she said desperately, "and I want to see her again before she dies."

His face remained as expressionless as a poker player's. "That doesn't explain what you were doing on that freight last night."

"I don't have any money," she blurted out, her mind working furiously. "I was going to hitchhike, but that could take forever, and I didn't have any time to spare. So that only left the train."

He arched a dark brow mockingly. "You really expect me to believe that?"

"Why not?" she retorted, lifting her chin. "It's the truth."

"Now why don't I believe you?" he asked softly as he advanced toward her, amusement curling one corner of his mouth as she backed up warily. "It might have something to do with the fact that that train you hopped last night was going south, not west. If you were in such an all-fired hurry to get to California, you should've at least made sure you were traveling in the right direction."

"I . . . I was confused. It was dark—"

"Well, you got that part right, at least. The rest is nothing but a pack of lies. Why don't I skip this line of questioning and tell you what I know about you, princess? It'll save us both some time."

Gabby blanched, her heart jerking in her breast as he seemed to stalk her across the hay. "You don't know anything about me." He couldn't!

"Oh, but I do." Pursuing her to the very edge of the bales of hay, he stopped just inches away from her. His eyes locked with hers as he reached out to finger the worn material of her jacket. "I know that whomever you got these clothes from outweighs you by at least seventy-five pounds, and he's hardly in your league. You're used to the feel of satin against your skin, not corduroy."

Trapped! He was too close to her, too close to the truth. Gabby felt her throat go dry. She tried to tell herself it was nothing more than fear. A man in his circumstances would probably do just about anything for money, including returning her to Baxter like a piece of lost luggage if he ever discovered her true identity. Her reaction had nothing to do with the feel of his hands on her clothes, on her.

"I—I stole the clothes," she admitted huskily.

"I don't think so. Last night you were nervous as a cat on that train. You haven't got what it takes to be a thief." She opened her mouth to argue further, but he stopped her by simply taking her hand and running his thumb across her palm. "Save the lies, Gabby...or whatever your real name is. I know class when I see it."

She couldn't have spoken if her life had depended on it. Slowly, incessantly, his thumb skimmed over her palm, back and forth, stroking her, heating the very blood that coursed through her veins. Too late, Gabby realized he was a man who knew how to touch a woman, make her melt. She willed herself to move, but her feet remained stubbornly still. Her heart hammering, she could only stare at him, caught in the snare of his glittering gray eyes.

Have you lost your mind, Austin? Let go of this child before you find yourself caught in something you don't want!

He heard the voice in the back of his head, listened to it, then ignored it and the heat that seemed to leap from her hand to his. His fingers tightened around hers. "Who are you, Gabby?" he demanded softly. "*What* are you?"

She gave him the only answer she could. "I'm just me," she said quietly. "Princess Di, Orphan Annie, nobody."

In the span of a heartbeat, his eyes turned frosty. "You're not going to tell me, are you?"

"No."

Her evasiveness was no more than he'd expected, but damn it, hadn't he proven to her that she had nothing to fear from him? Irritated, he snapped, "Fine. Then I'll leave you with your lies. I've got no use for them."

He was down the stacked bales of hay and striding across the pasture that surrounded the shed before Gabby's heartbeat could even begin to steady. Fighting the ridiculous feeling of being abandoned, she stared after his retreating back, watching as the sun, still low on the horizon, cast a long shadow before him. With every passing moment, his lean, hard figure grew smaller and smaller in the distance.

Before the silence of her own company could close in on her, Gabby deliberately broke it. "Fine," she muttered, awkwardly climbing down the bales of hay. "If that isn't just like a man! Comes to my rescue a couple of times and thinks he's entitled to my life story." She gave an unladylike snort. "Who does he think he is, anyway? Just because I won't tell him anything, he gets in a snit. Well, *ex-cuse* me! I didn't notice him volunteering any information about himself."

Working herself into a stew, she was convinced she was better off without him by the time she reached the ground and began to dust the hay from her clothes and hair. "I'm perfectly capable of taking care of myself. All I have to do is follow the railroad tracks to the next town, get myself some breakfast, then decide where I'm going from there."

But when she stepped out of the shed, she had no idea which way to turn to find the tracks. In the darkness of the night, she'd lost all sense of direction. The trees that surrounded the pasture all looked alike, a fact that didn't seem to disturb her former traveling companion in the least. His long legs had already carried him to the edge of the trees, and soon he would be lost from sight. He was, Gabby reluctantly admitted to herself, a man who always seemed to know where he was headed. She'd be a fool not to follow his lead, at least until they came to the tracks again or a town. Then they were definitely parting company! Cursing him and her own reluctance to strike out on her own, she started after him.

She had no idea how long they walked without taking a break. It seemed like forever. The sun rose rapidly in the clear sky, heating the air until the coolness that had chilled her during the night was only a memory. Struggling out of her jacket, Gabby tied it around her waist, then trudged on, silently cursing the man who kept a relentless pace a hundred yards in front of her.

When he came to a small stream and stopped for a drink, she almost sagged in relief. Keeping well out of his way, she dropped to her knees on the bank and cupped her hands in the flowing water. It was cool and clear and felt like heaven as she splashed it against her hot face. From the corner of her eye, she watched her companion fill a water bottle she hadn't even known he had, take a long swig and then fill it again. He had to know she was there, but he didn't even look at her, let alone acknowledge her presence. His face carved in stone, he capped the water bottle, rose to his feet, then forded the stream at its shallowest part without saying a word.

The hurt that coursed through Gabby surprised her. What was wrong with her? Hadn't she had enough pain and heartache from her own family without letting a total stranger slip past her defenses to hurt her? With a deliberately dismissing shrug, she turned back to the stream.

Pulling her medication from her purse, she took her time getting a drink, savoring the coldness of the water as it slid down her dry throat. Her eyes wanted to drift to Austin as he trudged up the small hill on the other side of the stream, but she kept them stubbornly lowered. It wasn't until she rose to her feet and started to cross the stream that she realized he had disappeared over the crest of the small hill and was now out of sight. She told herself she didn't need him. She couldn't need him. With need came dependence, with dependence vulnerability. And after the nightmare of terror she had suffered at Baxter's hands, she never intended to be vulnerable again.

But even as the thoughts registered, panic was • clutching at her stomach with hot fingers. Splashing across the stream, she hurried up the hill. A stitch burned in her side, but she pushed on, panting, trying in vain to subdue the irritation churning within her. Damn him, when had he become so important to her? He was just a stranger she'd met in the night. He might have come to her rescue, but he was hardly a knight on a white horse. If she hadn't been so breathless, she might have laughed at the thought. Any man who walked off and left a woman in the middle of nowhere without bothering to point her in the direction of civilization wouldn't know chivalry if he tripped over it! He'd made it clear he wanted nothing further to do with her. Well, that was just fine with her. But the panic gripping her didn't ease until she came to the crest of the hill and saw him doggedly walking down a two-lane dirt road on the other side. Glaring at his back, she fell into step a long way behind him.

Traffic on the road was practically nonexistent. In the span of a half hour, two pickup trucks had passed, each going in the opposite direction. Not even slowing down at the sight of the man walking on the side of the road with the girl so far behind him, they only kicked up dust before they disappeared from sight.

Wiping the dust from her face with the sleeves of her coat, Gabby was beginning to wonder if the road led anywhere when she heard another vehicle approaching from behind her. Seconds later, it slowed and a dusty red pickup pulled even with her. The driver, a middle-aged man in overalls and a red plaid shirt, leaned across the bench seat, rolled down the passenger window and gave her a friendly smile. "You picked a warm day for walking. Need a ride into town?"

Heaven. He was offering her heaven! "Oh, yes," she breathed with a grin. Reaching for the door handle, her fingers closed around it just as images from last night flashed before her eyes. The old tramp on the train, helping her, almost drooling over her. She shuddered. She could have been raped last night, and she was still trusting strangers.

Her fingers fell from the handle as if they'd been burned. Before she could be tempted to change her mind, she stepped back, forcing a smile. "N-no. I...thanks, anyway. I'd better walk. I need the exercise."

He frowned at her about-face. "You sure? It's a long way to town. You can ride in back if you want. I won't hurt you."

She took another step backward, her hands twisting together as she felt her smile freeze on her face. What if he wouldn't take no for an answer? "No, really, I'm fine," she insisted. "I'm not going all the way into town, anyway. Just down the road a bit. But thanks for the offer."

He studied her through suddenly narrowed eyes, allowing the truck to slowly roll forward as she started to walk again. "You look awfully young to be out here in the sticks by yourself. And I know just about everyone around these parts. You're not from around here." His blue eyes narrowed sharply. "You're not running away from home, are you?"

"No!" Her answer was too quick, too frantic and out before she could stop it. Idiot! she cursed herself furiously. He's already suspicious. You keep acting like a scared rabbit and he's going to know something's wrong. Stay calm!

Fighting the need to run, she stopped and forced herself to meet his probing eyes. Could he hear the pounding of her heart? "I...I'm visiting relatives. The creek runs through their property and I was exploring and—''

"And wandered farther than you'd realized," the older man said with a chuckle. "You must be Pete Hempstead's granddaughter visiting from New York. Is your mother with you? Gosh, I haven't seen Mary in years. How's she doing?"

Gabby managed a shaky smile. "She's just f-fine." Dear Lord, what had she gotten herself into? "She's going to be worried about me, though, if I don't get back pretty soon. What did you say your name was? I'll tell her I ran into you."

"Robert Townsend. If I didn't have an appointment in town, I'd stop by now to see her." Caught up in his plans, he didn't see the blood drain from Gabby's face. "Maybe I'll stop in on the way back."

"Yes!" She grabbed on to his suggestion like a lifeline. "You'll have time to talk then. I'm sure Mom'll want to see you."

He grinned, delighted. "Okay, then, I'll see you both in a couple of hours." Tipping his hat at her, he drove away.

Two hundred yards away, Austin stood in the shade of an oak that bordered the road, his hooded eyes trained on the small figure standing in the dust of the departing truck. She wasn't his responsibility. How many times had he told himself that since he'd walked away from her that morning? At least a thousand. And with every step, he'd found himself listening for the sound of her footsteps behind him. Even when he hadn't seen her, he'd somehow known, sensed, she was there. That was what worried him. He didn't want to be that aware of her.

His mouth tightened into a flat line, his eyes hard. The long, lonely days he'd been crisscrossing the country for his research were finally catching up with him, he decided. That was the only explanation. Why else would he be drawn to a child-woman who couldn't venture out of her rich, pampered world without being scared of her own shadow? Damn it, he wouldn't be sucked in by her big eyes and helplessness! Women today certainly weren't helpless or innocent. She'd just proven she had enough sense not to get into a vehicle with a stranger. He didn't need to keep constantly looking over his shoulder to see if she was all right.

Satisfied that he'd finally reasoned away the last, lingering traces of concern she'd stirred in him, he stepped back onto the road, following the rapidly settling dust of the truck. But not without first glancing over his shoulder to see that Gabby was following.

They walked for what seemed like hours, never drawing close enough so that either had to acknowledge the other's presence but always remaining within sight. Several trucks passed without slowing, but Gabby didn't even glance at them. Food. The lack of it had her stomach gnawing at her backbone; the thought of it was the only thing that gave her the energy to put one foot in front of the other. Images of steak and shrimp and chicken flitted before her mind's eye until she could almost swear she smelled them all.

Lost in the fantasy, she almost didn't see Austin suddenly veer off the road. Surprised, she watched him climb through a barbed wire fence with an ease that could have only come from practice and head for a group of trees just on the other side. Apples! Her stomach groaning with hunger, Gabby saw his lean fingers close around a dark red piece of fruit and pluck

it from the tree. Her mouth watered. Seconds later, he
settled under the tree with his prize as if he were preparing for the meal of his life.

Gabby moved quickly to the fence, only to hesitate. It was old and unkempt, the barbed wire saggy,
thick with rust, hanging between cedar posts more
from habit than anything else. Gingerly reaching out
to test the sharpness of one of the rusty barbs, she
looked across to the trees to find Austin stretched out
comfortably on the ground, mockery curling the side
of his mouth as he watched her.

"Need some help?" he asked casually.

Oh, how he would like that, she thought furiously.
He was just waiting for her to ask for help, to prove to
him once again that she had no business being out on
her own. Stiffening her shoulders, she gave him a
withering look. "No, thank you. I'd rather do it by
myself."

He shrugged, unconcerned. "Suit yourself."

He turned his attention to his apple, rubbing it
against his sleeve until it shone brightly, but Gabby
didn't doubt for a minute that he was watching her
every move. Ignoring him, she leaned down until her
back was parallel to the middle row of wire, then eased
one foot between it and the bottom row. Holding her
breath, she slowly slid the rest of her body through the
fence. She was almost through when a barb caught her
at the back of the waist, snaring her, leaving her awkwardly straddling the wire.

"Oh, no!"

Austin had been half expecting her soft cry of dismay. What he had not been expecting was the need to
go to her again, to extract her from the trouble she had
once again got herself into. He had to steel himself to

sit there and act as if he hadn't a care in the world. "Sure you don't need some help?" he asked as he settled more comfortably against the tree.

"No!"

Her curt answer fairly seethed with frustration and pride. He grinned in spite of himself. "There's no need to get hostile. Your jacket's all that's snagged. Untie it and you'll be home free."

She was out of the jacket and through the fence in a matter of seconds, which only infuriated her further. Resisting the urge to snatch an apple from a tree and throw it at his grinning face, she forced herself to ignore him as he had her at the creek. It wasn't easy. Sitting in the dappled shade, his black hair ruffled by the breeze that slipped through the trees and a wicked smile flirting with his mouth, he was a tempting devil. Gabby felt again the heat of his body as she'd lain next to him during the night, the feeling of safety that had enveloped her. Where had she ever gotten the idea that this man was safe?

Cautiously stepping around his outstretched legs, she quickly put the space of two trees between them. It didn't help. The apples that dangled overhead were all out of reach, and she had to jump several times to reach one. With every jump, she felt his eyes on her, watching her, studying her, touching her. By the time she grabbed an apple, her cheeks were as red as the fruit. Muttering under her breath, she dropped to the ground and deliberately kept her eyes on the apple as she polished it on her sleeve.

She had it up to her mouth, anticipation sweet on her tongue, when he leaned back and gazed up into the gnarled, untrimmed branches above them. "These trees look like they haven't been tended in years, so I doubt they've been sprayed. Better watch for worms."

Gabby's empty stomach turned over in protest. Jerking the apple back from her mouth, she stared at its smooth, unblemished skin in horror.

"Course, some people don't mind," Austin continued, cutting off a piece of his own apple with the same knife he'd threatened the hobo with last night. "It's just more protein." Popping the thin sliver into his mouth, he closed his eyes in ecstasy, savoring the juicy bit of it. "Damn, that's sweet! How's yours?"

If he hadn't been watching her as if he expected her to throw the apple down any second, she would have done exactly that. Instead, she was forced to take a bite. Swallowing the gag that rose to choke her, she took the tiniest bite she could manage.

"Well?"

Fruit, sweet and tart and wet, tasted like ambrosia on her dusty tongue, whetting an appetite that was already ravenous. She almost laughed in relief, until she remembered that there was no telling what lurked in the next bite. The apple slid down her throat like a lump of sawdust. "It's . . . fine."

Grinning, Austin sliced himself another piece. "I can tell you're crazy about it."

"If you're expecting accolades for a wormy apple, you're wasting your time," she retorted. "Under the circumstances, 'fine' is the best I can do."

He lifted a brow, his eyes dancing. "So the princess has a temper."

A temper? If she hadn't been on the verge of steaming mad, Gabby would have laughed at the suggestion. No one who knew her would have ever accused Gabriella Winters of having a temper. Her health hadn't allowed it. Yet in the span of less than twenty-four hours, this man had found innumerable ways to push her buttons and test her control. And she was getting damn tired of it. "For your information, Mr.—what the devil is your last name?"

His lips twitched. "LePort."

"Mr. LePort—"

"There's no need to stand on ceremony," he cut in. "Austin will do fine."

"I am not a princess!" she finally managed, drawing herself up, her brown eyes as dark as ebony as she glared at him. "And if I have a temper, it's only because you would test the patience of a saint!"

Austin hardly heard her. In the blink of an eye, she gave him a glimpse of the woman beneath her pixie exterior, a woman of passion and seething emotions. It was a picture he didn't want to see. Enough! he told himself furiously. This had gone far enough. If he started letting himself think of her as anything but a kid, he was asking for nothing but trouble.

He forced a grin that never reached his eyes. "My mother says the same thing, so don't feel bad. It's nothing personal."

"You have a mother?"

He couldn't help but laugh at her surprise. "Yeah. It's hard to get into this world without one." Rising to his feet, he tossed aside what remained of the core of his apple, then picked another, which he stored in his pocket. "You'd better eat that," he said, nodding at the barely tasted one she still held. "There's no telling where your next meal's coming from."

He headed back for the road before she'd realized he was calling an end to their lunch break, leaving Gabby staring blankly at the apple in her hand. She might live to regret it, but now that he was gone, there was no question of eating it. Throwing it down, she struggled through the fence again and started after him. Hungry or not, she knew it would be a long time, if ever, before she would be able to enjoy an apple again.

They had walked only a mile down the road when they came to a white split-rail fence that seemed to stretch into infinity. Slowing his pace, Austin studied it through narrowed eyes, noting the cracked and peeling paint, the occasional breaks in the weathered boards. The neat fields it encompassed were thriving and nearly ready for harvest, testifying to the fact that all the labor went into the farm work and little into keeping up appearances. Jingling the $3.32 in his pocket, he smiled at the way opportunity always seemed to present itself just when he thought he was going to have to break down and call his agent for a small loan to get him through the rest of his research.

The entrance to the farm was another half mile down the road. Simple and unpretentious, it opened onto a driveway that led to an old-fashioned farmhouse that could have easily housed a family of twelve. Without a moment's hesitation, Austin left the road and approached the house.

The man who answered his knock had the shoulders of a football player and the arms of a weight lifter. His plain, square face was weathered, tough and could have belonged to a man anywhere between forty and sixty. From his thinning gray hair, Austin judged him to be closer to the latter than the former.

Through the screen door, the farmer's eyes swept over Austin in a perusal that missed little. "Afternoon. What can I do for you?"

"I'm looking for work—"

"Sorry, son," the older man cut in before he could finish. "But I've already hired extra help for the harvest. I use the same people every year, and I just haven't got enough work for another hand. You might try down the road."

"How 'bout your fence," Austin persisted. "It looks like it could use some mending, and I'm good with a paintbrush."

There was no denying that the fence needed repair, so the farmer didn't even try. "I was planning on looking after that this winter, but..." He hesitated, once again studying Austin shrewdly. "You're one of those hobo fellas, aren't you?"

Austin bit back a grin at the description, taking it as the highest compliment. He worked hard to fit in with the men he was studying. "Yes, sir, I ride the trains whenever my feet get to itching."

"Well, I can't use you if they're going to start itching tomorrow or the next day," the older man said bluntly. "That fence is over two miles long, and if you start it, I expect you to finish it. That's going to take you at least a week or two, depending on the weather. If you got a problem with that, you can just keep on going."

"No, sir," he replied solemnly, banking down the smile that wanted to rise in his eyes. "I can handle that just fine."

"The name's Jones. Frank Jones. And you're...?"

"Austin."

The older man had obviously worked with hoboes before. He didn't press for a last name but looked past Austin to the gate, then nodded. "She with you?"

Austin almost groaned, not bothering to turn around. No! The denial sprang to his tongue, but the word never left his mouth as he sighed in defeat. "She seems to be."

"There's no free rides here," Frank Jones warned him. "She'll have to paint, too. Room and board and two bucks an hour. That's all I can offer you."

It was more than he'd hoped for. Austin nodded. "That'll be fine. Thanks."

"You can both start today. You'll find everything you need in the barn. That's where you'll be sleeping, too—I've only got a couple of quarters for the hired help, and they're already full. Supper's at six with the other hands. Don't miss it or there won't be nothing left."

"We'll be there," he promised, grinning.

But when he turned back to Gabby, the smile faded as he realized he'd just tied himself to her for the next two weeks. He must have been out of his mind!

Chapter 3

They painted for two and a half days before a thunderstorm forced them inside. Standing in the doorway of the barn, Gabby watched the rain sweep across the yard, thankful for the unexpected break. Ever since she and Austin had arrived at the farm, they'd spent most of each day face-to-face with nothing between them but a fence, he painting one side, she the other. She had no complaint with the work; in fact, she enjoyed it. For the first time in her life she was doing physical labor, enjoying the satisfaction of a job well-done. No, it wasn't the work she needed a break from, but Austin and the unsettling sense of expectation that throbbed between them whenever their eyes chanced to meet. And their eyes had clashed thousands of times during the past three days. Every time she'd looked up from dipping her brush in the paint, she'd found her vision filled with him.

Wrapping her arms around herself, she resisted the urge to glance back over her shoulder, where she was sure to find him in the shadowy depths of the barn. She knew he was as aware of her as she was of him, just as she knew he was watching her again with those brooding gray eyes of his. Why did he watch her? she wondered, staring out at the rain. It wasn't as if he gained any pleasure from it. Far from it. Invariably he would scowl and become short-tempered, until the tension between them was as fragile as hand-blown glass. How much longer did she have before it shattered?

The blare of a horn ripped through her musings as Frank Jones brought his pickup to a splashing halt beside the open barn door. Rolling down his window, he shot her a grin. "How about a ride into town?" he called over the steady pounding of the rain on the tin roof. "I've got your wages for the past two days, and you won't be doing any more painting today. If you need to do any shopping, this is your chance."

A trip to town. Gabby couldn't have been more thrilled if he'd offered her a trip to Paris. "Oh, yes! Wait, let me tell Austin...."

"I heard," he said quietly from behind her.

She whirled, her breath lodging in her throat as she found him so close her breasts almost brushed his chest. Something quick and hot slid into her stomach, as if she'd come too close to an open flame. Her hand fluttered to her throat and the pulse that suddenly raced there. "I—I didn't realize you were there."

He stared down at her with hard eyes, refusing to take the single step backward that would give them both some breathing room. What was it about this woman that irritated him so? Considering the monied background he was sure she was hiding, he'd expected her to be more of a hindrance than a help in painting the fence. But she'd thrown herself into the work without complaining once. He should have been relieved that it was going so well. He wasn't. He didn't want to like her; he didn't want to be so conscious of her every move. But he did and he was and he didn't like it one little damn bit!

Clamping his jaw on a curse, he shoved her purse at her. "Here's your purse. Let's go."

Surprised, she took it automatically. "You're going, too?"

"Yeah. I need another pair of jeans."

He didn't give her a chance to ask any more questions but strode past her into the rain. Jerking open the truck's passenger door, he waited impatiently for her to scoot into the middle before he climbed in next to her and slammed the door shut.

Gabby hardly had time to adjust to being sandwiched between the two men before the farmer shifted gears and turned the truck around in a tight circle. Caught off guard, she felt herself sliding, but there was nothing to grab on to. Seconds later, she slid into Austin, her thigh, hip and shoulder wedged intimately against his.

The silence that fell over the truck fairly sizzled. Against her thigh, Austin's muscles were as hard as stone. If she could have only found the words, she could have diffused the tension by teasing him about hogging the seat. But her voice was gone, dried up by the heat singeing her everywhere his body inadvertently touched hers. Stiffly pulling herself erect again, she prayed he couldn't hear the thundering of her heart.

"So how'd you two meet?" Frank Jones asked as he settled into the drive he knew like the back of his hand. "You know each other before you started riding the rails, or did you just find yourselves in the same boxcar and take up with each other?"

Alarmed that he should guess the truth, Gabby blurted out, "Before—"

"We chose the same car—"

Their words collided in midair, creating an awkwardness that was almost tangible. Seconds stretched into minutes; the only sound was that of the rain on the roof and the steady beat of the windshield wipers. Hot color burning her cheeks, Gabby tried to repair the damage. "We knew each other in Florida—"

"I ran into her three nights ago—"

Gabby wanted to shoot Austin for clinging to the truth, but she didn't even look at him as she ruthlessly continued, "I hadn't seen him since we took a freight down to Miami six months ago, then suddenly there he was, going in the same direction I was. Talk about a coincidence! I just couldn't believe it."

The story had *lie* stamped all over it. Stifling the urge to squirm, Gabby forced herself to meet the older man's speculative gaze. She held her breath, waiting for him to ask the questions that would trip her up, but it never came. Instead, Frank Jones only returned his attention to the road and commented, "There's the Catholic church steeple up ahead. Town's just around the bend." Gabby almost wilted in relief.

The town turned out to be Promise, Kentucky, population 2,010. It could have been any small town in America, untouched by the passage of time, looking as if it still belonged in the fifties. The courthouse sat in the middle of the town square, surrounded by businesses that no community could do without. A drugstore and café, the five-and-dime, a pool hall and theater with an Art Deco marquee. At the northwest corner, a dress shop and a men's store sat at right angles to each other, their windows filled with everything from jeans and boots to linen suits and lingerie.

Gabby had memorized all of Main Street in the time it took Frank Jones to find a parking space on the square. The rainy weather had freed all the area farmers from work, and the little town was thriving.

"Okay, here's your wages," the older man said as he counted out their money to them after he'd parked and they'd climbed out of the pickup. "I'll meet you back here at the truck in an hour and a half. Will that give you enough time to get what you need?"

"That'll be more than enough," Austin replied. "Thanks."

The minute the other man was out of earshot, Austin pulled Gabby out of the rain under the awning that jutted out over the drugstore and glared at her coldly. "Okay, Gabby, I want to know what the hell kind of game you're playing!"

Unprepared for the attack, she blinked in confusion. "'Game'? What are you talking about?"

"'I hadn't seen him since we took a freight down to Miami six months ago,'" he mimicked. "That's a damn lie and you know it. Why didn't you let me tell him the truth?"

Because the truth would have only led to more questions, questions she had no intention of answering. But she could hardly tell Austin that. Tugging at the fingers clamped around her arm, she gave up in defeat when he wouldn't release her and said stiffly,

"Because it's none of his business how we met or where."

"You're right," he retorted sarcastically. "The man just gave us a roof over our head, food to eat, not to mention a job. Why should he expect the truth from us?"

Gabby winced. "Austin, I'm not ungrateful—"

"Yeah, right. You just take it for granted that you're entitled to those things. Well, let me tell you something, sweetheart. Your daddy might be as rich as Rockefeller, but the rest of the world doesn't owe you squat."

She blanched. "My father isn't—"

"Save the lies," he cut in harshly. "I'm not in the mood for them. But I'm warning you, Gabby Whatever-your-name-is, one of these days I will find out the truth about you." Releasing her abruptly, he gestured at the money she still held in her hand. "That's not a bloody fortune, you know, so don't spend it on nonsense when you need clothes. And don't be late getting back to the truck."

"Yes, sir. No, sir. Whatever you say, sir," she snapped, but her sarcasm was wasted. He was already crossing the street to the men's store on the corner.

Damn him, she fumed as she headed for the women's shop. Did he think she was a child who had to be told how to spend her money when the only clothes she had were the ones on her back? Just because she'd grown up with money didn't mean she didn't know the value of a dollar. Her parents and Baxter had made it a point to see that she wasn't raised like a poor little rich girl who got everything she wanted, and she resented the implications that she was spoiled.

Lost in her thoughts, she was just lifting her hand to pull open the shop door when her eyes fell on the newspaper stand next to it. From the front page of the local paper, her own picture stared back at her.

Every drop of blood drained from her face. "Oh, no!" It couldn't be her! she silently cried, but another glance assured her that the dark, doelike eyes staring up at her from the black-and-white picture were her own. Glancing quickly around to make sure that Austin was nowhere in sight, she fumbled in her purse for a quarter, cursing when her shaking fingers couldn't seem to grasp any of the lose change. With jerky movements, she finally found a coin, dropped it into the machine and pulled out a paper.

Gabriella Winters, heir to the Winters cosmetic fortune, is still missing after two days of intense searching. Police have found no evidence of foul play but are not ruling out the possibility. Baxter Hawthorne, stepfather of the missing heiress and C.E.O. of Winters Cosmetics, is offering a ten-thousand dollar reward for any information leading to her return. She has been under a doctor's care for the past two months for paranoia and lately has been losing touch with reality. Anyone with information about her whereabouts should contact the Jefferson County sheriff immediately.

Stricken, the words blurred before Gabby's eyes and echoed in her head, slicing at her with the sharpness of a razor. Paranoia. Losing touch with reality. How could he? she thought, her breath catching on a sob. How could Baxter do this to her? He'd taken her private fears and made headlines with them, turning her flight into a circus, her sanity into a questionable commodity. How could she ever hope to persuade anyone that he was trying to drive her crazy after this?

So what are you going to do? a voice in her head taunted. Give up and wait for someone to find you and collect the reward?

No! If Baxter ever got her in his power again, she'd be lost. He'd let her get away from him once; it wasn't a mistake he was likely to make twice. She'd have to disappear so far underground that not even his reward could flush her out.

Snatching the paper back up, she looked at her own picture as if she were studying the face of a stranger. The photo had been taken at a charity ball last year. She was dressed in her mother's diamonds and a designer gown that had cost the earth and looked it. Pampered and sophisticated, she had a panache that belonged only to the very rich.

There was, however, nothing pampered, rich or even remotely sophisticated about the woman she had become. Dragging her eyes from the paper, Gabby glanced up at her image reflected in the store window in front of her. With her tattered clothes and equally tattered hair, her face free of cosmetics, she was everything that Gabriella Winters was not. Rough and coarse, with the haunted eyes that sometimes went hand in hand with poverty. Would anyone seeing her now make the connection between her and Gabriella Winters?

How desperately she wanted to say no! The life she'd left behind was part of another world, one she could no longer return to. But she couldn't lie to herself. She may have changed her hair and clothes, but the face that belonged to the woman in the picture was hers. Anyone who became the least bit suspicious of her would see the resemblance. She had to do something. Now! Crumbling the paper, she threw it into the nearest trash can and looked wildly around. There had to be a way to change her face....

Her eyes came to an abrupt stop at the drugstore. Before she'd even started toward it, a dozen possibilities were already spinning in her head.

The bell over the front door jingled as she stepped inside, drawing the eyes of the half-dozen people seated at the store's old-fashioned soda fountain. Gabby stiffened and quickly lowered her eyes, silently praying that none of them were reading the paper. Act normal! she told herself fiercely, but she'd never been much of an actress. How could she act normal when she felt as if *$10,000 Reward* was tattooed on her forehead?

Resisting the urgent need to duck her head, she moved unhurriedly to the makeup counter. A dozen different brands filled the display case, the most expensive of which was her own brand, Winters Cosmetics. For a timeless moment, she stared at the logo unblinkingly and knew that everything it represented was lost to her. Squeezing her eyes shut, she willed back the tears, the sense of loneliness that spread through her like a dark void. There was no going back now. Stiffening her spine, she ignored her own product and chose the discounted items, instead.

When she left the store ten minutes later, her eyes were shining with relief and an excitement she couldn't conceal. In the brown paper bag she clutched to her breast, she had everything she needed to create a new and improved Gabby. Tons of makeup, gaudy earrings, dye for her hair. Tonight she would do a complete make-over, and when she was finished, not even Baxter would recognize her if he passed her on the street.

I'm warning you, Gabby Whatever-your-name-is, one of these days I will find out the truth about you.

Austin's words suddenly echoed in her ears, chilling her soul. The excitement in her eyes gave way to a growing horror. He'd just spent the past two days across the fence from her, her face the first thing he saw every time he looked up. He knew every nuance of her visage, just as she knew his. If he saw the paper, he was bound to recognize her.

Would he turn her in for the reward? She paled at the thought. No, he wouldn't. He couldn't. He might only tolerate her intrusion into his life, but every time she'd needed him during the past few days, he'd been there, glaring at her, but helping her nonetheless. And then there were the times her skin seemed to burn whenever their hands, their bodies, accidently brushed. She'd seen his eyes narrow, his mouth tighten, as if he, too, felt something....

Suddenly realizing what she was doing, she jerked her thoughts back before they could go any further. It was time she woke up and smelled the coffee. No man was going to turn his back on ten thousand dollars for someone he thought was nothing but a bothersome teenager. If Austin found out about the reward, he'd turn her in so fast it'd make her head swim.

She couldn't let that happen. Her own need for clothes forgotten, she straightened her shoulders and made her way to the men's shop on the corner.

Austin was looking at shirts when he sensed her nearness. When, he wondered in annoyance, had he developed this early warning system where she was concerned? Every time she came within touching distance, a dozen different sensors went off in his body. It irritated the hell out of him.

Determinedly keeping his eyes on the rack in front of him, he flicked through the shirts without seeing any of them. "Finished your shopping already?"

Gabby's fingers tightened on the sack she held. "Y-yes. I didn't need much."

He snorted at that. "Yeah, right. You don't have anything but the clothes on your back, but you don't need much." Glancing up abruptly, his gaze zeroed in on the small package she clutched to her breast. "What's that?"

Gabby's knees threatened to shake as she suddenly remembered his order not to spend her money on any nonsense. But it was her money, she thought furiously. She'd worked hard for it, and she could spend it any way she liked. Refusing to cower before him like a child before the principal, her eyes never wavered from his. "My shopping."

"The hell it is," he growled, snatching the paper bag out of her hand before she'd realized his intentions.

"Damn it, Austin," she hissed, grabbing at the sack, "what I buy is none of your b—"

A low, harsh roll of curses cut her off in midsentence as he opened the sack and saw its contents. Makeup! Of all the harebrained, idiotic... Crushing the bag closed, his eyes snapped up to hers, impaling her. "How much did you spend on this junk?" he demanded icily.

"None of your—"

He took a step toward her before the words were even out of her mouth. "How much?"

Trapped by the clothes rack at her back and the towering strength of his body, Gabby had nowhere to retreat. He was so close she could feel the heat of his breath skating over her lips, weakening her knees. Her heart pounded heavily; her thoughts wanted to scatter under the force of his unbreakable gaze. The sparks that had been flying between them since the night they'd met were suddenly there, sizzling. She had only to remain stubbornly silent, and she would push him into setting them off like Roman candles.

"Ten dollars."

The two words came out low and husky. For what seemed like a lifetime, Austin just stood there, staring at her, his fingers curling into his palms to keep from reaching for her. If he touched her now, he wasn't sure if he would shake her or drag her into his arms. Two days' earnings, and she'd spent nearly a third of it on crap she had no use for, he thought in disgust, latching on to the anger that coursed through him. He should have known better than to think he could trust her with money. Women who'd been born with silver spoons in their mouths never gave a thought to where the next dollar, the next meal, was coming from.

"Take it back."

It wasn't a request, but an order. A very arrogant order that rang with the expectation of being carried out. Gabby stiffened, her eyes flashing. "In case you've forgotten," she said in a voice that was deceptively soft, "I don't need your permission to spend *my* money any way I want. I bought what I wanted, and I'm not taking it back. I couldn't even if I wanted to," she continued before he could argue with her again.

"Everything I bought was on final clearance and can't be returned."

"Well, great! That's just great. So how the hell are you going to get some clothes?"

Glancing past his shoulder, Gabby noticed they were beginning to draw the attention of the other customers, which was the last thing she wanted. "Austin, please," she said quietly, "there's no need to get all bent out of shape. I've still got over twenty dollars left. I'm sure I'll be able to find something on the sale rack."

"Yeah, I've seen what you buy off of the sale rack," he retorted. "This time I'm going with you."

Images of the newspaper stand outside the dress shop flashed before her eyes. "No! I mean, that's not necessary. I don't need you to watch over me like a—"

"Keeper," he supplied mockingly.

She shrugged. "Keeper. Warden. *Jailer.* Take your pick—they all fit. The point is, I'm not your responsibility."

"Tell me about it," he muttered under his breath as he clamped his hand around her wrist, then pulled her after him to the cashier to pay for the jeans he'd picked out earlier.

Before Gabby had a chance to douse the panic streaking through her like wildfire, they were outside and headed for the dress shop. Think! she ordered herself furiously. But there was no time. Austin's long legs made short work of the distance between the two stores, and with every step, the newspaper stand was drawing closer. In another few seconds, her picture on the front page would be clearly visible.

"Look!" she cried, pointing to the square. "Isn't that Mr. Jones going to the truck? He must be ready to go."

Frowning, Austin glanced over his shoulder just as he was reaching for the front door of the shop. "Yeah, that's him, but he's not stopping at the truck. Looks like he's heading for the café. Probably for a cup of coffee with some of his cronies." Pulling the door open, he motioned her ahead of him. "We've still got plenty of time left." He stepped inside right behind her and never even spared a glance for the newspaper stand.

Gabby almost laughed in relief, but her triumph was short-lived. The minute she moved to the sale rack at the back of the shop, she realized she'd made a mistake. Suddenly they were surrounded by lacy confections of lingerie. A silent Austin, his arms crossed over his chest and his face set in implacable lines, stood at her side like a wooden Indian, making her terribly conscious of the unexpected intimacies encountered when shopping with a man.

Fighting the blush that threatened to spill into her cheeks at any moment, she quickly flipped through the sale items and grabbed the first decent pair of jeans she came to on the rack. "These should do. I'll just try them on, and then we can leave."

"Those are designer jeans."

"Yes, I know. I've got two pairs just like them at home."

"Only two?" he mocked, taking the hanger out of her hand and hanging the jeans back up. "I'm surprised you haven't got a whole closet full of them. Find something cheaper."

His attitude about money was really starting to irritate her, Gabby decided with a frown. "Cheaper doesn't necessarily mean better quality."

Nothing but the best for the princess, he fumed. When was she going to realize that she was in the real world now? "In case you hadn't noticed, you need quantity, not quality," he drawled. "If you buy those, you aren't even going to have enough left over for a pair of underwear."

Heat fired her cheeks. "Could we leave my underwear out of this discussion, please?"

"Why not?" He shrugged, amused. "You seem to be. If you want to go around without any underwear, who am I to complain?"

"Austin!"

"What?"

Damn him, how could he look so innocent? "My underwear isn't any of your business," she hissed.

Common sense warned him to drop the subject, but there was no stopping the words that sprang to his tongue as his eyes locked with hers. "They are if you're not wearing any."

There was no amusement in his eyes now, only searing heat. Gabby felt the warmth of it, the danger, and struggled against it like a swimmer fighting the undertow. Her heart pounding, she jerked her gaze away, looking down blindly at the rack of clothes in front of her. "You're r-right. I'll find something cheaper."

But Austin was in no mood to stand by while she looked. Suddenly the shop was too small, his blood too hot. Angry at himself for ever bringing up the subject of underwear, angry at her for raising his temperature just by her nearness, he snatched a sweatshirt and a pair of plain jeans off the sale rack and thrust them at her. "Here," he snarled. "These should do. I'll wait outside while you try them on."

"No!" He couldn't go outside alone! She pushed the clothes back at him, along with some money she hastily dug out of her purse. "I don't need to try them on," she said quickly. "They'll fit. While you're paying for them, I'll get me some—" she looked around the lingerie that surrounded them and smiled weakly "—underwear."

It wasn't a subject Austin wanted to discuss. His jaw tight, he nodded curtly, then strode toward the checkout counter.

A little while later, they squeezed back into the pickup with their employer and headed for the farm. Their packages in their laps, their hips and thighs once again pressed close, they stared unseeingly out the rain-splattered windshield while the silence in the cab thickened.

Frank Jones settled more comfortably into the driver's seat and said casually, "Don't get to town much during the middle of the day. It's a nice change."

Silence was his only response.

Shrugging, he tried again. "Rain's supposed to let up tonight. Tomorrow it'll be back to the salt mines."

The wipers beat steadily against the windshield, the only noise in the ensuing quiet. Shooting a quick glance at his passengers, the older man frowned at their set faces. With a sigh of disgust, he gave up in defeat.

The rest of the ride home was accomplished in a silence that was interminable. Achingly aware of the slightest tensing of the other, Austin and Gabby both sighed in relief when the farm finally came into view. But once they had thanked Frank Jones for the ride into town and then ran into the barn, the tension that had filled the pickup only followed them inside. It was still several hours yet until sunset, but the heavy cloud cover had brought an early darkness, and the interior of the barn was filled with shadows. Overhead, the rain fell against the tin roof in a steady tap dance that was almost drugging in its monotony. Their eyes met for an instant, awareness flaring. They were alone, with nothing but time stretching out before them.

Swearing at the Fates, Austin stepped past her and flicked on the lights. It helped, but not enough. "If you don't dawdle in the bathroom, we've both got time for a bath before supper," he said curtly. "You're first. While you're in there, you can wash out those clothes you've got on and hang them on one of the stalls to dry. And don't use all the hot water. I'm not in the mood for a cold shower."

Gabby opened her mouth to tell him that's exactly what she thought he needed, but caution stopped her before the words ever left her tongue. He was itching for a fight. She could hear it in the terseness of his voice, see it in the inexplicable anger in his eyes, which was just barely held in check. Something was eating at him, something that all her instincts warned her to back away from while she still could. Tightening her arms around her packages, she carefully edged around him and hurried to the small bathroom next to the tack room.

Only when the door clicked shut behind her back did she realize she was trembling. What was he doing to her? she wondered wildly. He made her want . . . something, something no one else had ever made her feel, something she couldn't even allow herself to put a name to. It was all wrong. He was all wrong. He touched her and she trembled like a schoolgirl with her first crush. It had to stop! She was running for her life, and she couldn't let her emotions get wrapped up in any man, let alone someone like Austin.

Determined to put him out of her mind, she drew her bathwater and set about creating a new Gabby, one that was as far away from Gabriella Winters as humanly possible. Almost an hour later, she stared at the strange woman in the bathroom mirror and knew she'd succeeded. She'd cut her hair—again—and dyed it. Now as short as her ears and even curlier than before, it was a bright, brassy red. Touching it in wonder, Gabby laughed in delight. Why had she never experimented with her hair color before? She felt like a new woman, the same, yet somehow different. More daring. Adventuresome. Provocative? she mused. Maybe. The heavy makeup she'd applied certainly made her look older and more experienced, which was just what she'd been aiming for. For the first time since she'd stumbled across that paper in town, she could relax. With the right shading and contouring, she now looked nothing like her picture.

Humming softly to herself, she straightened up the bathroom, picked up the clothes she'd washed out and made her way to one of the stalls to hang them up. She was almost finished when she heard Austin behind her. "The bathroom's all yours," she said lightly, her eyes on the jeans she was spreading out on the top rail of the stall. "And don't worry, I left you plenty of hot water."

Hardly hearing her, he stared incredulously at her brassy red curls. "What the hell have you done to yourself?"

His angry snarl fairly shook the walls of the barn, but Gabby refused to let him shake her newly found confidence, as well. Smoothing a pant leg one last time, she turned, her smile not quite as steady as she would have liked. "It's the new me," she said gaily. "What do you think?"

For a long moment, he just stared at her, his gray eyes sweeping over her, growing colder with every change he noted in her appearance. "You look like a hooker," he finally said harshly. "Get back in the bathroom and wash it all off."

His words lashed at her like the sting of a whip. Surprised that he could hurt her so easily, all the joy fell from her face. "No."

"You'll do it or I'll do it for you."

Her chin came up at that. "You and whose army?"

It was just that simple. With four words, she set fire to a temper he hadn't even known he had until he met her. Swearing, he reached for her. "Just remember, you asked for it!"

She slipped from his fingers like smoke and turned to run. "No! Damn it, Austin, you're not my father! I don't have to answer to—"

His arm whipped around her waist, bringing her up hard against him. "No, I'm not your father," he growled in her ear, grunting as she pushed her elbow into his chest. "That's the whole damn problem!"

Cursing him, she squirmed and kicked and clawed until her breath was tearing through her lungs and her heart slamming against her ribs. With a last, desperate effort, she twisted out of his hands. But before she could take two steps, his fingers clamped around her left arm like a vice, jerking her back to him. "No!"

"Oh, yes—"

He broke off in surprise when the force of her weight colliding with his chest sent him staggering backward. He never saw the bucket on the ground behind him, and in the next instant he was falling into a pile of hay and dragging her down with him.

He landed on his back with Gabby sprawled on top of him, her face only inches from his. Shock vibrated through him and was echoed in the sudden pounding of her heart against his. Somewhere in the back of his mind, a voice warned him to let her go. Now! But she was too close, the feel of her in his arms too much like one of his fantasies. He saw awareness widen her eyes, felt her arms stiffen to push herself free. But it was too late. With a muttered curse, he tangled his fingers in her still-wet hair and pulled her mouth down to his.

Chapter 4

Heat. It poured through Gabby in waves, surprising her, stunning her. She wanted to protest, but the words wouldn't come; to struggle, but her bones were already dissolving, her pulse thudding. Her head ordered her to push out of his arms while she still could, but her heart whispered, *Stay*. Her fingers curled into the worn material of his work shirt, clutching at him for dear life as his tongue plundered her mouth. She'd been kissed before, by men she was convinced were more interested in her money than in her, but never like this. Never by a man who didn't want to, but couldn't seem to stop himself. He took her mouth with a raw hunger that seeped into her like the gathering clouds of a storm—dark, enticing and dangerous. Whatever walls she thought to erect were swept away in the thundering echo of her heartbeat.

Sweet. He groaned at the taste of her, his fingers tightening in her hair, his arm around her waist clamping her to him. He hadn't expected her to be so sweet, so soft in his arms, her mouth so eager under his. From the moment he'd met her, he'd known she was a mass of contradicting depths that a man could lose himself in if he wasn't careful, but nothing had prepared him for this. Woman and girl, wanton and innocent. Dear God, this was no child in his arms, but a woman, small and feminine, with a body that could tempt a man to madness. His hands, desperate to touch, moved over her, blindly searching over her new jeans and shirt for the sensuous curves beneath. At her soft gasp of surprise, of pleasure, desire clenched like a fist in his gut, drawing a growl from deep in his throat. She was so responsive, her kiss so giving, so bewitchingly untutored....

Woman. Innocent. Untutored.

The words clashed in his mind even as he realized he wanted her now more than he could ever remember wanting any woman after nothing more than a kiss. An *innocent* kiss, he thought as awareness suddenly raced through him, stunning him. Swearing at the effort it took to let her go, he wrenched his mouth from hers, his hands tangling in her hair again to hold her captive before him. His lips were only inches from hers. It took more concentration than he had to ignore the way her body lay sprawled on top of his. "How old are you?" he demanded tightly.

Shocked, breathless, her lips still throbbing, Gabby never thought to lie. "Twenty-six."

"Twenty—" He broke off abruptly, his mind reeling. Twenty-six! And he'd thought she was just a teenager! Feeling like a fool, he rolled her off of him and quickly rose to his feet to glare down at her. Damn it, he wanted some answers, and he wanted them right now! "Then why the hell are you traveling around the countryside pretending to be a kid?"

"I never pretended to be anything," she retorted indignantly. Refusing to let him glower down at her anymore, she scrambled to her feet and glared right back. "*You* decided I was a kid. Don't blame me because you thought I was a runaway. I never said anything to give you that impression."

"No, but you're sure as hell running from something," he tossed back. "What is it, Gabby? What are you running from? Did you rob a bank? Skip bail? What, for heaven's sake? A twenty-six-year-old woman doesn't hop trains with nothing more than the clothes on her back without a damn good reason."

"I . . . I—" Oh, God, she wanted to tell him! Clenching her fists, she told herself not to mistake the desire he'd stirred in her for anything but what it was. She couldn't start to trust him, couldn't let down her guard because of a kiss. But, oh, how she wanted to! "I have my reasons," she finally said huskily. "Let's just leave it at that."

He wanted to shake her, to kiss her senseless. But if he touched her now . . . Swearing, he refused to finish the thought and said instead, "I've got just one more question, then. Just how experienced are you?"

It was the last question she'd been expecting, the only one he could have asked that could be answered without words. A fiery blush singed her cheeks, telling him everything he wanted to know.

A muscle ticked along his jaw. "A virgin," he said flatly. "You're a virgin."

He threw the words at her like an accusation, but she only lifted her chin. "Yes."

So innocent, so proud. Grinding his teeth against the desire still heating his blood, Austin told himself there was no way in hell he'd touch her now. Trouble. Hadn't he known she was trouble from the moment he'd laid eyes on her? He should have listened to his instincts and walked away from her then and there.

He glared at her irritably. "Have you been hiding in a cave all your life or what? In this day and age, no one reaches the age of twenty-six without... without..."

She made herself finish his sentence. "Without making love?" She shrugged. "There were reasons."

"Which you have no intention of sharing with me. Fine," he said in disgust. "You keep your secrets, little girl. If you don't want to tell me, I'm not interested. Just stay out of my way, okay?"

He stormed past her and slammed into the bathroom, leaving behind a silence that seemed to vibrate with every beat of Gabby's racing heart. In the bathroom, the shower sprang on angrily. Heat cascaded through her body as she suddenly found herself bombarded with images of Austin furiously stripping off his clothes and stepping under the stinging spray. She could almost see the water streaming down his lean body.

"No!" Suddenly realizing what she was doing, she hurried into the tack room, which she had been using as a bedroom for the past two nights, shut the door and threw herself down onto the narrow cot that was squeezed up against one wall. Here the sound of the shower was muffled, the air filled with the pounding of her own heart as she fought to hold back the memory of his hard, demanding kiss.

What was she going to do?

Nothing in her past had prepared her for a man like Austin. She had never been the type of woman who could draw men like bees to honey. Sarah had always been the pretty one, the daring one, who could draw a man from across a crowded room with just a smile. When she'd married last year, after being in love countless times since she was sixteen, Gabby had felt no envy. She'd been too reticent, too wrapped up in her studies to become too strongly attracted to anyone. And always at the back of her mind was the fear of how a man would react to her "condition." So she'd retreated into her own world, and none of the tame, uninteresting men who'd found the nerve to come courting the wealthy Gabriella Winters had tempted her in the least.

From the lackluster kisses she'd received, she'd thought she wasn't the type to stir passion in a man. With just a kiss, Austin had shown her how wrong she was. But oh, what a kiss! Hot, wet, wildly seductive. Even now she could taste him on her tongue, feel his body grow hard as hers had melted like candle wax. If he'd decided to press for more than a kiss, she didn't know if she'd have been able to stop him.

She had to get away. He'd introduced her to something that was out of her league, tempted her with something she couldn't have. He could make her forget why she was running, forget why she couldn't trust him or anyone else. And that, more than anything, terrified her. He was a weakness she couldn't afford. She'd leave just as soon as they finished this job, she decided. Before he discovered who she was, before he had a chance to turn her over to Baxter, before he hurt her in a way no one else ever had. She wouldn't stop until she'd put the width of the country between them.

She closed her eyes with a sigh, convinced she'd made the right decision. But the relief she expected to feel didn't come. Instead, a lightning quick flash of pain streaked through her head and was followed almost immediately by a slight tingling in her left hand.

"Oh, no!"

She tensed, knowing it was the last thing she should do, but unable to stop herself as she recognized the old, familiar warning she always got before a seizure. It was always the same. The pain in her head, then a numbness in her hand, sometimes minutes, sometimes hours before she would suddenly find herself falling into a dark void of unconsciousness.

Her doctor had told her she was one of the lucky ones. Epilepsy could take many uncontrollable, violent forms, and she should be thankful that hers was so mild. But she didn't feel lucky whenever she woke from a seizure battling a lethargy that drained her and headaches that she could only escape in long hours of sleep.

Stay calm. Relax. Don't fight it and it'll go away.

The words flowed through her like a drug, easing the tension that gripped her. Through the years, she'd learned to control her condition to a certain extent, fighting it alone in the dark, private corners of her mind. But stress was her biggest enemy, always waiting in the shadows to yank her back down to reality whenever she made the mistake of thinking she had finally gained the upper hand. If she didn't stop the seizure before it began in earnest, she would once again lose the battle.

Slowly, deliberately, she cleared her mind of every thought, willing herself to calmness. Time and place slipped away, the only sound she heard was the beating of her heart. With a concentration that was vital, she turned all her attention to eliminating the tingling sensation in her hand. Only when it was completely gone would she win.

Twenty minutes later, she was somewhere between consciousness and sleep when Austin knocked on the tack room door. "You're going to miss supper if you don't get a move on it, Gabby," he said brusquely through the door. "You know the guys won't wait on you. C'mon, before everything's gone."

She jerked back to awareness, horrified. The tingling had stopped in her hand, but her head was throbbing and would continue to do so until she got some sleep. She couldn't let Austin see her this way! She couldn't handle any more questions, not now. And even if she had been hungry, the thought of enduring the inquisitive eyes of the other hands who would be at supper in the small mess hall behind the farmhouse was enough to kill her appetite.

Turning toward the wall, she pulled the cot's rough army blanket over her with closed eyes. "You go on without me. I'm not hungry," she called huskily, praying he would let it lie at that.

Austin scowled at the closed door. The woman was driving him nuts! One minute she was going up in flames in his arms, and the next she was hiding behind a door, refusing to face him. She was twenty-six years old, for God's sake! There was no reason to be embarrassed over a simple kiss.

If that was a simple kiss, a voice in his head taunted, *then the Grand Canyon's nothing but a hole in the ground!*

Cursing the thought, he jerked open the door and stepped inside. "Don't be ridiculous. You've got to eat—'' He broke off abruptly, his dark brows snapping together at the sight of her curled up on the cot in the dark. "What's wrong?"

"Nothing!" she said quickly, then winced as he flicked on the overhead light. "Austin, please, would you just go away and leave me alone," she pleaded as she turned her face into the pillow. "I'm not hungry."

He might have believed her if he hadn't caught sight of her pale cheeks and pain-clouded eyes before she turned away from him. His footsteps echoed hollowly against the wooden floor as he crossed the small room and came to a stop right next to the cot. His fingers itched to delve into her outrageously red curls, but he kept his hands stubbornly at his sides. "What's wrong?" he asked again, this time quietly. "Are you sick?"

She burrowed deeper into the pillow. "No."

"Don't lie to me, Gabby. I can see you're not feeling well." Unable to stop himself, he sat down on the edge of the cot and fought the need to touch. But it was a battle he knew he was destined to lose. Her vulnerability defeated him when nothing else could. Before he'd realized his intentions, he was gently rubbing her back. "Maybe I can help. What is it? Tell me."

During the past few days, she'd learned to deal with his anger, his rudeness, his hooded glances. She had no defenses against his unexpected concern, no weapons against the gentleness she'd never suspected lay beneath his stern exterior. Silly, weak tears flooded her eyes, and she could do nothing to stop them. "It's just a headache," she sniffed.

His fingers moved up to the nape of her neck and slowly kneaded the tenseness he found there. "A migraine?" he guessed.

It was as close to the truth as she could allow him to come. Sighing under the skillful working of his hands, she admitted, "I get them sometimes. It'll go away in a couple of hours."

If he hadn't come in, she would have lain there in the dark, suffering, and never said a word. What type of life had she come from, he wondered, that forced her to fight all her battles alone?

Rising to his feet, he ran his hand over her hair in a caress that was as soft as a sigh, then moved to switch off the light. "You just lie there and relax. I'll be back in a minute."

His long legs carried him out of sight before she'd even realized he was leaving, but within seconds, he was back. A dark shadow silhouetted by the light that streamed in through the open door, he moved to the cot, once again sitting down next to her. "Here. I brought you a glass of water and some aspirin," he said gruffly into the silence. "They're not strong enough to knock a migraine, but they should help some."

Gabby stared at the pills in his large hands, knowing they wouldn't help at all. But she didn't have the heart to tell him. Pushing up on her elbow, she took the water and popped the aspirin into her mouth. "Thanks." Giving him a weak smile, she dropped back down on the pillow and tried not to notice how his hip nudged hers. "You should go on to supper. There won't be anything left."

"In a minute." His hand came out of the darkness to push her hair back from her face. "Close your eyes."

"Austin, please—"

"Sh," he growled, pressing his fingers to her mouth. "I just want to make you more comfortable."

How could she be comfortable when the feel of his fingers against her lips made her ache deep inside? she wondered wildly, swallowing a sob. She didn't know herself when he was so near, touching her, stirring her senses with nothing more than the brush of skin against skin. Her heart was already pounding. She should make him move. The room was too dark, the cot too small and inviting. And the last thing she wanted was for him to be nice to her. But even as the thoughts registered, her eyes drifted shut with a will of their own.

Whatever she was expecting, it wasn't the cool, wet washcloth he slowly rubbed across her face. Startled, her eyes flew open. "What—"

"Easy," he whispered, sliding the cloth across her brow and temples. "It's just a wet rag. It won't cure your headache, but it'll make you feel better. Just close your eyes and enjoy."

It would have been impossible not to. He left no part of her face untouched, moving the cloth with feathery lightness over her hot cheeks, down her nose and around her mouth, dragging coolness across her flushed skin. She knew she should protest, but she couldn't seem to find the strength. Within seconds she was floating.

Austin watched the makeup come off with every sweep of the washcloth, revealing inch by inch the clear translucency of her skin. This was how she belonged—her face naked, unguarded, relaxed in pleasure, her lips parted on a sigh. All he had to do was replace the cloth with his mouth, and he could turn her sighs to moans.

His hand froze at her cheek, his palm cupping it as his thumb moved to her full lower lip. She was a virgin, he reminded himself, then cursed himself for needing the reminder. He'd kissed her, held her in his arms, but nothing had changed. He was a loner, a man who didn't have room in his life for ties. Before a woman had a chance to want anything deep or lasting from him, he always moved on—to another book, another lecture, another area of research. He wouldn't leave regrets behind him.

Releasing her, he rose quickly to his feet before he could be tempted to change his mind. "I'll bring you back something from supper," he said stiffly. "Here. Put this on your forehead and try to get some sleep."

For a long, silent moment, she ignored the washcloth he held out to her, her eyes searching his for the reason for his sudden withdrawal. But his face was in shadows, his shoulders rigid, the tension between them suddenly awkward. Gabby could almost see the kiss they'd shared replaying in his head, as it was in hers. Wordlessly, she took the cool cloth from him. "Thank you," she whispered in a voice that sounded nothing like her own. "If I'm asleep when you come back, don't wake me. It'll only make the headache worse."

She draped the cloth over her eyes and forehead, shutting him out. For a long, silent moment, he stared at her, then quietly moved to the door and shut it behind him on his way out.

All during supper, he told himself he'd done everything he could for her, so there was no reason to feel as though he had abandoned her. She was a grown woman and obviously well used to handling an occasional migraine. Alone. She didn't need him or his help; that, too, was just the way he wanted it. She might still be as innocent as the day she was born, but that didn't change the fact that she was some old man's rich little girl who had stumbled into his world by mistake. The sooner she was out of it, the better for both of them.

Satisfied that he'd finally put her out of his mind, he was determined not to rush back to the barn to check on her as soon as the meal was finished. A couple of the other hands were old hoboes who had, through the years, gradually become migrant workers who followed the crops by hopping the trains. He needed to sit down with them to see what kind of stories he could get out of them for his book. But ten minutes after the table had been cleared, he found himself heading for the barn.

He found her lying on her back just as she had been when he'd left her, the washcloth over her eyes, her face turned partially away from him. Setting the tray he'd brought her on a nearby barrel, Austin let his gaze roam over her. She looked so small under the rough army blanket, her cheeks still pale in the light that streamed in through the door, her breathing slow and steady as she slept. If she was still in pain, there was no sign of it on her face.

The relief that coursed through him should have been nothing more than what he would have felt for anyone who'd been suffering, but he knew there was a hell of a lot more to it than that. She was getting to him in ways he hadn't thought possible. When was the last time he wanted to hold a woman while she slept? he wondered. He couldn't even begin to remember. She was interfering with his work, damn it, intruding on his thoughts, his time, as if she had every right to claim a part of him!

What did he know about her? he wondered in growing resentment. Next to nothing. She was a rich twenty-six-year-old virgin running from something, something that always brought a haunted look to her eyes. Whatever it was, he would not get sucked into it! She could keep her problems and her soft skin and helpless brown eyes to herself, he decided as he turned and walked out. He had a deadline, and come hell or high water, he wasn't missing it because of a woman.

When Gabby woke hours later, the barn was pitch-black, shrouded in a silence that only comes with the dead of night. Disoriented, she lay unmoving, listening for Baxter's familiar snores down the hall. Instead, she heard the soft keening of the wind as it raced around the corner of the barn. The sleep clouding her brain like a fog parted, giving her glimpses of yesterday: her picture in the paper; a kiss that had lost none of its potency with the passage of time; the seizure she'd just barely prevented.

In the light of day, she knew the closeness of the three near disasters would once again tie her nerves in knots, but in the comforting shadows of the night, she didn't have the strength to worry. Her head was no longer hurting, the tingling in her hand had stopped, and she was starving. Tomorrow would take care of itself, but for now she had to find something to eat.

Throwing off the covers, she silently padded over to the doorway, then switched on the light. A tray of fruit and cheese sat on a barrel at the other end of her cot. Staring at it, Gabby felt hot tears sting her eyes. Austin had promised to bring her back something from supper, but fruit and cheese wasn't the normal fare for the hands. He must have told Frank Jones about her not feeling well and got it from him. A warm tide of emotion flowed through her as she settled back down on her cot and reached for an orange. Austin took every opportunity to make it clear he thought she was more trouble than she was worth, then turned around and went out of his way to help her. Would she ever understand him?

She'd hardly made a dent in the food when she felt his eyes on her. Glancing over her shoulder, she found him standing in the doorway dressed in nothing but jeans, which looked as if they had been hastily pulled on. Her mouth went dry at the sight of him. His black hair was tousled and unruly from sleep, his jaw shadowed with a night's growth of dark whiskers, his chest lean, powerful and bronze. But it was his eyes that made her insides soften like ice cream left too long in the sun. As hard as stone and diamond sharp, they burned with a heat that set the silence between them sizzling.

"Are you all right?"

The quiet question sent a shudder rippling down her back. She nodded, her voice gone, along with the peace of mind that had been hers when she'd thought he was sound asleep in an empty stall at the opposite end of the barn. Swallowing the orange slice that threatened to lodge in her throat, she struggled to break the continuing silence. "I'm ... much better."

Austin nodded. His eyes had told him the same thing the minute he'd stepped into the doorway. Her brown eyes were clear and free of pain, her cheeks flushed with a becoming color. The vulnerability that had made him ache to take her into his arms was gone, and in its place was a sleepy sensuousness that still made him ache to take her into his arms. If he had any sense, he'd get the hell out of her doorway before he did something stupid. But he never moved.

Unable to sit still under his penetrating gaze a moment longer, Gabby rose jerkily to her feet. "I forgot to thank you for the fruit. Would you like some?"

Eve, in all her innocence, couldn't have tempted Adam more sweetly. Austin stood firmly where he was and ground his teeth in frustration. "I don't think so."

His voice was like sandpaper rubbing across her nerve endings. The width of the room was still between them, but suddenly it was imperative that she put more emotional distance between them. "I've decided to head west just as soon as we're finished here," she announced tightly. "I want to see the Rockies. What about you? Where are you going?"

He didn't even hesitate. "Florida."

She should have been relieved, but all she felt was...empty. She wrapped her arms around her middle. "I see. Well, then, I guess we'll be parting company in a few days."

"Yes."

If he regretted it, there was no trace of it in his blunt reply. Ignoring the hurt that twisted her heart, she forced a smile. "There doesn't seem to be anything else left to say."

"No, I guess not. Just good night." And before either of them could change their mind, he stepped out of the doorway and shut the door, leaving her as she had always been. Alone.

The next three days passed in a whirlwind of activity. Now that they'd made the decision to part, it seemed as if Austin couldn't finish their painting job fast enough. He had them both up at first light and painting by the time the sun peeked over the horizon. Except for the briefest of breaks and lunches, they didn't stop until darkness forced them to. Even the weather cooperated, providing warm, dry days that were perfect for painting.

Before Gabby was ready for it to be over, the job was finished. Pleased with their work, Frank Jones paid them in full, then dropped them off at the small railroad yard on the east side of town that evening. Austin checked in the brakey's shack for the trains they wanted, and then there was nothing left to do but say goodbye. Shoving her hands into the back pockets of her jeans, Gabby hunched down into her jacket. "Well, I guess this is it," she said softly.

A hundred yards down the tracks, a yard switcher moved cars, breaking up trains to create new ones, while underneath their feet, the ground vibrated from the two-thousand-horsepower engines that were warming up for departure. Unobserved in all the activity, Austin pulled her into the dark shadows at the edge of the yard. "The brakey said the yard bulls are on the prowl because of a string of robberies, so be careful to stay out of sight until it's time to go." Releasing her abruptly, he nodded toward a long train of loaded cars on the far track. "That's your ride over there. You stay on that train, and it'll take you straight to Denver."

Deep inside her pockets, Gabby's hands curled into fists as she told herself this was for the best. But why did things that were for the best always seem to hurt so much? "When does it leave?"

"Ten minutes. They'll be hooking up the air hoses any second."

So she had no time to waste. Swallowing the lump in her throat, her eyes found his in the darkness. "Which one will you be taking?"

"The one the switcher's putting together now. It doesn't leave for another couple of hours."

She would be miles away before he even hopped his train. Horrified, she felt hot tears sting her eyes. No! She couldn't cry! Not now. Ever since they'd met, he'd made it clear he thought she was nothing but a spoiled baby who couldn't even run away from home without help. She couldn't let him see that it was tearing her apart to walk away from him. She knew the dangers of depending on anyone but herself. She didn't need him. Straightening her shoulders, she pasted on a smile the old Gabriella Winters would have been proud of. "I want to thank you for all you've done for me."

Austin stared down at her, his gray eyes shuttered. Even in the shadows he could clearly see her face, the heavy makeup that covered her clear skin, the black eyeliner that emphasized her impossibly large eyes, her mop of brazen red curls. Rage filled him. Damn it, did she know what she looked like? Did she know what kind of trouble she was headed for? Even without the makeup, a man had only to look at her mouth to crave the taste of it. With her lips parted in a smile, glistening with a lipstick that made them look wet and inviting, was it any wonder that it took all his self-control not to jerk her into his arms?

"No thanks are necessary," he said in a gravelly voice. Dragging his eyes from hers, he looked past her to where her train waited on the tracks like a dark shadow. "You'd better go before it's too late. They're almost through with the air hoses."

"I . . . yes . . . goodbye." Her whisper was as soft as the kiss she impulsively brushed against his rough cheek. She felt his start of surprise, his sudden stiffness, and suddenly the need to cling was more than she could bear. Forcing back a sob, she quickly whirled and walked away without looking back.

Head down, heart pumping, she hurried across the rows of tracks, darting in and out of shadows with abandon. Almost stumbling in her haste, she didn't slow down until she reached her train, and then only because she was too blinded by tears to see which boxcars were empty. Swearing, she dragged the back of her hand across her streaming eyes, only to stop dead at the sight of the brakeman heading straight for her, his lantern swinging in the night. She paled and glanced around wildly. But she was trapped. Caught between two trains with no empty boxcars to climb into, there was nowhere to hide.

Suddenly, without warning, an arm snaked out of the darkness to whip around her waist. Before she could even think to scream, a large male hand clamped over her mouth.

"Over here," Austin said in a low voice in her ear as he pulled her toward the train on their right. "Slip underneath."

She went limp at the sound of his voice, until she realized what he'd said. *Underneath!* He had to be crazy! If the train started to move, they'd be crushed.

"It's the only way," he growled, jerking her closer when she shook her head violently. "Damn it, Gabby, this is no time to be stubborn." And without another word, he pushed her head down and pulled her under the train with him.

The darkness was thicker here, cloying, the air as still as that before a storm. Her heart hammering, Gabby stared at the iron wheel that was right next to her head. Dark and threatening, it smelled of oil and dust and metal. Oh, God, what could she do if it started to move?

Austin felt her terror, the desperation as she clung to his hand with a strength he didn't think she was even aware of. But there was nothing he could do to reassure her now except hold her tightly. The brakey was growing closer with each step, his light destroying the darkness wherever it touched. He was checking the brakes on the Denver-bound train, but if he happened to glance around, to hear so much as the shifting of gravel under their feet, they would be caught.

Seconds stretched into an eternity, the brakeman's light growing so strong that Austin could see Gabby's whitened knuckles as her fingers tightened around his. Holding their breath, their nerves stretched taut, they waited to be discovered. But the other man never even looked their way. Humming softly to himself, he continued on down the line.

The minute he was out of earshot, they scrambled out from under the train. Shaking, Gabby whispered, "Oh, God, that was close! Suddenly he was right there in front of me and I didn't know what to do. How did you know I was in trouble?"

The light in his eyes was rueful. "Instinct."

It wasn't very flattering, but Gabby was too puzzled by his sudden appearance to notice. "What are you doing here? I thought you were going to wait across the yard for your train."

He'd thought the same thing until he'd watched her walk away. He'd told himself to let her go now that she was actually willing to leave him in peace, but then he'd seen the brakeman heading for her. The protectiveness that surged in him had had him hurrying to her rescue without a thought to the consequences. Rescuing maidens in distress was becoming damn habit-forming, but what was he supposed to do? She was a virgin painted up like a streetwalker, and he couldn't just turn his back on her. It wasn't as if he had to do the rest of his research on the train to Miami. He could do it anywhere.

He knew he was rationalizing, going in circles around a point he wasn't sure he was ready to face. He couldn't let her walk away. Not yet. But that was something he had no intention of telling her. "I've never been west, either. Maybe I'll go on out to L.A. and spend the winter there."

He was going with her. Relief shot through her, along with a happiness that was so close to joy it scared her. When had he become so important to her?

He lifted a brow at her silence. "If you don't object to sharing a boxcar with me."

Heat burned her cheeks. "Oh, no, of course not."

"Then we'd better find one quick," he said as the air brakes hissed. "This baby's leaving any second."

The train was heavily loaded, but they quickly found a car near the end of the line, its door opened wide to the yawning blackness inside. Throwing his pack inside, Austin hoisted Gabby up, then quickly followed. They hadn't even caught their balance when the train started to move.

Laughing, her eyes adjusting to the lack of light, Gabby turned to tell Austin how much easier it was to get into a boxcar when you had a man to help you. The words died unspoken on her tongue. At the opposite end of the boxcar, four pairs of eyes watched their every move.

Chapter 5

Damn!"

Austin's softly muttered curse was so low it was almost drowned out by the gathering roar of the iron wheels on the tracks, but Gabby heard it. A shiver raced over her skin. Suddenly the acrid scent of danger was in the air, the menace that radiated from the men who watched them almost tangible. Slowly, but with little subtlety, she drew closer to Austin.

"Get behind me," he said through his teeth, never taking his eyes from their companions. "In the corner."

Her heart banging against her ribs, she jumped to obey the terse order, backing up until her back was flush against the wall. Fear clutched at her throat. In the darkness that filled the boxcar, she caught the gleam of wine bottles in the men's hands as they stepped threateningly toward Austin. She didn't have to see their faces clearly to know that they were the type who turned ugly when they drank.

"She your woman?"

The question came from the biggest one, a towering giant, who Austin judged outweighed him by a good fifty pounds. He nodded. "Yeah."

His easy answer jolted through Gabby like an electric shock. He'd claimed her without blinking an eye, his ready stance daring anyone, including her, to make something of it. Her throat dry, her mind blank, she couldn't think of a single reason to protest.

The men they faced, however, had no such constraint. If they'd been sober, they might have heeded the warning glint in Austin's eyes, but the alcohol gave them false courage. The smallest one looked to his buddies for support, then sneered, "We don't hear her saying anything. Maybe she'd like a little variety."

Austin didn't even look at her. "Gabby?"

She blanched as four pairs of eyes turned hungrily on her. "No! I...I'm with him!"

It was not the answer they wanted. "Only because you haven't had us," the smallest one assured her with an evil grin. "Now why don't you come on over here and join us. Your friend can't protect you, since there's four of us and only one—"

"Two," Austin corrected silkily, sliding his switchblade from his pocket in the time it took one heartbeat to change to another. "And the lady carries a mean pair of scissors. By my calculations, that makes four against four." Swishing the blade in front of himself so they could see its sharp edge in the darkness, he flashed them a smile that was cold and deadly. "Since you're drunk, I'd say the odds aren't in your favor, gentlemen. Any bets?"

Gabby could almost swear she could hear the men's hearts pounding like a runaway train in the growing silence. Fascinated by the knife, they stared at it, dazed, until Austin jabbed it at them, silently demanding an answer.

"No!"

"Now wait just a minute—"

"We don't want no trouble...."

They backed up so fast, it would have been comical if there hadn't been such an ugly light in their eyes. Austin didn't relax his guard by so much as a flicker of an eyelash. "Then I suggest you go back to what you were doing and leave us alone. That way, we'll all get along just fine."

"Sure, if that's what you want."

"There ain't no need to get so damn touchy."

"We was just looking for a little fun."

They went back to their end of the boxcar like rats scurrying into the darkness, grumbling all the way. Shuddering, Gabby sank to the floor and tried not to imagine what their idea of fun was. If Austin hadn't been there...

"You all right?"

He moved to her side and took a position right next to her, his shoulder brushing hers as the swaying train picked up speed. She nodded, her smile shaky. "This is becoming a habit."

He frowned. "What?"

"Your coming to my rescue," she said in a low voice that didn't carry to the men across the car. "I don't understand it. I never got into trouble before I met you. But now, every time I turn around, I find myself in desperate need of a knight."

So she had noticed it, too, he thought as he stared at the men across the way, who had settled down to drink themselves into a stupor. Now he just had to figure out what the hell he was going to do about it. Determinedly keeping his eyes on the car's other occupants, he retorted, "It's called the Fair Maiden Syndrome. Women who live in ivory towers seem to be the most susceptible. Don't make the mistake of thinking I'm some kind of Prince Charming."

Was that what she was doing? Unconsciously living out a fairy tale and imagining herself attracted to something he wasn't? Turning her head, she studied his hard face in the darkness. No, he was no prince, and most of the time he was less than charming. It wasn't compassion that had driven him to come to her rescue, but something else, something he deeply resented but couldn't seem to control.

Any more than she could control the longing that swept over her whenever she thought of his kiss. "I'll remember that," she said quietly. "But just for the record, I'm not looking for a prince any more than you're looking for a princess."

The mocking lift of his brow clearly expressed his disbelief, but before he could say anything, his eyes narrowed on the drunks. He stiffened. "I hope to hell you've still got those scissors. It looks like you may need them."

Alarmed, Gabby's eyes flew across the boxcar. The men were still propped up against the wall, guzzling their booze, but they were now talking among themselves and shooting angry glances across the car. Fumbling for the catch on her purse, she quickly jerked out her scissors and inched closer to Austin. "You think they'd really try something?"

"Who knows?" He shrugged, his mouth flattening in disgust as he watched them swill the wine as if there were no tomorrow. "But I'm not taking my eye off them till we get off this train. If they make so much as a move toward us, they're going to regret it."

The men didn't make the mistake of leaving their end of the boxcar, but neither did they pass out, as Gabby had secretly hoped. Huddled in their corner as the train raced into the night, they ignored the steady, lulling motion of the car and stared unblinkingly at Gabby and Austin. They were waiting for them to fall asleep, she realized, stiffening. And her eyes were already heavy.

As if reading her mind, Austin said quietly, "It's going to be a long night. Don't get too comfortable or those guys'll be on us before you can blink."

Her body didn't need comfort to fall asleep when she was tired to the point of exhaustion after the past few days of frantic painting. Sitting up straighter, she unbuttoned her coat and let the cool night air rush in. She shivered, her head instantly clearing. But five miles down the track, her mind once again began to cloud with sleep.

Austin nudged her awake, cursing her softness as she leaned heavily against him, cursing the way he wanted to enfold her in his arms and pull her across his lap. What the hell was the matter with him? How could he continue to ache for a woman who was so obviously out of her element in his world? Hadn't he learned a long time ago that he couldn't expect a woman to view his work and the places his work took him the same way he did?

Once, when he'd still been working on his Ph.D., he'd made the mistake of taking a woman with him to the Indian reservation where he was researching his dissertation. He hadn't been in love with her, but they'd been lovers and he'd wanted her with him. He could still see her face when she'd discovered there was no electricity, no air conditioning, no shopping malls around the corner. Just as soon as she'd been able to get a ride, she'd hotfooted it back to civilization, where she belonged.

And Gabby was no different. She was here now only because something or someone had driven her away from her sheltered existence. He didn't doubt for a minute that she would run back to wherever she came from just as soon as the opportunity presented itself.

But that still didn't stop him from wanting to drag her off the train the first chance he got and kiss her senseless. Damn it, what was he going to do with her?

The question beat at him all through the night, echoing in his head like the monotonous drone of the wheels on the rails. Time ceased to exist. The hoboes ran out of liquor and began to nod off, but Austin never relaxed his vigilance. At his side, Gabby, too, sat stiffly, shivering in the cold that kept her awake, too tired to even speak. And still the train raced on.

The morning brought new problems. The hoboes, now rested from the sleep they'd snatched, could see what the night had hidden from them. With her bright cap of curly red hair and her innocence hidden beneath heavy makeup, Gabby had the look of a woman who would know how to please a man. Austin didn't have to look in a mirror to know that the exhaustion lining Gabby's face was reflected in his own and was more than visible to the hoboes. If they didn't get off the train soon, they were going to be in a hell of a mess.

It was two hours, however, before the screeching of the brakes ripped through the silence that had descended over the boxcar. Tension crackled on the morning air. His body stiff from the rigid position he'd kept all night, Austin struggled to his feet and pulled Gabby up beside him, instantly drawing the hoboes' attention from the gradually slowing scenery outside the open door. Propelling her to the other door, he glanced out and saw that the train was stopping to pick up some cars on a spur on the edge of a small town. "This is where we get off," he told her quietly. "The minute we stop, jump down and get away from the tracks as quickly as possible."

The brakes hissed one more time, bringing the train to a jarring halt. Glancing around for any railroad employees, Gabby quickly scrambled over the side to the dirt road that ran beside the tracks. She turned expectantly toward the town in the distance, but Austin stopped her, taking her arm as the four hoboes joined them on the road and eyed her hungrily.

"This way," he said, tugging her after him in the other direction.

"But—"

"Don't argue with me, Gabby," he snapped, glancing back over his shoulder to make sure the other men weren't following them. "We're going this way."

Her stomach growled, reminding her how many hours it had been since she'd eaten. She pulled at her arm, but his grip was like a vice. "Damn it, Austin, I'm hungry! Let go. I want to go into town and get something to eat."

"It's not your stomach you should be worried about right now, woman," he retorted with a scowl. "Come on."

Gritting her teeth, she stumbled after him and tried to hang on to her temper. He was doing it again, ordering her around like a child, taking charge of her without so much as a by your leave. The man was a damn steamroller.

"Look," she ground out, "I know you don't run into many woman riding the train, but I think I should warn you that Stone Age etiquette went out with the dinosaurs. You try dragging a woman around by her hair today and all you're going to get for it is a swift kick where it will do the most good. What's your problem, anyway?"

"You!"

"Me!" she gasped, finally jerking free of his hold. "Now just a darn minute! I never asked you to come after me. You were going to Florida, remember? Then the next thing I know, you're dragging me under a train, trying to get us both killed!"

"What I was doing was saving your butt. If I hadn't come along when I had, you'd be in jail right now with nothing to do but twiddle your thumbs for the next twenty days."

"I would have thought of something—"

"And would you have thought of something when you found our four friends waiting for you in that boxcar?" he demanded, nodding toward the hoboes, who had already disappeared from view. "You look like you're ready to take on anything in pants. What would you have done if one of them would have grabbed you?" he demanded, suddenly dragging her into his arms. "What would you have done when a man showed you just how much he wanted you?" Before either of them had a chance to think, he brought his mouth down hard on hers.

He told himself he was just teaching her a badly
needed lesson. She wandered around the countryside
without a thought to the dangers she was courting.
Images of the four hoboes cornering her in the boxcar, taking what they wanted from her, hurting her,
violating her, flashed before his eyes. His hands tightened on her, anger at her naïveté, fury at the need even
now tightening in him. It was time she learned the taste
of a man who would not be denied.

He gave her an openmouthed carnal kiss of raw
hunger. His tongue pushed past her soft, tempting lips
to the dark recesses within, boldly seeking out her
tongue and rubbing sleek and hot against it. When
surprise held her motionless, he crushed her closer,
one hand slipping down to the base of her spine, urging her against him. His mouth moved over hers, demanding a response, his tongue filling her, teasing her,
tormenting her. When he finally felt her shudder, felt
her hands crawl up his arms to cling to his shoulders
as if the ground shifted beneath her, it was suddenly
difficult to remember who was teaching whom a lesson.

The anger drained out of him, leaving only desire.
It burned in his belly like an inferno. Tearing his
mouth from hers, his lips raced over her face, the
curve of her cheek, her eyes, the stubborn tilt of her
chin. "If you think you're ready to handle a man,
handle this," he rasped against her ear as his tongue
gently deflowered it, then tenderly bit the lobe. Before she could do anything but gasp, his hand slipped
into her open coat and found her breast. "Handle
me," he murmured, taking her into his palm as his
mouth returned to hers.

Passion broke over Gabby like a storm that had been building for days, for years, pulling at her, threatening to drag her down into a dark, swirling tempest that began and ended with the man who molded her to him as if he would draw her inside him. Her mind emptied of everything but the feel of his hand at her breast, the hot, intoxicating taste of his mouth on hers, the aching need that made her thighs melt and her body go soft against his hardness. Her breath tore through her lungs, her heart racing against his palm. Could he feel the longing in her? The craving that turned her bones to water?

Somewhere deep inside her the voice of reason warned her she couldn't let this continue. He was right. She couldn't handle him; she couldn't handle the way he could make her ache for him when she'd never before ached for any man. But then his teeth nipped at her bottom lip, ripping a moan from her, and she didn't want anything to do with reason. She only wanted him. "Austin, please...."

His name on her lips was a plea he couldn't ignore. Tangling his fingers in her hair, he claimed her mouth again and gave in to the passion that was clawing at him with hot fingers. His hands moved over her, fighting the clothes that hid the silkiness of her skin from him. He had to touch her. Just once, he promised himself.

A half a mile down the road, the train whistle blew sharply, shattering a quiet that was filled with husky murmurs and soft, ragged breathing. Reality jolted Gabby back to awareness.

What was she doing? "No!" she cried against his mouth, unsure of whether she was protesting the kisses they'd just shared or her own return to sanity. Her

breath straining, her eyes desperate, she pushed out of
his arms. "I don't want this," she whispered. "I
can't." He made it too easy to forget why she was
running, why she couldn't trust anyone but herself.

It was a lie and they both knew it, but at the moment, it was easier for him to accept the lie than the
consequences. With eyes as cold as glaciers, he swore
silently at the effort it took not to reach for her again.
"We're both tired," he said flatly. "I suggest we get
some sleep before we do something stupid."

Watching him move into the copse of trees that
shaded the left side of the road, she struggled between tears and ironic laughter. She'd felt the earth
move, and all he'd felt was something stupid, something that he'd turned away from in favor of sleep. If
she hadn't been so tired herself, she might have
stormed after him and told him if she was going to do
something stupid, she certainly wouldn't do it with
him. Instead, she stumbled after him through the trees
and collapsed ten feet away from him under an old,
gnarled oak. Stretching out on the rocky ground as if
she'd been doing it all her life, she'd hardly closed her
eyes before she was asleep.

The sun was high in the sky when she awoke, the air
Indian-summer warm. At her side, Austin lay on his
stomach, his head pillowed on his arms, sound asleep.
Careful not to make a sound, Gabby eased to a sitting position, her eyes transfixed on his face. It wasn't
often that she got the chance to study him unaware.
His dark hair had tumbled over his forehead, giving
him a boyish look that he never would have tolerated
had he been awake. There was nothing, however, even
remotely boyish about the sensuous line of his mouth.

She could still feel his lips pressed to hers, his tongue stealing her will with a thoroughness that left her weak.

Biting back a silent groan at the vivid memory, she soundlessly pushed herself to her feet and deliberately turned her back on him. This was madness! She couldn't just sit there, staring at him like an infatuated teenager with a bad case of puppy love.

She'd only intended to take a short walk in the woods to stretch her legs and work out the kinks the jarring train ride had put in her back, but then she caught the gurgling murmur of a creek somewhere in the distance. Intrigued, her throat as dry as sand, she wandered farther into the trees.

The creek, when she finally stumbled across it, wound through the woods, catching the sunlight that peaked through the trees. Gabby stopped abruptly at the sight of it, a delighted grin spreading across her face. Five feet wide at its widest spot, it was shallow and clear, running over smooth, rounded rocks, except for the spot directly in front of Gabby. There, it curved around a huge boulder to form a pool that was deep and slow moving and warmed by the sun.

Dropping to her knees on the low bank, she pulled her medicine from her purse, popped a pill into her mouth, then cupped her hands in the water for a long, cool drink. Water splashed down her chin, wetting her shirt, making her suddenly conscious of the dust and dirt that covered her and the unseasonable warmth of the day. Biting her lip, she stared down at the inviting coolness before her and knew she wasn't going to be able to resist it. A quick glance around assured her that Austin was still asleep three hundred yards away through the trees, and no one else was in sight. Why not? she thought with a grin, and began peeling off her clothes.

Seconds later, she laughed in surprise as she eased down into the cool water. It flowed over her flushed skin like silk. Oh, God, this was decadent! And positively wonderful! Why hadn't anyone ever told her how free she would feel swimming without a suit? The pool was only four feet deep, and she had only to stand to have the water lapping at her breasts and the sun warm on her naked skin. Lifting her face to the clear sky and her arms wide, she fell back into the water with a giggle and let herself sink to the bottom before shooting back to the surface, gasping for breath. Sighing in pleasure, she dropped onto her back to float, her breasts poking impudently out of the water. A contented smile played with her mouth as she closed her eyes. She could stay like this for hours.

Austin found her just like that fifteen minutes later. Standing over the clothes she'd left in an untidy pile, he stood as if turned to stone, unable to drag his gaze away from her. Her eyes were closed, her red hair floating sensuously in the clear water, her pale skin gleaming in the sunlight. Drops of water clung to the curve of her breasts and their rosy peaks, drawing his eyes like a magnet. Full and soft and inviting, they were made for a man's hands. His hands.

And if he had his hands on her right now, he honestly didn't know if he'd finish what they'd started earlier or throttle her! When he'd woke and found her gone, he hadn't been able to stop the panic that hit him. His first thought that she'd wandered off by herself and run into the hoboes from the train had sent him scouring the woods for her like a maniac. With every passing second, he'd grown more agitated, more worried. And all the while she'd been playing in the creek as naked as the day she was born!

Closing his mind to the heat pooling in his loins, he crossed his arms over his chest and scowled at her. "What the hell do you think you're doing?"

She jumped in surprise at the angry snarl and promptly floundered and sank. Water surged into her mouth and nose. Choking, she burst back to the surface, her hair dripping in her face, a red-hot blush stinging her in cheeks. "Austin! I—" She broke off, gasping at the almost physical touch of his eyes on her naked breasts. Groaning in dismay, she hastily sank back into the water till her shoulders were covered. "I—I thought you were sleeping!"

"Obviously," he growled, glaring at the sweetly lifted breasts that teased him through the clear water. He took a step toward her, realized what he was doing and snapped his eyes back up to hers, determined to keep them there. "What would you have done if one of the winos off the train had found you instead of me? Or the owner of this land? Are you trying to get raped, or what?"

"No, of course not—"

"Then what the hell are you doing?" he thundered. "Do you think a man can come across you naked and not want you?"

Suddenly they weren't talking about just any man, but him. She felt his eyes drop to her breasts, talking about just any man, but him. She felt his eyes drop to her breasts, stroking her beneath the coolness of the water, heating her from the inside out. She shivered, crossing her arms across her chest even though she knew it was too little protection, too late. "I'm sorry," she said huskily. "I didn't think."

"You'd better next time or you're going to be in over your head before you know what hit you."

Her arms tightened as images of him holding her, loving her, sweeping her into a dark world of passion flashed before her eyes. The hammering of her heart echoed deep inside her. Unconsciously, she licked her suddenly dry lips. "Yes. I will."

The slide of her tongue across her lips was almost his undoing. Turning his back on her abruptly, he snapped, "You'd better get out of that water before you freeze to death. You're starting to turn blue."

He took one step away from her clothes and planted his feet like an oak sinking roots. Gabby stared at his broad back and knew it was the only privacy he was going to give her. Gathering her courage, she waded cautiously out of the creek. He didn't move so much as a muscle, though she knew by his sudden tenseness that he was aware of her every movement behind him. Achingly vulnerable, she reached for her underwear.

Austin stared unblinkingly at the tree in front of him and found himself assaulted by the unexpectedly teasing sound of her getting dressed. The glide of silk panties over her thighs and hips, the jerky whisper of jeans over wet legs, the rasp of a zipper, the snap of her bra and the adjustment of straps over her shoulders. Piece by piece, his imagination tortured him with the image, stretching his control to the breaking point. It shattered when he heard her fingers fumbling with the buttons of her shirt.

Before he'd even realized his intentions, he whirled to face her and caught her with her shirt open down to her waist, the pink gossamer material of a bra that was nothing more than a promise peaking out at him from the parted material. He had, he decided instantly, two choices. He could either button her shirt immediately or strip it and the rest of her clothes from her and give in to the desire tearing him apart. Even as he reached for her, he wasn't sure which choice he was going to make.

Gabby froze at the touch of his fingers on her shirt. Her breath caught in her throat, she stared down at his hands, unable to move, to even lift her eyes to his. Could he hear her heart banging against her ribs like a sledgehammer? she wondered wildly. One touch, that's all it would take. One touch of his hand on her breast, and she wouldn't be accountable for her actions.

She waited an eternity, but the touch she held her breath for never came. Muttering under his breath, he jerked the edges of her shirt together and buttoned it as if she were a particularly bothersome child. If her heart stopped and his fingers trembled when the back of his knuckles brushed against her breasts, they both studiously ignored it.

When he was finished, he couldn't drop his hands away from her fast enough. "There," he said curtly, stepping back. "Now let's get the hell out of here. I'm hungry."

They walked into the small town of Weiner, Arkansas, without saying a word, each achingly aware of the other. Even if Gabby could have thought of something to say to break the tension between them, his set face would have stopped her. Wisely holding her tongue, she spoke only to order herself a hamburger at the local Dairy Queen.

The silence couldn't last, however. The minute they stepped out of the restaurant, he shot her a frown.

"What do you want to do? Find work around here somewhere or go on?"

Gabby didn't need to look at a map to know that they were still too close to Kentucky, too close to Baxter. "Go on," she said quickly. "We have enough money to last awhile, don't we?"

He nodded. "If we don't blow it on something stupid," he said, looking pointedly at her purse, where she'd stashed her makeup. "We'll have to wait until dark to catch another ride, so we might as well kill a few hours in the local jungle. Come on."

"Jungle?" she repeated, hurrying after him. "What are you talking about?"

"It's a . . . campsite where the hoboes hole up while they're waiting for the next train. There's bound to be one near the tracks somewhere. We can get the schedule there and catch up on the latest news."

They found an old sawmill and warehouse near the tracks, which looked as though they hadn't been used for years. Concealed by low, hanging trees and a wall of wild bamboo, they walked by it twice before they saw the narrow path almost hidden in the undergrowth.

Edging closer to Austin's back, Gabby followed him through the brush to a clearing of hard-packed earth. Not knowing what to expect, her eyes widened in surprise at the sight of the shanty town of huts that had been constructed under the trees. Packing cardboard, sections of thick paper, surplus wood and crates had been confiscated from the railroad through the years to create a community of sorts within spitting distance of the tracks.

At one end of the clearing, a bonfire was sheltered from the wind by a twisted hackberry tree. A grizzly old man, standing in the doorway of the nearest hut, warily watched them approach. He nodded at them stiffly. "What you folks need?"

Austin wasn't surprised by the man's suspicions. In his months of riding the rails, he'd discovered that the real hoboes could spot an outsider at first glance, regardless of how they were dressed. Information was only volunteered after an old-timer was sure you weren't there to run him off or turn him in to the yard bulls.

Smiling easily, Austin explained, "We're heading west, and we were hoping you could tell us when the next train leaves. We haven't been through here before and weren't sure if it was safe to ask at the brakey's shack."

"Well, now, that depends on whose shift it is," he drawled, rubbing his whiskered jaw. "If my memory serves me right, Clark's on days right now, and he can be mighty touchy. If his wife's been giving him trouble, he'd just as soon sic the bulls on you as look at you."

"Then we'll be sure to stay out of sight," Austin assured him. "When's the next ride out?"

The old man, sensing a kindred spirit, grinned. "There's a hotshot going through at eleven on its way to Kansas City. Used to catch it myself whenever I got a hankering for barbecue. They got real good food in Kansas City."

Austin's lips twitched. "Sounds like you've traveled around a bit."

It was the only encouragement the hobo needed. "Oh, yeah," he said with a sigh, a dreamy expression clouding his faded blue eyes. "I seen it all over the years. If I had some coffee, I'd invite you in and tell you all about it."

It was the hint Austin had been waiting for. The minute he'd seen the older man, he'd suspected he could supply all the information he needed to tie up his research. Digging quickly into his pocket, he glanced at Gabby. "Would you mind going back into town?"

She hesitated. The last thing she wanted to do was go into the cardboard shack behind the old man, but something in Austin's eyes told her he really wanted to talk to this man. Her fingers closed around the money he held out to her. "Cream and sugar?" she asked dryly.

He grinned. "Yeah. Thanks."

She slipped back through the brush, but they never noticed. Pulling up an apple crate, the hobo motioned for Austin to sit. "Yeah, I've seen a lot of changes over the years. When I first started hopping the trains back in the thirties, hoboes watched out for each other. They'd leave signs on the sides of barns and mailboxes telling each other where they could get a meal."

Austin leaned forward. "What kind of signs?"

"Well, like a chair meant you could get a sit-down supper. If one of the legs was broken, that meant you had to work for it. And if it had a cross on top, you might as well get ready 'cause you was gonna get a sermon along with the food." He shook his head sadly. "Most of those signs are gone now. Even the hoboes are different. Back then you'd find all sorts of craftsmen riding the trains. Wood-carvers, stonemasons. Hell, hoboes built half the courthouses and city squares in the South. They weren't bums, just men who wanted to be free. They'd carry everything they needed on their back and sleep wherever they laid their head, no matter what the weather was doing. You won't see that today, no sir.''

Snatching up the newspaper at his feet, he shoved it into Austin's hands and pointed to the picture under the headlines about an early blizzard in the plain states. "Look at that! Six inches of snow and I'll bet the Sally's full of tramps. Sissies," he said in disgust. "The Salvation Army's for people who're down on their luck, not dudes like us, who don't care about nothing but riding the trains. People just ain't got any independence anymore."

Austin scanned the article on the freaky weather and frowned. "Looks like this storm caught everybody by surprise. And it's heading this way."

"Yeah, it was supposed to be here tomorrow, but it got stalled in Nebraska. If you're going to Kansas City, you better find yourself some heavier duds. You'll freeze in what you got on."

"Yeah, well, maybe we'll find someplace around here to hole up until it blows through," Austin replied thoughtfully. "I wouldn't want to be caught in a boxcar when it hits."

He started to hand the paper back to the old man when his eyes snagged on a caption near the bottom of the page. "Heiress Still Missing." Normally, he would have skimmed over the story without really seeing it, but the name at the very beginning of the article reached out to grab him. He froze, the words of the short article driving into his head as he read:

Gabriella Winters, heir to the Winters cosmetic fortune, is still missing after an extensive five-day search. There has been no hint of foul play. Be-

cause of Ms. Winters's unstable mental condition, her doctor and family now fear she has
suffered some type of breakdown. She is on
medication. The reward for information leading
to her whereabouts has been raised to twenty-
thousand dollars by her stepfather, Baxter Hawthorne.

Next to the story was a picture of Gabby.

Chapter 6

It was her. There was no doubt in his mind. The makeup and the shorter, dyed hair certainly changed her appearance, but the woman who stared back at him from the picture had Gabby's big, too-innocent eyes, her stubborn chin, her sensuous smile. Damn it, what was Gabriella Winters, with all her millions, doing hopping the train like a common tramp? And what the devil did her family and doctor mean about her mental condition? He had just spent the better part of a week with her, and if she was unbalanced, he was the king of Siam! What the hell was going on?

"I'm back," Gabby sang out as she entered the clearing. "Sorry it took so long, but I passed a bakery on the way and couldn't resist it. Hope you like doughnuts."

Austin swore under his breath and hastily dropped the paper back to the ground. "Yeah, that's fine," he said quickly as he rose to his feet and took the sack of doughnuts from her so she could pass around the coffee. "But we'll have to hurry. We've got to ask around and see if we can find work before dark."

Gabby frowned in confusion. "Work? But I thought we were taking the next train west."

"You'd do better to stick around here for a while, gal," the older man said as he took the Styrofoam cup of coffee she handed him. "There's a nasty storm blowing this way, and you don't want to get caught in it."

Austin watched the emotions flicker across her expressive face. He had to bite his tongue to keep from asking her the myriad questions demanding answers in his brain. She didn't trust him any more now than when they had first met. If he pushed her for the truth, she would run from him just as she had from her family. And the last thing he wanted from her was fear. Watching her through narrowed eyes, he said, "I thought we'd stay here for a week or so, till the weather gets back to normal. If that's okay with you."

If she hadn't been so surprised that he was actually consulting her, she might have wondered why. As it was, she could hardly say she preferred to move on without explaining why. She shrugged unconcernedly. "We don't seem to have much choice in the matter."

"Smart girl," the hobo said in satisfaction. "People hereabouts are friendly. This is rice country, so you shouldn't have any trouble finding someone who needs an extra pair of hands, especially this time of year. You might try asking one of the waitresses at the café if they know anyone who could use you. They always know what's going on."

"We'll do that." Draining the last of his coffee, Austin offered the older man his hand. "Thanks for your help. We appreciate it."

"No more than I appreciate the coffee, son," he said, chuckling. "Good luck to you."

Just as the old man had predicted, a waitress at the café knew of two local farmers who were short-handed. One was a widow who had broken her arm three days before and the other was a man and his wife who had just had twins and were swamped with work. Since the new parents lived just on the outskirts of town, Gabby and Austin went there first.

As they approached the large, modern brick home surrounded by neat fields of rice and soybeans, Gabby's steps grew slower and slower as her heartbeat seemed to grow louder and louder. Had all her make-up washed off in the creek? she wondered wildly. She should have taken time to repair it. What if she was recognized? She grew pale at the thought and hastily finger combed her hair down into her face. Would Austin think she was out of her mind if she insisted on putting on fresh makeup before meeting the farmer and his wife?

"What's wrong?"

Austin's sharp question cut into her musings like the crack of a whip. Her eyes flew to his. "I . . . nothing."

"Are you having second thoughts about working here?"

"No." How could she possibly explain? "I . . . I don't like having to ask strangers for help."

Was that it or was she afraid she might be recognized? "Everyone needs help of one kind or another

during their life," he replied, watching her closely.
"It's nothing to be ashamed of."

"I'm not ashamed. It's just—"

"What?"

If I can't even trust my own family, how can I possibly trust a stranger? The words hovered on her tongue, but she'd already said more than she wanted to. "Nothing. I just haven't had much experience at this." Glancing up at the solid wooden door of the farmhouse, she stopped halfway up the walk, motioning for him to take the lead. "Since you're the one who seems to know what you're doing, I'll let you do the honors."

"Nothing to it," he predicted, striding past her and up the steps to the front porch.

The woman who answered the door was far too old to be the mother of newborn twins. Guessing her to be one of the babies' grandmothers, Austin said, "I'm looking for Mr. Thompson. We were told in town that he was looking for hired help."

The older woman pursed her lips, her deep-set brown eyes missing little as they swept over Austin, then moved to Gabby, who stood at the bottom of the porch steps. "My son and daughter-in-law have gone into town to the doctor," she finally said, bringing her sharp gaze back to Austin. "I'm not sure when they'll be back. Are you two married?"

The question was thrown at him like a dagger, catching him flat-footed. He hesitated, but the suspicion darkening the older woman's eyes told him there was only one acceptable answer he could give. "Yes."

Behind him, he heard Gabby's almost silent gasp, but the woman didn't even spare her a glance. Her mouth tight with disapproval, she said tartly, "Then maybe you ought to get your *wife* a ring. There's no work for you here." With one last censuring stare at Gabby, she shut the door firmly in his face.

If he hadn't been so furious, Austin would have laughed at the irony of it. The meddlesome old woman had practically labeled them lovers, though she couldn't have known Gabby was as pure as the driven snow. His face set in grim lines, he turned away from the door and grabbed Gabby's hand. "Come on."

His grip would leave a bruise on her wrist, but it was the hard resolve in his eyes that robbed her of breath. She hurried to keep up with his long legs, her heart suddenly beating like a drum. "Where are we going?"

"To get a ring."

"See anything you like?"

Gabby stared down at the rings before them, trying to choke back the panic rising in her throat. They'd been to the town's four antique stores in search of an inexpensive ring and had finally ended up at the costume jewelry display in the flower and gift shop. And in every shop, Gabby's protest had been the same. "This isn't necessary, Austin."

"Trust me. It is." Scowling down at the assortment of rings, he said curtly, "You pick one or I will."

One glance at his set face told her he wasn't going to budge on this. Damn him, why was he being so stubborn? "This is ridiculous!" she hissed, turning her back on the salesgirl who was watching them curiously from across the shop. "Just because one dried up old woman jumped to the wrong conclusion—"

"She was only thinking what every other woman in this town will be thinking when they see us together," he growled in a voice as low as hers. "This is the Bible Belt, and people expect us to be married if we're traveling together. If we're going to get a job, then you're going to need a ring. Now pick one.''

It wasn't a request; it was an order. Feeling trapped, Gabby hesitated, but the fierce light in his gray eyes was as strong as the pull of the moon on the tide. ''The plain gold band,'' she said huskily, knowing she was making a mistake.

He plucked it up off the imitation black velvet before she could change her mind and strode to the cashier at the front of the store. Drawing a five-dollar bill from his wallet, he handed it to the girl and waited for his change. As they left the store seconds later, the bell on the door chimed merrily.

Outside, the small town was fairly hustling with activity. The rice harvest was already well under way, and grain trucks were lined up at the big concrete cooperative dryers near the tracks. Austin never noticed. Stopping on the sidewalk in front of the shop, he turned abruptly to face Gabby. ''Give me your hand.''

Her heart skipped a beat. Linking her fingers behind her back, she tried to reason with him. ''Austin, please—''

Without a word, he reached behind her and grabbed her left hand. The ring, too big for her slender finger, slid over her knuckle easily and wobbled into place.

Unable to drag her eyes away, Gabby stared at the gold-tone band as if she'd never seen her finger before. She told herself it was just a necessary prop in a game they were forced to play. It could be taken off as easily as it had been put on, with just as little emotion. It meant nothing, absolutely nothing.

Why, then, did she feel as if he'd just claimed her, just branded her as his? she wondered, swallowing to ease her suddenly tight throat. And why did it feel so right?

Austin frowned down at her bent head and felt himself tense as he half expected her to tear the ring off her finger. What the hell did he care, anyway? he thought irritably. A piece of cheap costume jewelry wouldn't mean anything to the rich Gabriella Winters, even if it had been bought to protect her reputation. If he had any sense, he would tell her he knew who she was and end this farce once and for all. She could go back to her daddy, and he could go to the swamps and write his book. They'd both be back in their own worlds and happy as clams.

Yeah, right, he thought, forcing back a cynical snort. The only thing wrong with that little scenario was that he knew he wasn't going to put her out of his mind by simply putting her out of his life, and he couldn't forget the fear he saw in her eyes every time he urged her to go home. What had happened to her to haunt her so? He would find out, he promised himself, and not from a newspaper story, but from her. He wanted her trust, more, he realized, than he should.

"Let's go," he said gruffly, shattering the silence that stretched between them like a chasm. "The other farm's west of town. We'll have to hurry if we're going to get there before dark."

After that, there didn't seem much to say. Whether they wanted to admit it or not, they'd stepped over an invisible line, and it was too late to go back. Silently, they headed out of town.

The sinking sun was just reddening the horizon when they reached the Widow Beauchamp's farm. Unlike the other farms they had passed, where combines cut the golden rice and shot it up into grain buggies that followed along behind, the Beauchamp fields were silent, undisturbed but for the wind that softly rippled through the golden grain.

Glancing skeptically at the old wooden house, which looked as if it were deserted, Gabby said, "Are you sure this is the right place? It doesn't look like anybody's here."

"The waitress said the first house on the left past the bayou," he replied, waiting till she joined him on the porch before knocking sharply on the door. "This has got to be it."

The woman who answered the door was tall and rawboned, her mousy brown hair streaked with gray and gathered in a clip at the nape of her neck. Dressed in a pink large-sleeved duster, she cradled her right arm to her generous bosom, the sling that hooked around her neck helping to support the cast that stretched from the tips of her fingers to past her bent elbow. She wasn't a pretty woman—years in the fields had toughened and weathered her skin—but her open face was lined with a character that would draw the eye quicker than beauty. Behind black-rimmed glasses, her brown eyes were sharp and direct.

"Yes? Can I help you?"

"We're looking for work," Austin said, drawing Gabby closer to his side and linking his fingers with hers. "My name's Austin, and this is my wife, Gabby." The lie fell smoothly from his lips even as his fingers tightened around Gabby's. "We were told in town that you could use some help."

"Help?" She chuckled. "I think I'm going to need a heck of a lot more than that to get this dang crop in. Nothing short of a miracle's going to do much good." Pushing the screen open, she stepped out onto the porch and motioned to four wicker rockers cozily arranged at the far end. "My name's Ida Beauchamp. Have a seat and let's talk."

As they settled into the rockers, she nodded at her arm, the lines mapping her expressive face deepening as she scowled in disgust. "As you can see, I've got a broken wing. We had a storm go through here last week, and the high winds almost tore the shingles off the roof. I was up there nailing them back down when I lost my balance and fell. It was a stupid thing to do," she admitted ruefully, "but if that's the only stupid thing I do in my life, I'll do all right."

Austin's lips twitched at the image of her on the roof pounding away. "You're lucky you didn't break more than your arm."

"If I was lucky, I wouldn't have broken it at all. I couldn't have picked a worse time. That storm blew the rice down. If I don't get it out of the water soon, it's going to start sprouting again, and I'm going to have a real mess. And if that's not enough, my hired hand's in the hospital with a sick gallbladder." Tilting her head to the side, she studied Austin through narrowed eyes. "What do you know about rice farming?"

"Not much," he admitted readily, liking her blunt approach. "But I grew up on a farm in Kansas, and I can tell you all you want to know about growing wheat."

"You know how to run a combine?"

"I did fifteen years ago. I haven't done it since I was a teenager."

She grinned, her brown eyes twinkling behind the lenses of her glasses. "It's not something you're likely to forget. What about you, Gabby?" she asked suddenly. "You ever farmed?"

Gabby hesitated, struggling with the truth. She'd never been much of a liar, and instinct warned her it would take a master fibber to put one past this woman and get away with it. "My family raised horses," among other things, she silently added, "but we never worked the land."

"Well, that's okay. All you'll need to do is drive the rice buggy behind the combine. You shouldn't have any problem with that. I'll also need your help in the house with the cooking and washing. I haven't been able to do much with just one arm." She turned back to Austin. "You have any references?"

"We worked for Frank Jones in Promise, Kentucky, painting his fence," he replied. "In fact, we just finished it yesterday. I can give you his number if you like."

For a long, thoughtful moment she considered the suggestion before shaking her head, satisfied. "No, I don't think that'll be necessary. If I haven't learned how to judge people by now, I'm an old fool. If you want the job, it's yours. I can give you room and board and two hundred a week, and you'll earn every penny of it. I've got a hundred acres of rice waiting to be harvested. After that, we start on soybeans. Course, my hired hand should be back by then, but if he's not, I'll need your help."

Austin grinned. "When do we start?"

"Last week would have been perfect, but right now'll do," she said, smiling broadly as she rose to her feet. "The grain trucks and all the equipment are in the workshop out back. Everything will need to be cleaned up and checked out to make sure it's running okay. While you're doing that, I'll show Gabby the kitchen, and she can start cooking supper."

Cooking! Agitated, Gabby jumped to her feet. "Mrs. Beauchamp...I—"

"Just call me Ida, dear, everyone does," she cut in as she swept past her into the house. "We don't stand on formality around here. Come on in."

Rooted to the spot, Gabby stared helplessly after her, watching through the screen door as she headed for the back of the house. Frowning, Austin stood and said, "What's wrong?"

Her eyes, dark and defensive, turned to his. "I can't cook."

His first instinct was to laugh in disbelief. "You're kidding," he scoffed. She had to be kidding. Almost everyone over the age of twenty knew how to cook something. "I'm sure Ida doesn't expect you to be a gourmet chef. Just stick to something simple."

"Like boiled water?" she retorted. "I might be able to handle that without burning up the pot or kettle or whatever it's boiled in."

The amusement fell from his face at her confused tone. "You're not kidding."

"No," she said flatly. "I'm not." She wasn't likely to kid about something that everyone else took for granted. She could quote *Beowulf* in Old English, but she'd never even fried an egg. Even if there hadn't been a hired cook in the house for as long as she could remember, she would have been protected from the possible dangers of the kitchen just as she had been from everything else.

Austin stared down at her and started to ask her where she'd been all her life when he suddenly remembered who she was. What was he thinking of? Of course she wouldn't know how to cook! With her money, why should she sweat over a hot stove when she could hire someone to do it for her?

"Just hum a few bars and fake it, then," he suggested finally. "There's bound to be a cookbook somewhere in the kitchen. It'll tell you everything you need to know."

He made it sound so easy. But minutes later, when she found Ida waiting for her in the big, old-fashioned kitchen, panic tumbled into her stomach. How was she going to carry this off? she wondered wildly. Resisting the urge to bolt, she forced a smile. "What would you like for supper?"

"Oh, something quick, since it's so late," the older woman said lightly. "I've thawed out some hamburger meat. How 'bout hamburger gravy, fried potatoes and biscuits? I'll—" The ringing of the phone somewhere in the front of the house cut her off in midsentence. "Let me get that, then I'll be right back and show you where everything is."

She bustled out, leaving Gabby standing aghast in the middle of the kitchen floor. She'd never heard of hamburger gravy, and even if she could manage the potatoes, she didn't even know where to begin in making biscuits! She had to find a cookbook!

She whirled, her heart pounding, and glanced frantically around the kitchen. Cabinets lined two walls, their glass-paned doors showing their neatly stacked contents. Dishes, glasses, groceries. There wasn't a cookbook in sight. Rushing over to a drawer next to the sink, she jerked it open, but it only contained silverware. Swearing under her breath, she shoved it closed and pulled out the larger one underneath it. Kitchen towels filled it to the brim.

"What are you doing?"

The question came from right behind her and froze Gabby in her tracks. Oh, God, now what? How could she possibly explain this?

"If you're looking for valuables, dear," Ida said in amusement, "you won't find them in the kitchen."

"Oh, no!" Her cheeks hot with embarrassment, Gabby whirled and tried not to squirm under the older woman's probing stare. "Please, I wasn't looking for anything to steal. I . . ." She hesitated, struggling for an explanation, but the only thing she could come up with was the truth. "I was just looking for . . . a cookbook."

"'A cookbook,'" Ida echoed in astonishment. "But—"

"You might as well know now. I don't know how to cook. *Anything*," she added miserably. "That doesn't mean I won't try, but I don't even know what hamburger gravy is."

Ida's lips compressed, holding back a grin at the forlorn announcement. "It's not something you're likely to find in a cookbook." She chuckled. "Where are you from?"

Louisville. The answer was almost out before she could stop it. Biting her tongue, Gabby was surprised at how badly she wanted to confide in this woman. Hadn't she learned by now that it was dangerous to trust so easily? "I'm from up north," she lied huskily. "New England."

If Ida noticed she didn't have a New England accent, she kept it to herself. "And your mama never taught you to cook?"

"My mother died when I was sixteen. We always had a cook."

She nodded, suddenly understanding how Gabby could wear her baggy clothes as if they were designer originals. "Well, that explains it, then. I'll just have to teach you." Taking a seat at the round claw-foot table that dominated nearly half of the room, she propped her cast up on the smooth, polished surface and motioned to a cabinet next to the stove. "The skillets are in there, and the meat and potatoes are in the refrigerator. We'll put the potatoes on first, then start the gravy."

As easy as that, Gabby knew she had found a friend. A slow smile spread across her face. "I hope you know you're taking your life in your hands. This could turn out to be a real disaster."

Behind the lenses of her glasses, Ida's brown eyes twinkled merrily. "If I can fall off a roof and only suffer a broken arm, it's going to take more than your cooking to kill an old war-horse like me. Let's get started."

The cooking lesson, far from being a nightmare, turned out to be more fun than Gabby ever expected. Ida gave her step-by-step instructions as patiently as a teacher presenting the alphabet to a first grader for the first time. As she learned how to peel a potato and cut it into cubes for frying, she had to laugh at her own awkwardness in wielding a knife. Canned biscuits were popped into the oven while Ida explained how her mother had discovered hamburger gravy during the depression, when she'd only had a small amount of meat and milk to feed a family. Standing at Gabby's side as her mother had once stood at hers, Ida taught her how to brown the hamburger meat, then sprinkle flour over it and brown the flour slightly before adding the milk to make a cream gravy. By the time it was ready, so was everything else.

Her cheeks flushed from excitement and the heat from the stove, Gabby pulled the biscuits from the oven as if she had been doing it all her life. Placing them on the table with the other food, she laughed in delight and gave Ida a quick hug. "I didn't burn anything. I can't believe it! Thank you!"

"See, I told you there was nothing to it," she said, returning her hug. "Call that husband of yours. If he's been working as hard as we have, he's bound to be starving."

Austin didn't need to be called twice. Seconds later, he walked into the kitchen, his hands greasy from working on one of the trucks, and stopped dead at the sight of Gabby standing next to the table full of food. Her brown eyes as bright as her smile, she looked like a new bride who had cooked her first meal for her husband. Austin stared at her and knew if she'd really been his bride at that moment, nothing on earth would have stopped him from walking up to her and sweeping her into his arms.

But she wasn't his bride, and Ida Beauchamp was standing right next to her, looking every bit as proud as Gabby. Both of them were obviously waiting for his reaction. His eyes went to Gabby's. "You do that all by yourself?" he asked softly.

Her smile deepened. "Ida coached me through it."

"It smells good."

"Well, we wouldn't be eating it if it didn't," Ida drawled, chuckling. "Before we're through, she's going to be a first-class cook. Let's eat."

"Let me wash my hands, and I'll be right there," Austin said as he moved to the kitchen sink. "Don't start without me."

The meal that followed was the best any of them had had in a long time. The food was plain but good, the conversation nonstop and interspersed with laughter. Ida, too long alone, was in her element, regaling them with old stories from the past that sounded new again when told to strangers. Before they knew it, they'd finished off every morsel of food Gabby had cooked.

"Damn, that was good," Austin said, pushing back from the table with a wide grin and rising to his feet. "I haven't eaten like this since I left Kansas, and it's a good thing, too. I'd be as big as a house."

Gabby's eyes went to his lean hips encased in snug jeans, the memory of the feel of him against her as he'd kissed her rising up to warm her cheeks. From what she remembered, there wasn't an ounce of fat on him anywhere. "I don't think you have anything to worry about," she said huskily.

"If anything, you could use a little fattening up," Ida added bluntly. "Farm work takes a lot out of a man. And a woman, too. Look at me," she teased, drawing their laughter.

"You're beautiful and you know it," Austin tossed back as he headed for the back door. "And speaking of work, I'd better get back to that truck. I think I can finish it up before bedtime."

He left them to the chore of cleaning up, but it only took Gabby a matter of minutes to put the dirty dishes in the dishwasher. Wiping the counter and stove clean, she dried her hands on a dry dish towel, then turned to Ida with a smile of satisfaction. "There, all done. Is there anything else you'd like me to do tonight?"

"No, tomorrow's soon enough to start the housework. I'll just show you to your room and get you some clean sheets." She turned into the hall and pushed open the door to a room right off the kitchen. "There's a connecting bath with plenty of clean towels in the closet," she said as she switched on the light. "If there's anything else you or Austin need, just let me know. My room's upstairs."

Gabby stared at the iron bed pushed up against the far wall of the Spartan room, unable to think of a thing to say as Ida handed her the clean sheets. Of course they were expected to share a bedroom. Ida thought they were man and wife. But a double bed! She'd never thought, never even considered—

"Gabby? Is everything okay?"

She jerked her gaze back to the older woman and found Ida frowning at her in concern. "What? Oh, yes, everything's fine." Flustered, she ran her hand through her hair. "I . . . I guess I'm just tired."

"Then I'll let you get some sleep," she replied. "Tomorrow's going to be a busy day. Good night."

The door shut quietly behind her, but Gabby hardly noticed. Clutching the sheets to her breast, she cautiously approached the bed. What was she going to do? she wondered wildly. She'd agreed to wear the ring, to play the part of his wife, but she couldn't sleep with him! That was carrying the charade too far. If she made the mistake of getting into that bed with him, it would be all too easy to forget that the ring on her finger wasn't real, that he wasn't hers. She couldn't lie next to him, feel his nearness, his heat, without going quietly out of her mind.

She had to do something! Striding quickly to the closet, she pulled open the door to find several blankets neatly stacked on the top shelf. She sighed in relief. She'd make a pallet on the floor, and Austin could have the bed. It was the only logical solution. She would pick it up every morning, and Ida would never have to know.

Austin stood outside the closed bedroom door, his hand hesitating on the doorknob. *Well, go on,* a voice in his head jeered. *You can't stand out in the hall all night!*

He swore under his breath, wanting to kick himself for even suggesting that they pretend to be married. He'd solved one problem only to create a much bigger one. As sure as Superman had X-ray vision, he knew there was a double bed on the other side of that door, a double bed that Ida naturally expected him to share with Gabby. How the hell was he going to do that without making love to her?

It was going to be damn hard. Scowling at the double meaning, his fingers tightened around the doorknob. There was no help for it. He'd just have to convince Gabby that he wasn't an animal and spend the rest of the night praying that he didn't act like one. His jaw rigid, he knocked softly on the door and stepped inside.

He didn't know what he expected, but it wasn't the sight of Gabby down on her knees making a pallet on the floor. Across the room, clean sheets were turned back invitingly on the bed. The *double* bed.

Shutting the door with a soft, ominous click, he leaned back against it and watched as she hurriedly smoothed down the blankets and quickly rose to her feet to face him. His eyes fell to the pallet before lifting back to her face. "What's that?"

There was nothing in the quiet question to set the nerves in her stomach jumping, but they did, nonetheless. Stiffening her spine, Gabby struggled to keep her voice as calm as his. "My bed."

While he'd been sweating bullets out in the workshop over sharing the damn bed, she'd been calmly working out a solution. For some reason, that irritated the hell out of him. "You don't trust me?"

Startled, she felt her cheeks turn as red as her hair. "No.... I mean yes! Damn it, Austin, it isn't a matter of trust...."

"Good," he growled softly. "Because you can trust me. Come here, Gabby."

Her heart jumped into her throat. "Austin—"

"If it isn't a matter of trust, then you can come here, can't you?"

She was trapped as neatly as a rabbit in a snare, and they both knew it. "I can't," she whispered. "Please..."

"Then I'll come to you." He crossed to her in three strides and came to a stop directly in front of her. Her dark, bottomless eyes begged him in ways she couldn't possibly be aware of, and it took all his self-control not to jerk her against him and fall with her onto the bed. "If you trust me, then you know I would never do anything to hurt you, don't you?"

He wasn't the one she was afraid of. Unable to get a word through her suddenly dry throat, she nodded.

"So I can touch you without you being afraid of me?"

No! a voice in her head screamed, but it was too late. "Yes."

The word was hardly out of her mouth before he was gently tracing the blush in her cheek. The tips of his fingers were rough, her skin like satin. With merely a touch, he stole her breath.

He felt her stiffen, but the pressure of his fingers on her face stayed as soft as a whisper. With infinite slowness, he learned the curve of her brows, the pert tilt of her nose, the angle of her jaw, the sensuous line of her mouth. Over and over again, he committed every inch of her to memory, until her lips were parted and his fingers trembling for more than just a caress.

She swayed toward him unwittingly. His muscles bunching with the need to reach for her, Austin ran a finger under her jaw and tilted her chin until her mouth was only a heartbeat away from his. Smoky gray eyes glittered down into hers. "And you trust me to kiss you without hurting you, don't you?"

Mesmerized, she couldn't move, couldn't think of anything but the throbbing of her lips for the touch of his. "Y—"

His mouth covered hers before she finished the word. This kiss, unlike the others he'd given her, was as soft as his touch, as unthreatening as a kiss of greeting, of hello. Her eyes closed with a sigh, her mind clouded. No, there was no threat here, only a pleasure that was soul destroying. With a murmur, her arms stole around him as she crowded closer, seeking his heat. How could she have known that his kiss could be so undemanding, so safe?

Dragging his mouth from hers, his fingers dove into her wild curls, holding her before him until her eyes slowly lifted to his. "See, it's just a kiss," he whispered. "You can trust me even if we take it deeper."

This time he gave her no time to answer, but dragged her up on tiptoe and into his arms, his mouth covering hers with a groan. He was hot for her, aching, the sweet, hungry thrust of her tongue driving him half-mad. He was the one with the experience, but with a sigh, a touch, she aroused, seduced, made him need.

His hands moved to the buttons of her shirt, only to fumble like a teenager with his first woman. Swearing, he broke off the kiss and scowled down at the offending garment. Curling his fingers in the material, his muscles tightened to rip it from her body.

What the hell was he doing?

He froze, staring down at his hands, the fire in his blood burning in his eyes. Was this how he proved to her that she could trust him? By ripping her clothes from her and taking her where she stood?

A muscle jumping along his jaw, he struggled for a control that was balanced on a double-edged sword that could slip at any second. But he didn't release her. He couldn't. Molding her hips to his, he lifted his head abruptly and trapped her in his gaze. "I want you," he rasped fiercely, his breath hot against her lips. "Feel what you do to me. I can't remember the last time I wanted any woman this badly, but that doesn't mean I'm going to take you like some Neanderthal. Now tell me *I'm* the one you have to be afraid of if we sleep in the same bed."

Dazed, Gabby could only stare at him, her heart racing in time with his. Her arms were tight around his waist, her stomach and thighs cradling his hardness, her blood raging.

He saw the dismay that widened her eyes and released her with an angry expletive. Turning his back on her, he stripped off his sweatshirt and threw it across the room, then unzipped his jeans with a savage jerk. Pushing them off his hips, he stepped out of them and kicked them aside without once looking in her direction. "If you want to sleep on the floor, you're welcome to it," he said coldly. "Don't expect me to talk you out of it."

Chapter 7

When she crawled, shaking, onto her pallet, Gabby tried to convince herself that she'd made the best of an untenable situation. But it was a long night, and the day that followed was even longer. Austin treated her as if she'd insulted him and took every opportunity to avoid her. He was up in the morning and out in the workshop working on the equipment before she'd found the strength to rise from her hard bed. Meals were silent, hurried affairs thick with tension. Most of his conversation was reserved for Ida and centered around the parts he needed for the different vehicles. When he deigned to notice Gabby, his jaw always seemed to turn to granite, his eyes to ice. As soon as he could decently excuse himself, he hurried back out to the workshop.

When he finally came to bed the next night, it was hours after Gabby had once again retreated to the safety of her pallet. Exhausted, but too tense to sleep, she lay with her eyes closed and listened to the whispered sound of him stripping off his work clothes. Seconds later, the bed's old springs groaned softly in protest as he slipped between the sheets. The beating of her heart ticked off seconds, minutes, an eternity. She knew from his breathing he wasn't asleep, but if he was aware that she wasn't, either, he gave no sign of it. Turning toward the wall, he shut her out as easily as if he'd slammed a door between them. He didn't move the rest of the night. She knew because she lay awake for hours, her ears attuned to his slightest movement.

The next morning, however, when she awoke to find Austin gone again, his sheets rumpled as if he, too, had spent a restless night, she knew she was going to have to do something to end the tenseness between them. Distracted for the past few days by the conflict between them, she'd taken her medication absently, all her thoughts on Austin. But now, as she stared down into the brown plastic container that held her medication, that was a luxury she could no longer afford. She had one pill left.

Sinking to the side of the bed, her face ashen, she stared at it in disbelief. How had this happened? She hadn't had time to get the prescription refilled before she'd made the sudden decision to run away from home, but she'd thought she'd had enough pills to last her awhile. Dear God, what was she going to do? She couldn't go to a strange doctor for more medication without having to answer a score of awkward questions. But she couldn't do without her pills, either, not for any extended period of time. She was already under far too much stress where Austin was concerned.

Without her medication, she was sure to have a seizure.

Think! she told herself fiercely. She had to have her medication, and the only way she was going to get it was by going to a local doctor. That would take money, especially if he insisted on giving her a complete neurological exam before giving her a prescription. She had some cash in her purse, but it would never be enough.

She felt panic start to creep through her like a snake in high grass and forced herself to calmness. There had to be a way. Austin had some money left from their painting job, though she didn't know how much. She'd just have to borrow it and hope there'd be enough for both the doctor and the prescription. Now all she had to do was find a way to ask him for the money without telling him what she needed it for.

The problem nagged her all through breakfast and the discussion of the day's work. Austin, speaking to her only once, requested her help with the harvesting after she finished her duties in the kitchen. By the time she headed out to the workshop, she still didn't know what she was going to say to him.

He was leaning against the tractor, impatience the only expression on his impassive face as he watched her walk toward him. Pushing himself erect, he was all business as he said, "I'll drive the combine, and you pull the grain buggy behind me with the tractor. Once it's full, you'll dump it in the truck and take it into town to the dryer. Hopefully, the lines won't be too long in town, and you won't be gone that long—"

She stiffened. "I can't."

"What do you mean, you can't? Gabby, I can't do the harvest by myself—"

"I can't drive."

He wasn't in the mood for games. After two nights of listening to her toss and turn, of wanting her until he ached, his temper was on a short leash. "That isn't funny, Gabby."

"It wasn't meant to be," she replied defensively.

Setting his hands on his hips, he scowled at her in growing puzzlement. Would the woman never cease to surprise him? "First you don't cook, and now you don't drive. Would you like to tell me what's going on here? Every teenager I know got his license the minute he turned sixteen. Why didn't you?"

Because I have epilepsy. Because epileptics can't get a driver's license unless they've been seizure free for three years. Because I haven't gone a year without a seizure, let alone three.

The frustration and pain of it was there in her eyes, but the habits of a lifetime kept the truth locked away in her own mind. "I just...couldn't," she said finally. "I was never interested, so let's just drop it, okay?"

Secrets, he thought, frowning at her. She had so many damn secrets. And so little trust. What had happened to her to make her so leery? "No, we're not going to drop it," he said flatly. "Are you afraid to drive? Is that why you don't have your license?"

"No—"

"Good. Then it's time you learned how." He reached for the door to the cab of the tractor and pulled it open. "Hop in."

"But...Austin, I don't have my license! I can't!

"You don't need a license to drive the tractor here on the farm. All you need is a couple of lessons and a little practice steering. By the end of tomorrow, you'll be driving this tractor like you've been doing it all your life."

Did he have any idea how he was tempting her? He was holding out a piece of forbidden fruit to her, and she wanted oh, so desperately to reach for it. But doubts kept her stubbornly where she was. "What if I hit something?"

"Like what?" he retorted. "I'll take you out in one of the fallow fields, and you can practice to your heart's content. There aren't even any fence posts for you to hit. Come on, Gabby," he urged her softly. "Anyone who's got the guts to hop a freight train can surely learn how to drive. You're a gutsy lady. Take a chance."

She stared into his eyes and knew she was going to do it. He had more faith in her than anyone else ever had. How could she continue to doubt herself when he didn't? "You'll make sure I don't hit something?" she asked, glancing apprehensively at the tractor.

He grinned. "I'll be right there beside you the whole time, I promise."

It was the first time in days that he had smiled at her, the warmth she saw in his eyes melting the last of the coolness between them. Her heart suddenly light again, she climbed awkwardly into the tractor's small cab. Seconds later, Austin joined her, squeezing into the space that had been designed for one. At the feel of his hip against hers, her thigh against his, memories of what had happened the last time they'd touched stole into the cab.

His eyes straight ahead, Austin said gruffly, "The tractor has a standard transmission, but all you'll need to know is how to get it into first gear, since you won't be going very fast." He pointed out the clutch and brake and gas pedal, then told her how to start it. "Okay, turn the key."

With trembling fingers, she did as he instructed, then laughed in spite of herself when the engine chugged to life and a puff of diesel smoke belched from the exhaust pipe. She turned brown eyes wide with anticipation on Austin. "Now what?"

"You put it in first and see if you can get this baby to move." He placed her right hand on the gearshift, then covered her fingers with his and molded them to the knob. He felt her tense, but his eyes stayed on their joined hands. "Like this," he said quietly, and maneuvered the stick shift down into position, letting her feel the way the gears clicked into place under her fingers. "That's first. Got it?"

"Y-yes."

"Now comes the fun part. Slowly let the clutch out as you give it gas."

He didn't warn her that it would die if she gave it too little gas or let the clutch out too fast. She found that out for herself. He didn't warn her that it would buck like a bronco until she learned to do it smoothly. But he was right about one thing. It was fun!

Gabby couldn't remember the last time she had laughed so much. They stopped and started and stopped again, until the tractor's jerky progress had them both chuckling. Tension flew right out the cab's open window, but they were enjoying themselves too much to notice.

The lesson ended before Gabby was ready for it, but the newfound peace she and Austin had achieved continued for the rest of the morning, through lunch with Ida and into the afternoon as they started harvesting. She didn't fool herself into thinking that it would last—everything would change the minute they went to their separate beds that night—but for now it was a peace she needed desperately. All too soon she would have to find a way to ask him for the rest of his money without telling him what she needed it for, then somehow get to town and a doctor.

The opportunity came two hours after lunch, when they'd harvested enough rice to fill one of the grain trucks. Surveying the full truck with a frown, Austin wiped his dusty forehead with a handkerchief before shoving it back into his pocket. "I'll have to take it into town to the dryer since you don't have your license and Ida can't handle the truck with her broken arm. You might as well take a break. There's no telling how long I'll be gone."

"I'll go with you," she said quickly. While he was waiting his turn to dump the rice, she would be free to find a doctor. "I need a few things from the store." How was she going to ask for the money? "I seem to be a little short of cash," she fibbed jerkily, unable to meet his eyes. "I... Could you lend me some until Ida pays us at the end of the week?"

He lifted a brow in surprise. She had to have some of the money she'd earned painting left. What was she up to? "How much do you need?"

"Twenty," she said, holding her breath, and prayed it would be enough.

Without a word, Austin reached into his back pocket and pulled out his wallet. He handed her a five. "That's all I've got. I knew we'd be getting a job, so I gave that old hobo in town some money to get him some groceries. His arthritis has been acting up, and he hasn't been able to work."

Gabby stared at the money in dismay. It was so little and she needed so much! Blindly, she reached for it. She'd have to ask Ida for an advance on her salary. It was the only option she had left.

"Is that enough?" Austin asked.

He was watching her like a hawk; she could almost feel the touch of his eyes on her. Avoiding his gaze, she nodded and turned to walk around the hood of the truck to the passenger side. "Yes, thanks. I guess we should be going before it gets any later."

The seizure, when it hit her, came without warning. A bolt of electricity, too strong for the circuits in her brain, shot through her head. She stiffened, then her hand lifted to her forehead, only to stop halfway there as if frozen. Before she could do anything but whisper a stricken "Oh, no," the darkness was descending on her like a cloud of doom from hell. Without another sound, she tumbled headlong into unconsciousness and crumpled to the ground.

"Gabby!"

Her name a hoarse cry on his lips, Austin ran to her side, his hands shaking as he dropped to his knees and reached for her. Half-afraid to touch her, he turned her on her back, his heart stopping at the sight of her bloodless cheeks. "Gabby?" Urgently cupping his hand to her face, he shook her slightly, but not even an eyelash twitched in response. Alarmed, he fumbled frantically with her clothes, loosening them, searching for a pulse.

"There's got to be a pulse," he muttered fiercely. The taste of fear bitter on his tongue, he jerked back the collar of her shirt to run his hands over her exposed throat. Against his fingers, her heartbeat raced strong and steady. His shoulders sagged in relief. The story in the newspaper had said she was on medication. Thank God it wasn't for her heart!

Which meant it had to be something else. Gently pushing her hair back from her face, he willed her eyes to open. "Wake up, sweetheart," he said huskily. "Tell me what's wrong." But she never moved. Helplessness coursed through him. Damn it, a woman didn't just drop unconscious without a damn good reason! What was wrong with her?

At a loss as to what to do, he sat back on his heels and studied her, fighting a panic that urged him to snatch her up and race her to the nearest hospital. Her breathing was irregular, strained, then even as he watched, it began to steady and deepen, as if she had slipped into sleep. Feeling for the pulse on the side of her neck again, his eyes zeroed in on a chain that encircled her neck and disappeared inside her blouse. With one tug, he pulled it free. A tag attached to the chain fell into his hand.

EPILEPSY. ALLERGIC TO PENICILLIN.

Stunned, Austin stared at the medical ID necklace. Another secret revealed to him, another one of the countless mysteries that made up Gabriella Winters solved. How many more dragons was she hiding from him, fighting alone?

Gently tucking the necklace back inside her blouse, he couldn't take his eyes from her pale face. God, epilepsy! He knew next to nothing about it, not even how to help her. And that was what infuriated him. He wanted to hold her, to protect her, but he didn't even know if he should touch her. Why hadn't she told him? he wondered. Was she so scared of him and whatever she was running from that she couldn't even trust him with that tiny bit of information? They were practically living in each other's pockets, for God's sake! She should have warned him, told him what to do in case of a seizure....

If I'm asleep when you come back, don't wake me up. It'll only make the headache worse.

Her voice floated out of his memory as images of the night she'd had the migraine flashed before his eyes. Had she really had a migraine or had that, too, had something to do with her epilepsy? Just now, before she'd collapsed, she'd started to grab her head. When she came to, would her head once again be killing her?

The thought of her in pain twisted his gut. There had to be something he could do for her. Maybe Ida would know.... But even as he started to rise to his feet, the still, silent figure drew him back to her side. He couldn't leave her there alone. And he wouldn't move her and risk waking her. That left him only one choice: to stay with her until she regained consciousness.

Moving to the truck, he retrieved the jackets they had shed earlier and hurried back to her. The full force of the cold front sweeping in from the northwest wasn't due to reach them until later that evening, but the temperature had already started to drop so that it was cool in the shade. Covering her with the jackets as gently as if she were a sleeping child, Austin settled down beside her, his eyes trained unwaveringly on her pale face.

The blackness lifted slowly, like a fog gradually burned off by the bright rays of the sun. Gabby stirred, awareness returning in jumps and starts. A cool breeze whispered over her face, carrying the scent of winter. Something covered her, blocking out the creeping coldness. Beneath her back and head, the ground was hard and unyielding. Exhausted, her body drained of every ounce of energy, she had to fight just to open her eyes.

Gray. It was the only thing she saw, the only thing she wanted to see upon waking. The gray of Austin's eyes. Not the cold gray he sometimes blasted her with when they argued, but the rarer, warmer gray of dawn that heated her blood whenever he kissed her. When he looked at her like that, he could do anything he wanted to her and she couldn't find the strength to resist.

Stretched out beside her on his side, his head propped in his palm, he leaned over her to tenderly trace the color that gradually returned to her cheeks. "Are you all right? You gave me quite a scare."

Disoriented, she blinked in confusion; and in that split second, her memory came rushing back. Hot, weak tears filled her eyes. "Oh, no!" she whispered, stricken. Did he know? Unable to meet his eyes, she turned her face away and realized she was still lying where she must have fallen, and it was his jacket that warmed her. "I...I must have fainted," she said thickly, and prayed he would accept the lie.

His hand molded her cheek, gently forcing her eyes back to his. "I found your medical ID necklace, Gabby," he said quietly. "You should have told me about the epilepsy."

The tears filling her eyes spilled over her lashes. "It's not something you just announce to the world," she said, choking up. "It scares most people and makes them uncomfortable."

"I'm not most people," he replied as his fingers caught the tears rolling down her cheeks. "I'll admit you did scare the hell out of me, but it was only because I didn't know what to do to help you. Talk to me, honey. You don't have to fight this alone, you know."

Her throat constricted; her fingers reached for him. She told herself she could have handled his shock, his uneasiness. But he accepted in an instant what she had shared with no one but her family, and the last of her defenses crumbled. With a murmur of distress, she turned into him and buried her face against his chest, needing to lean on him just this once.

"I ran out of medicine this morning," she mumbled. "I've been worrying about it all day, and too much stress always brings on a seizure."

So that was what she needed the money for! His arms slipped around her, cradling her close. "You should have told me," he chided. "I would have taken you into town to a doctor, and you would have saved yourself all this."

Her fingers curled into his shirt. "A strange doctor's going to ask a lot of questions."

Questions that might lead her stepfather right to her. It was the closest she had come to admitting that she was running from a past she didn't want to catch up to her. A week ago, three days ago, he would have been pressuring her for more information, but now all he wanted was to hold her and protect her.

His fingers stroked her back, soothing her. "Then we'll just have to come up with some answers that satisfy him," he retorted. "Don't worry about it. I'll find a way to get you your medicine." He pulled back enough so he could see her face. "How do you feel?"

"Tired." She sighed, her smile shaky. "It'll take about twelve hours of sleep for me to get my energy back. It always does."

"Then I'd better get you to a doctor, then home to bed." Rising quickly to his feet, he drew her up beside him, then lifted her into his arms and strode around to the passenger side of the truck.

She wanted to cling to him but forced herself to let him go as she eased her onto the seat. "What doctor?" she asked in alarm. "Austin, please, there are things I can't tell you or a doctor...."

He could have said she'd told him more in the past few minutes than she had in all the days he'd known her, but he only patted her hand and slammed the truck door. "Weiner's a small town, and Ida's lived here all her life," he said as he joined her in the cab. "She's bound to know someone who'll give you a prescription without asking too many questions. We'll stop at the house and see if she has any suggestions."

He had them back at the house before Gabby could even begin to think of a story to tell Ida, but she needn't have worried. Over her protests, Austin carried her in the house and had an explanation ready when a worried Ida met them at the door.

"My Lord, what happened?"

"She's all right," Austin assured her as he gently deposited Gabby on the couch. "She has epilepsy and she had a small seizure out in the field." Giving Gabby a reassuring smile, he turned to the older woman. "She needs her prescription refilled. Do you know someone who would renew it for her?"

"Well, yes, of course, but wouldn't it just be easier to call her doctor? He could call the prescription in over the phone."

Austin hated lying to her, but he had no other choice. "It's not that simple," he said reluctantly. "Gabby's father doesn't approve of me, so we ran off and got married. She doesn't want him to know where we are."

"And you're afraid your doctor might tell him where you are?" Ida guessed, frowning in concern at Gabby.

She nodded. It was nothing less than the truth. "He's an old family friend. He would feel honor-bound to tell Dad."

"He wouldn't if he'd seen the two of you together," the older woman retorted tartly. "Anyone with eyes can see that the two of you belong together." She moved to the phone. "Let me call Dr. Caldwell. He's only a family doctor, but he's a good man, and I've known him most of my life. I know he'll help you. I'll just tell him you're my niece from California who's come to help me while my arm heals. He's never met her, so there shouldn't be any problem."

She placed the call while they listened, explaining to the doctor how her niece Gabby had left California in such a rush she'd forgotten her medicine. When she hung up a few minutes later, she was smiling. "He said to come on in and he'll fix you right up."

Any fears Gabby had that Dr. Caldwell would probe into her past vanished the minute she saw him. A large, gruff man who was pushing seventy, he had a thick head of hair that had once been as red as Gabby's dyed curls but was now frosted with gray. He also had the kindest green eyes she had ever seen. Patting her shoulder, he welcomed her and Austin into his office as if he had known them all his life.

"Come in, come in," he said eagerly, motioning them to the chairs in front of his desk once they had introduced themselves. "Ida said you were on phenobarbital, so I went ahead and wrote out the prescription except for the name," he continued as he seated himself behind his desk and reached for a pen. "She didn't mention your last name."

Her mind a blank, Gabby looked helplessly at Austin. "LePort," he said huskily. "Gabby LePort."

"LePort, hmm?" the older man mused as he filled in the rest of the prescription, then slid it across the desk to her. "Don't recognize the name, but that's not surprising. Ida's got so many nieces, it's hard to keep track of all of them, especially since they all live out of state and don't get back to see her too often. Who's kid are you?"

Beneath her makeup, Gabby paled. Ida had said she'd known the doctor for most of her life. He probably knew the names of all of her brothers and sisters. "Actually, I'm her great-niece," she said quickly. "By marriage. Her husband and my grandfather were brothers."

He frowned. "I didn't realize John had a brother."

Oh, God, she'd made a mistake! "They didn't get along very well," she lied again as she grabbed the precious prescription and stuffed it into her purse. "They tended to avoid each other as much as possible." Rising quickly to her feet, she gave the older man a shaky smile as he and Austin both stood. "We won't take up any more of your time, but I want to thank you for seeing me on such short notice, Dr. Caldwell.

I don't know what I would have done without this prescription.''

The frown still darkening his lined face gave way to a smile. "It's my pleasure, dear. I'd do anything for Ida. We go back a long way. If you have any more problems while you're in town, just let me know."

"We will," Austin said, offering his hand. "Thanks, Doctor."

Her smile frozen in place, it took all of Gabby's remaining strength to precede Austin out the door. Once they were outside, she leaned against the wall like a wilted flower. He took one look at her and slipped his arm around her waist. "Come on," he said gruffly, urging her across the parking lot to the truck. "We'll stop at the pharmacy, and then I'll get you home."

"What about the rice?" she reminded him as she let him help her into the cab. "You should go on and dump it at the dryer while we're here."

"The line's forty-five minutes long. I'll come back. You need to be in bed."

She wouldn't have minded the wait, but he'd made up his mind and there was no changing it. Twenty minutes later, they were back at the farm and he and Ida were hovering over her as if they expected her to collapse at any moment. It was a feeling she was all too familiar with.

"Please, could we just forget this afternoon happened?" she pleaded, even though she knew it was impossible. "I'm all right. Or I will be as soon as I get some rest."

Austin's eyes narrowed at the tiredness and defeat he heard in her voice. "We'll forget it when you don't look like you're going to blow away in a good, stiff wind." He opened the door to their bedroom. "Nap time."

She would have liked nothing better than to crawl into bed, but she couldn't. "It's only an hour till supper. I have to start it now, or we won't be eating till midnight."

"Oh, no you don't," Ida said flatly. "Tonight we're having canned soup and sandwiches, and the only help I need is opening the cans. Austin can do that when the time comes. You go to bed. We'll call you when everything's ready."

They had everything neatly worked out, and she didn't have the energy to argue with them. Without another word of protest, she did as she was told. Five minutes later, she was asleep.

She awoke an hour later, her head thick and groggy, needing something to eat and more sleep. Austin took one look at her and steered her to the table, then he and Ida joined her. Hot vegetable-beef soup cleared her head long enough for her to notice that the cold front had finally arrived. Outside, the wind whistled around the house and fogged the windows.

"I see the front finally came in," she said quietly, breaking the cozy silence as she finished her soup.

Ida nodded. "Came through about an hour and a half ago. Weatherman says it'll blow itself out by late afternoon, but tonight's going to be pretty cool. Have you got something warm to sleep in?"

"Just a cotton shirt."

"I figured as much," the older woman snorted. "You'll freeze to death in that." Rising from the table, she stepped into the washroom attached to the back of the kitchen and pulled a just-dried flannel gown from the dryer. "Here. Go put this on while it's still warm and get into bed with you. Austin'll do the dishes.''

Gabby couldn't help but laugh at Austin's look of surprise. ''I think you'd better tell Austin. It looks like he's the last to know.''

''I just did.'' Ida chuckled. ''Now go on before that gown gets cold. You've got no business being out of bed.''

She was right. The small amount of sleep she'd gotten wasn't nearly enough, and Gabby could already feel her small burst of energy starting to drag. Thanking Ida with a kiss on her weathered cheek, she stepped into the bathroom to change.

By the time she reached the bedroom, her head had begun to throb, and she wanted nothing so much as to lie her weary body down and not move for hours. Closing the door behind her, she stopped short at the sight of Austin spreading blankets on the bed. She didn't have to look past him to the closet, where she stored the blankets she used for her pallet, to know that they were the same ones. The slow pounding of her heart seemed to echo in her chest. ''Austin...''

He straightened abruptly, unable to drag his eyes away from her. The red plaid gown Ida had given Gabby was two sizes too big for her and covered her from her neck all the way to her toes. As shapeless as a flour sack, it successfully hid every curve she had, yet somehow managed to make her look as sexy as hell.

Steeling himself against the need to go to her, he said flatly, ''You're not sleeping on the floor tonight, so don't even think about arguing about it. You're taking the bed.''

''And where are you sleeping?''

"With you."

The hard look in his eye dared her to argue. All she could manage was, "I am?"

He nodded, his jaw set in stone. "You're damn right. I'm not in the habit of forcing myself on sick women or virgins, you know. You happen to be both, so there's nothing for you to worry about. You're perfectly safe."

Somehow, she knew she was. If he had proved anything to her today, it was that she could trust him to protect her. Even from himself. Pushing herself away from the door, she crossed the room to him, not stopping until she was directly in front of him. "I always knew you were a knight," she said softly, a crooked smile playing around her lips. Standing on tiptoe, she placed her hands on his shoulders to balance herself, then brushed his rough cheek with a kiss. "Thank you for taking such good care of me."

His hands were reaching for her when she whispered good-night and turned to the bed. If she knew he watched her as she crawled between the sheets, she gave no sign of it. Closing her eyes with a sigh, she drifted almost immediately into sleep. Dumbfounded, Austin didn't know if he should be flattered or insulted that she found him so safe.

Chapter 8

It was a dream. Just like one of his fantasies. The scent and feel of Gabby in his arms, her back snuggled against his chest, her bottom warm against his loins. Drowsily, he drew her closer, enchanted with the illusion. Soft. God, she was soft. How could a dream be so soft? The thought nagged at him, threatening to drag him into consciousness, but the need for the dream woman in his arms was too strong. Sighing in pleasure, he buried his face in her curls, then pressed a kiss against the back of her neck as his hands went searching.

Under the covers, his fingers found the hem of her gown. The bare skin of a slender thigh beckoned. There was no thought of resisting the temptation, no thought at all. His palm slid up the length of her, caressing, stroking, loving the way her silken skin warmed under his hands.

Beneath his fingers, she stirred. A soft murmur parted her lips, her hips nudged him. His low growl of approval muffled against the back of her neck, he trailed his lips over to her ear as his hands grew bolder. He explored her slowly, leisurely, as if he would learn all her secrets through touch alone. The curve of her hip fascinated him. The dip of her waist tantalized. Higher still, the warm, satin softness of her unrestricted breasts drew his hand like a magnet. Cupping her gently, his thumb brushed across the crest once, twice, then stayed to linger as the nipple tightened sweetly.

He thought he heard her groan, but his blood was beginning to heat, and he couldn't be sure. So real. So responsive. Against his palm, her heart raced, matching his beat for beat. On the distant edges of his consciousness, dawn was but a blur of misty light, time without meaning, which didn't dare to intrude on his fantasy. The dream would last as long as he touched, tasted, claimed. Seduced by the thought, he turned her in his arms.

Gabby came awake to find her body humming and her bones as fluid as warm, thick honey. Awareness hit her all at once. Somehow her gown had ridden up past her waist, her bare legs were tangled with Austin's, his arousal was hard and hot against her stomach. Stunned, she didn't even have time to blink before his hand molded to her jaw and turned her mouth up to his.

Even as his tongue swirled lazily into her mouth, wooing her with a thoroughness that left her weak, Gabby knew he was more than half-asleep. Moaning his name against his lips, she struggled to hang on to her rapidly disappearing common sense, telling herself she wasn't ready for a physical relationship when she was only just now starting to trust him. But her body wasn't interested in the workings of her mind, only the magical skills of his mouth and hands. When his fingers abandoned her breasts to slide down her stomach, seeking the heat of her passion, she could only gasp, anticipation squeezing the air from her lungs.

It was the sound of his name on her lips the second time that jolted him completely awake. His eyes, heavy lidded and sensuous, opened to find hers waiting for him. Dazed, he saw that her lips were wet and parted from his kiss, her brown eyes nearly black with a passion that matched his own. But it was the tight knot of desire in his gut, begging for release, that had the breath hissing through his teeth in a curse. How the hell had he let this happen? Just last night, he'd assured her she was safe with him. So much for his promises, he thought in disgust. If he hadn't awakened when he had, he'd have taken her without a thought.

Gabby saw only the regret darkening his eyes and misunderstood. Embarrassment and hurt washed over her. Suddenly, she couldn't get out of his arms, out of his bed, fast enough. She pushed against him, her legs tangling with his.

Austin's sharply drawn breath cut through the awkward silence like a knife. His fingers clamped down on her hips, holding her against him, holding her still. "Gabby, honey, you're not helping matters," he growled, closing his eyes as he struggled for control. "Just . . . give me a minute."

Her heart slamming against her ribs, she froze.

Dragging in deep breaths, he forced his thoughts to anything else but the woman in his arms. The book he would soon have to retreat to the swamps to write, the work waiting for him in the fields, the cold front that chilled the morning air. But that only brought him back to Gabby and the bed they were sharing. Did she realize what a joke she was making of the self-control he had always prided himself on?

Opening his eyes suddenly, he saw that she did. They were both achingly aware of the need she had stirred in him, a need that hadn't lessened in the least. "I didn't mean for this to happen," he said tightly, his mouth still only inches from hers.

"I know." Oh, God, she didn't want to talk about it. Tearing her eyes away from his, she stared at his naked chest, but that only made her want to touch him. Muttering a curse, she slammed her eyes shut, trying to close her mind to the feel of him against her. It was impossible. "Let's just forget it," she whispered huskily. "Tonight I'll sleep on the floor again—"

"Do you really think that's going to change anything?" he asked quietly, tilting her chin back up until she was forced to meet his eyes.

Heat singed her cheeks. "Austin...I'm not looking for a lover. Not now. You don't know anything about me—"

"I know enough. For now, anyway," he added under his breath.

"No, you don't," she argued, "but it doesn't matter. My life is a mess, and you're a complication I can't afford."

A rueful grin tilted up one corner of his mouth. "Welcome to the real world, sweetheart. I wasn't looking for a lover, either, but I seemed to have found one. Now what are we going to do about it?'' He saw the panic hit her eyes and could have shaken her. "After what just nearly happened, do you really think I'd rush you into something you're not ready for?''

The color in her cheeks deepened. "I just haven't h-had much experience at this.''

"If you were experienced, we wouldn't be having this discussion,'' he pointed out dryly. "I want to make love to you. No, let me rephrase that. I'm *going* to make love to you, but not until you want it as badly as I do. Do you want me, Gabby?''

It was a bald question that demanded a bald answer. And something in his eyes warned her she wasn't getting out of that bed until she gave it to him. She swallowed, forcing moisture into her suddenly dry throat. "Yes, but—''

"A 'but,''' he groaned, lifting his eyes to the ceiling in silent supplication. "How did I know a 'but' would be tacked onto that yes? That's something we're going to have to work on. Starting right now.''

In the blink of an eye, he had her flat on her back, his mouth on hers. The languid heat of his earlier kisses was gone, replaced by a hunger that was scorching in its demand. He didn't woo her but took her mouth as he longed to take her body, driving out all thoughts but those of him, sweeping aside all tastes and feelings except those that centered around him. His hands moved over her, hot and wild and intoxicating, until she was shuddering and clinging to him, stardust streaking through her veins.

He could have her now, before she ever knew what hit her. The thought ate at him, pushing him to the edge. But just as surely as he knew he tasted surrender on her tongue, he knew he'd lose her if he didn't stop now. Time. He'd promised her time, and by God, he was going to give it to her.

Dragging his mouth from hers, he scattered kisses against the side of her neck, the harshness of his breathing matching hers in the early morning quiet. "You're driving me crazy, woman," he rasped against the pulse racing in her throat. "If we're going to take things slow and easy, one of us better get the hell out of this bed. Now!"

He rolled away from her only enough to let her escape if she wanted to. Her insides still quivering, Gabby scrambled from the bed on unsteady legs and tried to tell herself she was doing the right thing. But her heart didn't believe it.

Her toes curling against the cold floor, she quickly snatched up her clothes and backed toward the door, unable to take her eyes from Austin still lying in the bed. The covers pulled only to his waist, he seemed immune to the cold as he watched her every step with eyes that were still smoldering with passion. With his black hair disheveled from sleep and her fingers and his jaw darkened with stubble, a more experienced woman than Gabby would have found it difficult to walk away from him when her body still throbbed for a relief only he could give. "I'll...get dressed...in the bathroom," she stuttered, and escaped into the hall while she still could.

After that, their relationship was undeniably changed, though outwardly work seemed to dominate their lives. From early morning till late in the afternoon, they worked together bringing in the harvest, and all their conversations seemed to be limited to the

never-ending repairs on the truck, the next field they
would tackle, the long lines at the dryer in town. But
with their eyes, they spoke of things better left unspoken: Gabby's continued presence in Austin's bed two
days after the cold front was just a memory; the long
nights they lay in each other's arms before they slept,
talking politics and favorite foods and movies, carefully avoiding any mention of the events of the past
that had brought them together or the future that
would rip them apart; the slow, drugging kisses with
which Austin awoke her each morning.

He'd promised her time, and he gave her that and
more. He wooed her as carefully as a man woos his
first and only love, touched her when she least
expected it, a brush of his hand against hers, body
against body, gone before she could do anything but
gasp. A carved jack-o'-lantern appeared on the bedroom dresser one night, surprising her, delighting her.
The next night, she walked into the darkened bedroom to find it alight with candles, the flames casting
out the darkness with their golden glow. Touched,
enchanted, something deep in her heart seemed to
give, a wall tumbled, and she knew that the sweet torture that colored their nights and made their days
bearable couldn't go on for much longer. She was
weakening, melting, her resistance crumbling more
with every passing day.

But it wasn't until he woke her three mornings after her seizure without the kisses she had grown to
expect that she realized she loved him. Stunned, she
could only lie there, staring at him as he climbed out
of bed and pulled on his pants, the knowledge ex-
panding inside her chest until it filled her all the way
to her toes. She loved him. How had it happened?

When? Only days ago she'd been steeling herself to leave him. Now she couldn't imagine life without him.

"Come on, woman," he growled, his voice still husky from sleep as he popped her on the hip. "Out of that bed. Today's the big day."

She looked at him blankly. Had he read her mind? "'Big day'?"

"The Rice Festival," he reminded her, slipping on a clean shirt. "Don't tell me you forgot."

The Rice Festival was an end-of-harvest celebration that drew tens of thousands of people from all over Arkansas to the small town of Weiner every year. There was a parade and carnival and music, as well as two days of arts and crafts, contests and entertainment. The local paper and all topics of conversation in town had centered on nothing else for days.

It was the last thing Gabby wanted to think of now. Did he know she loved him? Had he even begun to guess? And where, dear God, did they go from here?

The teasing glint in Austin's eyes faded to a frown as she just continued to lie in bed staring at him as if she'd never seen him before. He took a step toward her, suddenly afraid. "Gabby? Are you all right?"

Startled, she looked up to find him standing over her. Heat flared in her cheeks. "What? Oh . . . yes, of course. I guess I was thinking about something else."

He arched a brow at the sight of the soft flush that tinged her creamy skin. Now what had she been thinking about to make her blush? Fascinated, he perched on the edge of the mattress next to her, then stretched his arm across her to place his hand next to her hip as he leaned toward her. His eyes delved into hers. "Something or someone?"

She couldn't tell him that she'd been foolish enough to fall in love with him! He'd given her no indication that he wanted that from her, and she doubted that he ever would. Hadn't he warned her that he was a loner? She cast her mind frantically around for something to say and blurted out the truth without thinking. "It's just that every morning you've kissed me awake—" Appalled, she broke off and closed her eyes with a groan. "I can't believe I said that."

Austin grinned and fought the need to crawl back into bed with her. So she was just as addicted to their morning kisses as he was, he thought smugly. Did she have any idea what it cost him to let her go morning after morning? "Maybe I'd like you to kiss me for once," he said softly, giving in to the temptation to stroke her hair. "If you want me, show me."

It was such a simple request. And loaded with dynamite now that she knew how much she loved him. But she couldn't have ignored it any more than she could have willed her heart to stop pounding. Right or wrong, she loved this man, and she had to show him, even if she couldn't say the words.

Her eyes locked with his, she slid her hands up his arm, over muscles that were suddenly tense, to his shoulder and then to the back of his neck. With a gentle tug, she brought him down to her.

She should have been nervous, at the very least uncertain. She'd never made love to a man, never tried to seduce one. And that was what she wanted to do, she realized as her mouth met his. Seduce him. She wanted to make him ache as she had ached, set his blood singing as hers had sung, to pleasure him in a way that only a woman in love could. She didn't know how to begin, but it didn't matter. Nothing mattered but now, this moment and the sparks that were already sizzling between them.

She tried to kiss him as he had kissed her for the past two mornings, slow and easy and languid, as if they had all the time in the world. But her emotions were too volatile, the little control she'd had shattered by the love coursing through her. Her tongue swept over his mouth as her arms tightened around him, a desperation unlike anything she had ever known driving her past thought.

She felt his shudder as she took the kiss deeper, heard his groan as her teeth nipped at him, and wanted to soar. Need drove her now, raw and pulsing and as sharp as a knife. Her mouth hot and wild on his, she tugged impatiently at the shirt that he'd pulled on, her fingers aching to touch him. All of him. Wrenching her mouth free of his, she muttered a dark curse as she whipped the shirt from his back and tossed it away. Before it could float to the floor, her hands were exploring him in wonder, her mouth sliding down the hard column of his throat to taste him.

Beautiful. It was the only word she could think of to describe the hard, lean muscles that sculptured his chest, the power that lay just beneath the surface. Murmuring his name, she rained kisses across his shoulder, down to the flat plane of his stomach and back up again to the tempting darkness of his nipples.

A groan ripped through his throat at the hot flick of her tongue on him, teasing him, destroying him. She moved over him like wildfire, burning him with her heat, setting him aflame until even the short, gasping breaths of air he was able to drag into his lungs seemed scorched with the scent of her.

He clutched at her, desire hot needles in his blood as he tried to clear his head for just a moment. Dear God, what had he done? He'd asked for a kiss and unleashed a wanton who wanted him as badly as he wanted her. For days, he had waited for a sign that she wanted more from him than the kisses he struggled to keep under control every morning, until he thought he would go crazy with the need for more. Now she was giving it to him, giving herself to him so sweetly she stole his breath, and there wasn't time for the type of loving he intended to give her their first time together.

Swearing, he dragged her mouth up to his and gave her a ravaging kiss before sitting up abruptly and pulling her up with him. His breathing as rough and uneven as hers, he locked her in his arms and buried her face against his chest. Lowering his chin to the top of her head, he murmured, "Woman, you certainly pick your moments. Do you know what time it is?"

Her arms tightened around his waist. "Time for you to make love to me," she whispered huskily against his throat as her heart still pounded against his. "I need you, Austin."

He groaned and pressed a kiss to her hair. Did she know how difficult she was making this? "Ida will be downstairs in five minutes. When I make love to you, I want all night."

All night. It sounded like heaven. She'd been so alone for so long, he was something she'd never thought she'd have—a man of her own to share the long, lonely darkness between sunset and dawn. He didn't speak of forever, only a night, but she hadn't expected him to. Their time together was moments stolen out of a dream that couldn't last. But for a little while, she could love him and pretend that it was for an eternity. It would have to be enough.

Pulling back, her eyes met his. "Tonight?"

He nodded, already counting the seconds and cursing them. "Tonight," he promised huskily, and wondered how he was going to make it through the day.

Gabby was convinced that she would spend the rest of the day fantasizing about the evening, but she never got the chance. From the moment she stepped out of the bedroom and into the kitchen, time seemed to slip into fast forward and she didn't have a minute to sit down, let alone daydream. Breakfast was cooked and gulped down, then Austin was pushing back from the table and quickly striding toward the door. "The parade doesn't start until eleven, so we've got time to start on that last rice field. If we're lucky, we may even be able to finish before the festival starts."

"Sorry, Austin," Ida said as she carried her plate to the sink, "but I'm going to have to steal Gabby away from you this morning. I need her help in the kitchen."

He nodded. "All right. I'll just use the hopper attached to the combine instead of the grain buggy. I'll see you ladies later." His eyes, smoky with promise that warmed Gabby like a caress, met hers in the instant before he stepped out the door.

"We haven't got much time, so let's get busy," Ida said as she hurried to the pantry and began pulling sugar and flour and cocoa from it. "Get the pie pans and the mixing bowls. You're going to enter a dessert in the rice-cooking contest."

"What!"

"Now don't panic. I worked up the recipe last winter. I've been trying to win that contest for the past twenty years, but the best I've been able to do is honorable mention. This year I think I've come up with a real winner. I'm not going to miss it just because of a dumb broken arm."

Behind the lenses of her glasses, the older woman's eyes were bright with determination and hope. Gabby's heart sank. During the past few days, she'd learned the basics of southern cooking, but she was nowhere near ready to enter any kind of a contest. "Are you sure you want to do this?" she asked uncertainly. "What if I foul it up? I'd feel terrible if you lost because of me."

"Don't be ridiculous," Ida snorted. "If we lose, it won't be because of you but because the judges don't know a good thing when they taste it. Come on, enough of this nonsense. Let's get started."

If Gabby had learned anything since coming to work for Ida, it was that there was no denying her when she spoke in that drill sergeant voice of hers. Sighing in defeat, Gabby felt a half smile tug at her mouth. "Has this recipe got a name?"

Ida grinned. "Chocolate crunch pie. And you're going to love it."

She was right. An hour and a half later, her clothes and face splattered with flour and chocolate, Gabby poured a creamy chocolate filling into the crunchy rice pie shells Ida had helped her make. Unable to resist, she swiped her finger around the inside of the empty mixing bowl and carried the chocolate she'd gathered to her mouth. Her eyes closed on a groan of pure pleasure as the mixture dissolved on her tongue. "Oh, God, Ida, that ought to be outlawed."

The older woman took her own swipe at the bowl and sighed in satisfaction. "Tastes just like mine." Laughing, she gave Gabby a bear hug, cast and all. "Hot damn, Gabby, we're going to win, you just wait and see! When the judges taste this, they're going to think they died and went to heaven."

"What do you mean 'we're' going to win?" Gabby laughed as she scooped up the last of the chocolate clinging to the bowl. "I just followed your directions. It's your recipe. You deserve all the credit."

"Nonsense," she scoffed. "The judges will take one look at my arm and know I couldn't have possibly made this by myself. We'll enter it under both our names."

"But—"

"No arguments," she interrupted, excitement dancing in her eyes as the back door opened to admit Austin. "We haven't got time. Here's Austin now." She moved toward the hall. "We've got to get ready to go. The Rice Tasting Center opens at the Catholic Hall at eleven. Don't dawdle."

Austin watched her hurry out of the kitchen before turning his eyes back to Gabby. A grin stretched slowly across his face as he noted the chocolate smeared on her cheek. "What's going on?"

"We're entering a pie in the rice-cooking contest," she explained. "It's Ida's recipe, but she insists on putting my name on it, too, since I had to cook it for her. She thinks we're going to win."

"That good, huh?" he teased as he crossed the room to her and stopped just short of the pies on the table. "Do I get a taste?"

He was so close she could see the mischief dancing in his eyes. Her heart skipped a beat as her smile answered his. "If I let you cut into one of those pies, Ida would kill us both. And we already licked the bowl clean."

His gaze moved to her cheek, stroking her. "You missed a spot," he murmured huskily. Before her hand could move to it, he leaned closer, his breath warming her skin. "Let me get it."

His lips settled on her cheek in a kiss so soft she might have imagined it but for the flick of his tongue slowly working at the chocolate. Heat tumbled into her stomach, melting her knees. She closed her eyes weakly, swaying toward him even as she protested, "Ida will be down soon.... Austin, please...."

"Don't say that," he growled, his lips sinking to her throat. "The only way I can please either one of us right now is to take you into our bedroom and keep you there the rest of the day."

"Ida—"

"I know, I know." Jerking back abruptly, he shoved a package into her hands to keep from pulling her into his arms. "Here. I bought this for you in town the other day. I thought you might want to wear it to the festival."

Surprised, she clutched the sack to her as if it contained the Hope diamond. "You bought me clothes? But why?"

He could have told her that he was tired of seeing her in clothes that were two sizes too big for her, but he only shrugged and offered, "I just thought you might like something new. I hope it fits. I had to guess at the size."

Opening the sack, she pulled out a black skirt and matching black-and-white sweater. They weren't expensive, but she knew it must have taken all the money he'd had left after he'd taken her to the doctor to pay for them. And they were just her size. Running her hand over the checked design of the sweater, she felt hot tears sting her eyes. "Oh, Austin...."

If a single tear reached her cheek, he knew she'd be in his arms when Ida came down the stairs. Forcing a grin, he teased, "You're not going to get all mushy on me, are you? 'Cause then I'll have to kiss you, and we'll never get to town in time to enter that pie in the contest."

She choked on a laugh, blinking furiously. "We can't have that. Ida would never forgive us." Standing on tiptoe, she gave him a quick kiss on the mouth, which ended before it had begun. "Thank you," she said softly. "I'll go change."

The day that followed was one that Gabby knew she would remember always. There wasn't a cloud in the sky to rain on the parade, and the town was fairly overflowing with people from all over the state. The whole community had thrown itself into the festivities, and laughter and music floated on the air along with the tantalizing scent of food from the food booths.

It was a perfect day for a party, a perfect day to be in love. After the pie was entered in the contest under both their names, Ida caught up on all the gossip with some old friends, and Austin and Gabby were left to their own devices until the judging of the cooking contest. Hand in hand, they strolled through the crowd, laughing at the antics of a clown act on one of the two stages that had been set up for entertainment before wandering over to the carnival, where hawkers dared anyone who walked by to try their hand at the games of skill.

It was a dare Austin couldn't resist. He knocked down milk jugs with a baseball, pitched pennies into dishes, shot free throws with a basketball. And at every game, he won. Loaded down with the stuffed animals he won for her, Gabby finally laughingly begged him to please stop.

As the day passed, the crowd thickened, but all Gabby saw was Austin, all she felt was his fingers linked with hers, his hip and thigh brushing hers. They laughed together as they watched the lip sync contest, gazed into each other's eyes as they fed each other cotton candy. And when they finished and Austin pulled her into his arms to press his mouth to hers as if he were starving for the taste of her, Gabby nearly melted with the sweetness of it. She clung to him, unaware of the crowd that jostled them, the laughter, the interested eyes of strangers. If he wanted to kiss her in front of God and the whole town, she wouldn't offer one word of protest.

When he finally drew back, the taste of her and the candy still on his tongue, his grin was wide with satisfaction. "That's the best thing I've tasted all day."

"What?" she teased, her brown eyes twinkling. "Me or the candy?"

His grin broadened. "What do you think?"

"I think you're hedging. Maybe you need another kiss to decide the issue."

"And maybe we need to find Ida before I drag you off into the bushes and make mad, passionate love to you," he countered. "What do you think?"

He was teasing, she thought, studying the wicked grin curving his mouth. But then her eyes lifted to his, and the heat she saw there made her mouth go dry. "I think we'd better go find Ida," she said breathlessly, dragging a laugh from him. "While we still want to."

They found Ida just outside the Catholic Hall, waiting impatiently for them. "There you are!" she said in relief, grabbing each of them by an arm and dragging them inside. "Hurry up. They're about to announce the winners."

Austin grinned. "Why, Ida, if I didn't know better, I'd think you were nervous, and I can't imagine why. Gabby said you were sure you were going to win."

"Hush!" she shushed him, laughing in spite of her best attempt to appear stern. "We are going to win, but I don't want the whole world to know it before the fact. There's nothing worse than a cocky winner."

"Oh, look," Gabby said, drawing their attention to the front of the crowded room, where a microphone had been set up. "They're getting ready to make the announcement."

The man who stepped up to the microphone introduced himself as the president of the rice company sponsoring the contest. "As you know, we've been having this contest for many years," he told the anxious spectators, "but I think this year's entries were the best ever. Picking the winners was a tough job, so if you don't win, it was only because you were up against some stiff competition."

"Get on with it," Gabby muttered, clutching Austin's hand.

"The winners are—"

Ida grabbed Gabby's free hand. "This is it!"

"In the salad category, for her rice and tomato salad...Hester Weatherspoon." A startled cry went up from somewhere near the front, and everyone laughed. "In the bread category, for her rice hush puppies...Marjorie Peters." This time a shriek ripped through the expectant silence and was followed by wild applause. "In the meat category, Mike Hopkins for his shrimp creole casserole." When there was no response, the announcer looked out into the crowd in concern. "Isn't Mike here?"

"Yeah," someone said from the back, laughing. "He passed out!"

Laughter rippled through the room, but Ida hardly noticed. Her fingers tightened on Gabby's. "Desserts are next."

But when the next category was announced, neither Ida's nor Gabby's name was called. It wasn't until then that Gabby realized how much she wanted Ida's recipe to win. Turning to the other woman, she tried to console her. "Oh, Ida, I'm sorry! Please don't be discouraged. You heard the man say how tough the competition was."

But Ida's eyes were still on the announcer. "It's not over yet. He hasn't announced the grand prize winner."

"And now for the grand prize winner." A hush fell over the room. "I told you already how good the entries were, and I wasn't exaggerating. But all of the judges agree that picking the top winner was the easiest and best-tasting decision they ever made. Ladies and gentlemen, the top prize for this year's rice cook off goes to...Ida Beauchamp and Gabby LePort for their chocolate crunch pie!"

"My God, we did it!" Ida said numbly. "We did it!" With a screech, she grabbed Gabby and danced a jig.

Stunned, Gabby laughed until the tears ran down her cheeks. "I can't believe it. I just can't believe it."

Austin let out a rebel yell that could have been heard in the next county, then pulled them both into his arms for a kiss and a hug before quickly releasing them and pushing them toward the front. "Go on, you two. Go collect your prize."

Towed along by Ida, Gabby was halfway to the front before she remembered that the last thing she wanted was to be the center of attention. But it was too late. Ida reached the microphone and insisted Gabby share the limelight with her. Resisting the urge to fidget, Gabby stood at her side, deferring to the older woman to accept the three-hundred-dollar prize for them and do all the talking. Agonizingly aware of all the eyes on her, studying her in curiosity, Gabby almost wilted when it was finally over. But even as she stepped out of the building into the gathering twilight, she couldn't help worrying. Had anyone recognized her?

Only half-aware of Ida and Austin's jubilation, she never saw the man who stepped in front of her until she crashed into him. Before she could fall, strong hands reached out to grab her, steadying her. "Oh, God, I'm sorry," he apologized quickly, his sharp brown eyes searching her face. "Are you all right? I didn't mean to knock you out of your shoes."

She stepped back into the comforting wall of Austin's chest. "No, no, I'm fine," she said quickly, embarrassment climbing her cheeks. "It was my fault. I wasn't watching where I was going."

"Well, if you're sure you're okay..." With another muttered apology, he disappeared into the crowd.

"Earth to Gabby," Austin teased in her ear as he slipped an arm around her waist. "Come down out of the clouds, sweetheart, before you get trampled."

"She's got a right to be walking on air," Ida said, the grin on her face looking as if it had been permanently carved there. "If I was a few pounds lighter, I might be up there with her myself!"

"Oh, don't give me that, Ida Beauchamp," he tossed back. "I bet you can float when you want to. Let's go find a dance floor and find out."

"A dance floor?" she repeated, her skepticism belied by the interest sparkling in her eyes. "Why, I haven't danced in years."

"Then we're going to correct that right now. There's a big band playing at stage one, and we've got some celebrating to do."

And celebrate they did. The beat of the old Benny Goodman and Glenn Miller tunes was as mesmerizing as the music of the Pied Piper, drawing people from out of the shadows to dance under the stars. Her foot tapping, Gabby saw Ida swept away by the farmer who lived down the road from her, and in the next instant, Austin was pulling Gabby into his arms. Laughing, her feet hardly touching the ground, she followed his steps perfectly.

"I've been wanting to do this ever since we left the farm this morning," he said as he twirled her toward him and caught her close.

She blinked in confusion. "What? Dance?"

"No, get you into my arms," he retorted, flashing her a grin. "I should have thought of this sooner."

She felt his thighs firm against hers and said huskily, "Anticipation is good for the soul."

His eyes narrowed as he backed her away from the crowd and into the dark shadows on the sidelines. Dragging her still closer, he swayed to the music, content just to hold her. "And what would you know about anticipation?" he teased.

"Only what you've taught me. It makes sleeping...difficult."

His grin tilted ruefully. "Try impossible," he suggested. "Especially when you're in my arms."

In the darkness, she moved until her body was flush with his. "I never knew it could be like this," she whispered as the rest of the world withdrew to the very edges of her awareness.

"Just wait, sweetheart," he promised, his eyes glowing in the darkness. "The best is yet to come."

They danced and danced, drawing out the anticipation until they both ached with it. Ida searched them out in the shadows to tell them that she was leaving the truck for them and catching a ride home with friends. As soon as she was out of sight, they were once again drowning in each other's eyes. They could have danced minutes, hours; neither noticed the passage of time. But when they had each had enough of the intoxicating torture, the knowledge was there in both their eyes.

Dropping his arms from around her, Austin took her hand. "Let's go home."

Chapter 9

By the time they reached the farm, Ida had already gone to bed. The house was quiet and dark, the only light the one she had left burning for them in the kitchen. Shutting the back door quietly behind them, Austin took one look at Gabby's face and knew she needed some time alone. "Why don't you go on and get ready for bed," he suggested in a low, rough voice that seemed to belong to the night. "I'm going to check and make sure everything's locked up."

Her heart thudding, Gabby escaped to the bathroom to change into her gown. It wasn't until the door shut behind her and she was alone with nothing but her thoughts that she realized she was shaking. Had he seen how nervous she was? Was that why he had insisted on checking the locks when they both knew that Ida never went to bed without making sure everything was secure?

Staring into the mirror over the old-fashioned pedestal sink, she winced at her pale, wide-eyed reflection. The apprehension darkening her eyes was far too close to fear. Oh, God, he must think she was a fool! Twenty-six years old and trembling at the thought of making love with the man she loved. Somehow she would have to show him that it wasn't him she was afraid of, or even herself, but her own inexperience. She'd never had much confidence in her own sexuality, but it hadn't mattered. No one had ever made her heart thunder in her breast or made her long for something she couldn't even put a name to. Until now.

A rueful smile curled one corner of her mouth. How ironic that now, when she had nothing more than flannel to tempt him with and hands that were growing rough with work, she found herself in love. If she had run into him in her other life, as Gabriella Winters, she would have come to him in silk and satin, with skin to match. But then again, Gabriella would have never had a chance to meet a man who owned nothing but the clothes on his back, whose only mode of transportation was the trains he illegally hopped. She would rather miss the silks and satins than miss Austin.

And he was waiting for her. Suddenly needing the feel of his arms around her, she hurriedly stripped off her clothes and pulled on the gown. She had no perfume to scent her skin, only the clean smell of lavender soap as she quickly washed the heavy makeup from her face. When she was finished, there was no artifice to the woman who stared back at her from the mirror. With her heart in her eyes and her courage in her hands, she headed for the bedroom.

He was already there, standing in the glow of the single candle he'd placed on the nightstand. Still dressed in the shirt and jeans he'd worn to town, his eyes were dark gray embers in the sculptured hardness of his face. Clutching the skirt and sweater she'd taken off, Gabby faltered to a stop just inside the door, her breath leaving her lungs in a rush. The candle flickered, as if with her sudden doubts, setting the deep shadows in the corners dancing. Helplessly, her eyes met his in the silence that stretched between them.

Before she could struggle to find his name, to tell him of her worry of disappointing him, he stunned her by saying, "I don't want to hurt you."

"'Hurt me'?" she echoed, confused. "Why would you think that you would?"

"Because you make me crazy," he said simply. "And I want to make this special for you, and I don't know that I've got that much control."

If she had any last lingering doubts about loving this man, they vanished as she realized he was just as nervous as she was. She stepped toward him, unable to stay away any longer. "I know there's going to be a certain amount of pain the first time," she said softly as she stopped just inches from him. "I'm not worried about that. I just don't want to disappoint you."

The flame from the candle seemed to jump from the wick into his eyes. "It'll never happen," he assured her huskily as he pulled her into his arms. "Trust me."

"With all my heart," she answered simply. Her arms circled him, bringing him tight against her. The impatience that had been pulling at her all day stilled at the touch of his fingers on her cheek as they slowly skimmed over her as if he would absorb her into his skin. Go slowly, he urged her without words. Linger.

Savor. There was so much to taste, to feel. With a sigh, she let the tension drain out of her, making room for the pleasure.

She turned to honey in his arms, soft and hot and flowing. Murmuring her name, he fought to keep the kiss light and his arms from crushing her to him. Every time their eyes had met during the long day, he'd pictured her like this, melting all over him with her sweetness and the world held at bay by the closed door and the night. Now he had hours to love her, an eternity to lose himself in her. How would it ever be enough?

His breath shuddering through lungs that suddenly couldn't get enough air, he drew back, but only for an instant. Capturing her face in his hands, he tilted her chin, changing the angle, and settled his mouth on hers as if he could spend hours just kissing her. His tongue teased, then flirted with hers, coaxing a response from her that sent heat shooting into his stomach.

Too fast, he thought hazily, sharp needles of desire already pricking him. He was taking it too fast. She'd waited so long for this, he wouldn't give her wham, bam, thank you, ma'am. She deserved fireworks and comets, and he wanted to be the one to give them to her.

Dragging his mouth from hers, he rained moist kisses across her cheek and down her neck, nudging aside the lacy collar of her gown to taste the pulse hammering at the base of her throat. "Sweet," he murmured. "Did I ever tell you how sweet you are? I've got to touch you."

Dizzy, aching, her head spinning, Gabby never noticed how busy his fingers were at the buttons that trailed almost down to her waist until the front of her gown parted, revealing her to his hands and eyes and mouth. She gasped and looked down to see his dark hair in vivid contrast with the whiteness of her breasts as his mouth journeyed to a rosy crest. His mouth latched on to her, suckling. His name a soft, keening cry on her lips, she arched into him, her fingers grasping his hair to hold him close as her knees threatened to buckle.

Again, he took his mouth from her before the pleasure could become too intense, the pain of holding back too sharp. Lifting his head, he traced her with his hands, heating her as his fingers circled a nipple lazily, dipped to her waist, then slid back up to find her shoulders still hidden under the warm flannel. With a simple movement of his wrists, he sent the gown sliding to the floor in one long caress of her body. Lowering his head, his mouth captured the breath that rushed between her parted lips as he picked her up and carried her to the bed.

She was floating, even after her bare back settled against the sheets, caught up in a dream as she watched with passion-heavy eyes as Austin undressed. Bathed in the light of the candle, he dropped his shirt to the floor and stood before her in nothing but jeans, which did little to hide his arousal. In the next instant, even the jeans were gone, and he was climbing into the bed with her.

Heat against heat, heart against heart. With whispered sighs and moans, they moved into each other's arms and drifted deeper into a world where the only reality was the fire slowly building inside them. He touched her before she felt the need to ask, knowing without words where she wanted his hand, his mouth.

Following his lead, she did likewise, exploring him tentatively, glorying in the hard, masculine beauty of him with a shyness that nearly shattered his tightly reined control.

When they were both feverish, hot, desperate for more, he took her over the first crest with his hands alone. Before she even had time to catch her breath, he was kissing her again, parting her thighs, entering her so slowly, so gently, tears streamed from her eyes. Horrified that he'd hurt her, he froze, the muscles clenching in his jaw as he fought for control. "Oh, God, sweetheart, I'm sorry—"

"No!" Her legs twined around him, holding him close, her smile tremulous as she pulled him back down for a kiss. "Don't stop now," she whispered. "You didn't hurt me. I just never expected it to be so beautiful."

His fingers unsteady, he brushed the tears away from her hot cheek and planted a kiss there. No woman had ever moved him more. "You're the one who's beautiful."

"If I am, it's only because you make me feel that way. Love me," she murmured, arching into him sweetly and destroying the last of his control. "Completely. I don't want to miss anything."

He could have told her then that together they'd already found what some people never discovered in a lifetime, but he couldn't find the words. Groaning her name, he did as she asked and let the passion sweep them away.

The morning sun was just creeping into the bedroom when Gabby woke to find herself held close in Austin's arms, as if, even in sleep, he couldn't get

enough of her. His chest was a wall of solid heat at her
back, his arm a heavy weight locked around her middle. Smiling dreamily, she covered his arm with hers
and hugged him to her, images of their loving flashing against her closed eyelids. How could she have
known by just looking at him that there was such tenderness in him? He'd loved her so gently, so thor-
oughly, she hadn't wanted the night to end. If they
could just have a few more hours, they could pretend
that they were alone in the house and had nothing to
do but lie in bed and enjoy each other. Giving in to the
need, she slid her hand over his and silently urged his
fingers to her breast.

"Little wanton," he growled in her ear, closing his
fingers over her possessively. When she started in surprise, he only chuckled and nuzzled her neck. "I think
I've created a monster," he teased. Before she could
begin to guess his intentions, he flipped her onto her
back and brought his mouth down to hers with a hunger that stunned them both.

He wanted her. Again. It still surprised him how
much. Last night, he'd seeped himself in her until he
hadn't known where he ended and she began, until the
scent and taste of her surrounded him and clouded his
brain. It should have been enough, but the memory
only made him want her more in a dozen different
ways.

His hands tightened as his body did. "I want you,"
he groaned against her soft, giving mouth. "Right
now. I can't seem to get enough of you."

It was an admission he hadn't expected to make out
loud, one she hadn't expected to hear. Lifting her hand
to his face, she ran her fingers over the rough stubble

that shadowed his jaw, loving the friction it created as her eyes smiled into his. "The feeling's mutual."

Her cheeks were already chafed from his beard, like patches of fever on her tender skin. Running her finger around her kiss-swollen mouth, his eyes met hers. "You should have told me I was rubbing you raw," he murmured. "I keep forgetting how sensitive your skin is."

"I didn't want you to stop kissing me," she replied, grinning. "Things were just getting interesting."

"Oh, so you want interesting, do you?" he said with a laugh, suddenly levering himself up and pulling her after him out of the bed. "I'll give you interesting. You can watch me shave, and then I'm going to drive you crazy in the shower."

Stark naked, he tugged her toward the door, ignoring her giggling protest. "Austin, have you lost your mind? We can't step out in the hall like this! What if Ida—"

From out in the kitchen, they suddenly heard the unmistakable sounds of coffee being made. Ida made it every morning the minute she came downstairs.

Reality, sharp and intrusive, stood between them like an unwanted guest. Austin bit back a curse. What the hell was he thinking of? There would be no hot shower with Gabby, no long morning spent with her in bed. Last night, wrapped in her arms, it had been easy to slip into a world of fantasy that was populated only by the two of them. But now, in the cold light of day, he was forced to admit that nothing had changed. She trusted him enough to make love with him, but not enough to tell him who she was, what she was running from. If the fears that still haunted her

urged her to once again flee across the country, there
was nothing he could do to stop her, nothing he could
do to help her.

Just the thought of that happening had his hands
tightening on her. "Gabby, we have to talk—"

The morning farm report suddenly droned from the
radio in the kitchen, then increased in volume as Ida
turned it up slightly. Austin's terse curse mixed with
Gabby's chuckle. "That's a hint, in case you didn't
notice," she said quietly as she snatched up her gown
and struggled into it. "We'll have to do this—"

"Later," he grumbled, pushing her toward the door
while he had the strength to let her go. "I know, I
know. Duty calls. Go take your shower."

Later, Gabby never knew how she cooked breakfast without burning half the food. She was much
more comfortable around the stove than she had been
a few days ago, but her attention kept sliding to Austin. Dressed in a blue flannel work shirt and jeans, his
jaw freshly shaved and his hair combed, he sat at the
kitchen table and appeared to be reading the morning
paper. But Gabby wasn't fooled. Every time her eyes
drifted to his, he was watching her with a hunger that
had nothing to do with food. Bedroom eyes. She'd
heard of them all her life, but it was only now that she
knew what the saying meant. He had only to look at
her with those smoky eyes of his and she found her
thoughts tangling with images of last night and intimacies that still left her breathless.

He knew what he was doing to her—she could see
the knowledge in the slow smile that curled just the
corner of his mouth before his gaze once again
dropped to the paper. Cursing him, loving him, she

longed to turn the tables on him and heat his blood
with one long look. But Ida was sitting across from
him at the table, watching the two of them with
knowing eyes. Struggling to act as if their relationship were no different than it had been the day before, she turned her attention back to her cooking.

During breakfast, the work for the day dominated
the topic of conversation, just as it did every morning. Austin had finished the last of the rice harvest
while Gabby and Ida were making pies the day before, and the soybeans wouldn't be brought in for
several more days. That gave them all a chance to
catch their breaths and turn their attention to other
work that had been put on hold during the harvest.
Austin announced his intention of replacing a leaky oil
pump on one of the trucks. With Ida's help, Gabby
planned to tackle the laundry after she took care of the
dishes.

The day promised to be a routine one . . . until they
finished breakfast and carried their plates to the sink.
Gabby was already starting to rinse the dishes when
Austin crossed to her and turned her into his arms to
give her a slow, lingering kiss. When he finally lifted
his head, he was grinning and she was clinging to him
helplessly. "See you at lunch," he whispered, then
headed for the coat rack next to the back door, where
his jacket was hung.

"My, my." Ida chuckled as she leaned back against
the counter and leveled teasing brown eyes on Gabby's glowing face. "Last night certainly put you two
in a romantic mood. You should go dancing more
often."

"I couldn't agree more," Austin said, his gray eyes
flashing wickedly. "There's something about holding

a woman under the stars that goes right to a man's head." Shrugging into his blue jean jacket, he pulled open the back door and gave Gabby a wink. "See you later."

When Gabby only stood there, staring after him, Ida laughed and patted her on the shoulder. "You're lucky he's yours, honey. If he wasn't married, half the women in the county would be after him."

Unconsciously, Gabby fingered the ring on her left hand. The claim she had on Austin wasn't as strong as the gold band she wore, and it was fake. The brightness went out of her eyes at the thought. But before the day could be completely ruined for her, she remembered that there was nothing artificial about the care and gentleness he had shown her last night and this morning. Then, there had been no one there but the two of them, no one he had to pretend for. The need he had for her had been as real as hers for him. As long as she could hang on to that, nothing else mattered.

The morning flew by, as did her chores, but she hardly noticed the work itself. Standing in the sunshine, the wind whipping at her hair and cheeks, she found a quiet contentment in hanging the just-washed clothes on the lines that were set up on the opposite side of the house from the workshop. Hanging Austin's clothes next to hers felt right, as if she really were doing this for her husband instead of her lover. A peace unlike any she had ever known flooded her, bringing a smile to her lips to match the one in her eyes. She was so full of joy, she wanted to hug the whole world.

As she hung up the third load, she felt eyes on her, watching her every move, and almost laughed out loud. Austin. Every time she'd stepped out the back door, he'd seemed to sense it and would look up from his work on the truck to find her. He never said a word, but the message in his eyes had needed no words. The promises she'd seen there had set her heart thundering.

The fine hairs at the nape of her neck tingled, warning her that this time he had followed her out to the clothesline. Grinning to herself, she hung up the last shirt in the load, then whirled, half expecting him to be sneaking up on her. He was just walking around the corner of the house.

Her hands settled on her jean-clad hips, her grin smug as she watched him approach. "And just what do you think you're doing?"

His hands were greasy, but that didn't stop him from walking right up to her and wrapping his arms around her, though he was careful not to touch her with his fingers. Resting his forehead against hers, he flashed her a rakish smile. "I'm looking for a redhead to run away with. What do you say, sweetheart? Want to make a quick trip into town with me for a new oil pump?"

When he smiled at her like that, she would have walked to China with him if that's what he wanted. But the laundry room was still knee-high full of dirty clothes. "Oh, Austin, I'd love to but I've still got a ton of laundry to do. I can't just run off and leave it when there's so much to do."

"You can't, huh?" he teased, rubbing his nose against hers. "What if I make it worth your while?"

The bottom seemed to drop out of her stomach at the sudden deep timbre of his words. Her arms slipped around his waist. "How?"

"How about a strawberry sundae at the Dairy Queen?"

So he wanted to play games, did he? She bit her bottom lip, pretending to consider, then shook her head regretfully. "Can't. I'm watching my weight."

"So am I," he tossed back, leering at her playfully. "You know, I've never known a woman to turn down a sundae before. Especially strawberry."

She almost laughed. "I'm not most women, in case you haven't figured that out yet. Try something a little . . . hotter."

His arms tightened around her. "Hotter, hmm? How about a chili dog?"

This time there was no holding back the laugh. "You know, for a smart man, you're remarkably obtuse. It's not food I'm interested in."

"Then maybe you'd like to stop in the woods on the way back and neck," he growled, swooping down to nip at the sensitive lobe of her ear, then tease it with his tongue. "Think about it. All alone in the woods in the pickup. There's an old quilt in the workshop I could throw in the back."

Did he know how he was tempting her? The laughter in her eyes gave way to regret. "What about the laundry?"

"It'll still be here when you get back?" he replied hopefully. At the shake of her head, his smile turned rueful. "Well, so much for my irresistible charm. I guess I'll have to make the trip to town alone, huh?"

Her lips twitching, she stepped out of his arms before she could change her mind. "Looks that way."

The single step he took toward her made a mockery of the distance she had put between them. Grinning devilishly, he reached out and ran a greasy finger down her nose. "Stubborn wench, I'll see you at lunch," he promised as he stepped past her. "Think about me while I'm gone."

She thought of nothing else from the minute he drove out of the yard. As she returned to the laundry room and pulled clean sheets from the washer, she determinedly told herself she couldn't possibly be missing him already. He'd just left. But she was. She started a load of jeans and found herself wondering where he was on the road to town, if he'd passed the woods yet and thought of her. If she'd gone with him, would they have even made it into town? Shaking her head at the images that played before her mind's eye, she quickly picked up the basketful of wet sheets, then stepped outside.

She had one sheet on the line, whipping in the wind, when she thought she heard a car drive into the yard on the other side of the house. Was Austin back already? Her heart pounding, she dropped a wet pillowcase back into the laundry basket and started around the house, the beginnings of a smile stretching across her face.

But the car that had pulled up before the house was a plain white Ford sedan, not Ida's pickup. And the man who got out wasn't Austin. He was as tall as Austin, but heavier, with a hard, rugged face that was dominated by sharp brown eyes and a cynical mouth. Standing next to the car, his thick brown hair ruffled by the wind, there was something vaguely familiar about him, but Gabby couldn't quite put her finger on where she had seen him before. She didn't think he was one of the many friends Ida had introduced her and Austin to yesterday at the festival, but she couldn't be sure.

She started toward him hesitantly. "Hi. Can I help you?"

Before he could answer her, another car suddenly drove into the yard and parked behind the Ford. Gabby only had time to note that it was a silver Mercedes before two men stepped out of it. She paled, recognition almost stopping her heart. Baxter and Dr. Edison Hill, her doctor.

"No!"

Her horrified whisper was whisked away by the wind, but Baxter Hawthorne heard it. He winced as if she had slapped him, the attractive age lines that usually enhanced his blunt, good-looking features deepening. Dressed in a navy three-piece suit that looked incongruous in the rural setting, his thick white hair disheveled, he stepped toward her, his eyes taking in at a glance the changes in her. "Gabriella, sweetheart, don't be that way. I've been so worried about you."

Her eyes flew from him to the doctor, who was approaching cautiously on her other side. Dr. Ed had always been her friend, someone she'd trusted with her life. A small man with kind eyes and a narrow, scholarly face, his hands were as gentle as his smile. But he had been the one who gave her the medication with the penicillin in it, and she couldn't trust him any more than she could her stepfather.

Struggling for control, she took a step back, then another, tears welling in her eyes. "I don't know how you found me, but I'm not going back," she said, choking up. "And don't think you can make me. I'm not a child you can drag home for running away. Damn it, stay away from me!"

Edison Hill stopped in his tracks at her sudden cry, his green eyes loving but sharp as they noted how close she was to terror. "It's all right, Gabriella," he said quietly. "You know we're not going to hurt you. We're just here to help you."

A sob rose in her throat as her fingers curled into her palms. She couldn't let them calm her with quiet words that were only meant to trick her. "Do you think I can't see what you're doing? I've seen the papers! You want everyone to think I'm going out of my mind so you can get control of my money."

Only three feet away from her, Baxter took another step toward her and held his hand out to her, his blue eyes filled with reproach. "Sweetheart, you're not thinking clearly. When have I ever tried to hurt you? I love you. Don't you know I wouldn't harm a hair on your head?"

Confused, wanting desperately to believe him, she searched his square face for the lies she knew had to be behind his words, but she saw only concern in his eyes and a pain that was as real as her own. Oh, God, how could she believe him? How could she not?

"No!" The corner of the house brought her up short, stopping her retreat. "No, I don't know anything anymore," she said on a note of rising hysteria, tears now streaming down her face. "I can't trust you, and I'm not going back. I can't! No, don't touch me—"

But it was too late. His arm was around her, his familiar scent surrounding her as he pulled her against his chest. Terrified at getting pulled back into a world of soft smiles and lies, she struggled to free herself even though she knew it was too late. He was a bear of a man, and although his hold was gentle and sought only to keep her from becoming too hysterical, she was too upset to notice. "No. Let go! I won't let you do this!"

"Easy, baby, calm down. You know it isn't good for you to get this upset."

When she only struggled harder, her breath now tattered sobs, he looked helplessly at the doctor.

"I'm going to have to give her a sedative," Edison said quietly.

Gabby stiffened, the panic gripping her abruptly turning to horror. "No!"

"It'll just calm you down, honey," the older man assured her as he opened his medical bag and quickly prepared a shot. "We'll talk when you wake up."

"No...*no!*" she moaned as she felt the prick of the needle in her arm. Her heart pounding madly, the drug raced through her system, dragging her down into a darkness from which there was no escape. In seconds, her eyes grew heavy, her body leaden, and she couldn't fight it. Austin. Where was Austin? It was her last thought before she went limp in her stepfather's arms.

Alarmed by the cries that had just reached the back of the house, Ida stepped out on the front porch just in time to see Gabby sag in the arms of a stranger. Carrying the shotgun she'd retrieved from the study, she snapped it up into position, resting it against her cast. "What the hell's going on here?" she demanded harshly. "You better have a damn good explanation, mister, or you're going to find yourself talking to the sheriff."

Baxter settled Gabby more comfortably in his arms and didn't even lift an eyebrow at the shotgun staring him in the eye. "I've already talked to Sheriff Hawkins, Mrs. Beauchamp, so you can put that gun away. I'm Baxter Hawthorne, Gabriella's stepfather, and I've come to take her home."

"If you've got to knock her out to get her to go with you, then I'd say she doesn't want to go," she retorted tartly. "Does her husband know about this?"

"She hasn't got a husband. The man she was with is just someone she's been traveling with."

Stunned, Ida almost dropped the nose of the gun. "That's a lie. It has to be."

"No, ma'am, it's not." He nodded toward Edison Hill, who was closing up his medical bag. "This is Dr. Hill, Gabriella's doctor. He was treating her for paranoia when she ran away weeks ago. We've come to take her home so she can get the medical treatment she needs. If you don't believe me, go call the sheriff. He'll verify everything I've just told you."

"But she seemed perfectly fine," Ida protested. "There must be some mistake."

He nodded, not the least surprised. "Gabriella is very adept at concealing her emotions. Now, if you'll excuse us, I'd like to get her home. It's going to take a lot of care to get her back on her feet."

He carried her to the Mercedes and tenderly laid her on the back seat. Seconds later, he and the doctor drove away. As Ida watched, another man she had only just noticed standing next to a white Ford got into the car and followed the Mercedes down the road.

Ida didn't wait to see more. Hurrying back into the house, she rushed to the phone and quickly called the auto supply store in town. Austin might not be Gabby's husband, but Ida knew he would have never let those three men carry her off. Cursing herself for not making them wait until he returned, she sighed in relief when she finally heard a familiar voice on the other end of the line. "Buddy, this is Ida. I'm looking for Austin, my hired hand. Is he there?"

"He was about twenty minutes ago," the clerk drawled. "But we didn't have that oil pump he needed, so I sent him on over to Fred Bailey's place in Newport. They should have what he needs."

"Thanks. I'll try there," she said, and immediately hung up before he could start a long-winded conversation. But when she tried Fred's place, Austin had just left without the part and without saying where he was going. Swearing, she reached for the phone book and called every auto parts store within a thirty-mile radius, leaving a message for Austin to call her immediately if he happened to come in. After that, all she could do was wait.

Ten miles away, the Mercedes and Ford stopped at a small runway that was owned and operated by a crop-dusting company, where Baxter's private jet awaited them. As the doctor carried a still-unconscious Gabby to the plane, Baxter approached the man who stepped from the Ford and held out an envelope full of cash to him. "I want to thank you for finding her for me, Nick. You did a good job."

Nick Bonadero took the money reluctantly, his eyes narrowed on the small figure being carried into the plane. "Is she going to be all right?"

"She will be now that she's going to get the treatment she needs," the older man said confidently. "You don't need to worry about her anymore. She's my concern now, and I'll take good care of her." Reaching into his pocket, he pulled out a set of keys. "Here are the keys to the Mercedes. Drop them off when you turn in your rental car in Memphis, and they'll send someone to pick it up."

Without another word, Baxter turned and boarded the jet. From his position by the Ford, Nick watched the plane take off and head north, the image of wide, haunted brown eyes destroying the satisfaction he usually found in a job well-done.

Chapter 10

Barreling along the road to the farm as if he'd been driving it all his life, Austin glanced down at the carnations that lay on the seat next to him and grinned ruefully. Flowers! What would Gabby and Ida say when he showed up with an armload of carnations for them? They'd probably think he had lost his mind, and he couldn't help wondering if they might be right. When he'd seen that kid selling carnations on a corner in Jonesboro, he'd stopped and bought every flower he had before he could check the impulse. When was the last time he'd acted so sentimentally? He couldn't even begin to guess.

Up ahead, he caught sight of the farmhouse and unconsciously increased his speed, although he was already well past the legal limit. He'd told Gabby to think of him while he was gone, but he was the one who hadn't been able to push her from his mind. As he'd rushed from one town to another looking for that damn oil pump, all he'd been able to think about was how long it was going to take to get back to her. The half hour he'd planned on being gone had stretched into two hours, and that was too damn long.

Laughing at his own impatience, he pulled into the yard and cut the engine, half expecting Gabby to come flying around the house to him when she heard the truck. But there was no sign of her, so he quickly gathered up the flowers, intending to slip in the back door and surprise her.

He never got the chance. Just as he stepped out of the pickup, the front door flew open and Ida came hurrying down the steps to him, her usually tanned cheeks as white as a sheet, her hair streaming behind her as if she'd been running agitated fingers through it. "Austin! Thank God you're home! Gabby—"

Alarmed, the flowers fell from his arms, forgotten as he grabbed Ida's shoulders. "What happened? Has she had another seizure?" he demanded roughly, his eyes rushing past her to the house. "Where is she?"

He would have moved past her, but her fingers latched on to him, holding him before her. "She's gone!" she cried. "Her father showed up with a doctor and another man and took her home."

Gone. She was gone. The loss that went through him left him numb. Last night, he'd spent hours holding her, loving her. How could she be gone? Unconsciously, his fingers tightened on the older woman's shoulders. There had to be a mistake. "Damn it, Ida, what do you mean they took her home? She was running away from Baxter Hawthorne. She would have never gone with him willingly."

"I didn't say 'willingly,'" she replied cautiously, bracing herself for the explosion she knew was sure to come. "By the time I reached the front porch, Gabby was as limp as a rag in her daddy's arms. They must have drugged her."

Ida had never seen fury like the kind that transformed Austin's face at that moment. His jaw became set in granite, his eyes turned cold and deadly with rage, and the curses that rolled off his tongue widened Ida's eyes. Quietly, she told him everything Baxter Hawthorne had told her, including his claim that Gabby and Austin weren't really married. "I don't care if you're married or not," she said flatly. "I know you care about that girl, and you would have never let them take her if you'd been here. I threatened to call the sheriff, but Mr. Hawthorne said he had already talked to him. I'm sorry, Austin, but there was nothing I could do."

Violence still pulsing in his blood, he clamped his teeth on an oath, his mind torturing him with the image of Gabby lying helpless in the arms of her stepfather. "It wasn't your fault," he said quietly, finally regaining control of his anger. "It's true, we aren't married. I'm sorry we had to lie to you, but Gabby was running from something she wouldn't even tell me about. Whatever it was, it terrified her." His hands dropped from her shoulders to clench into fists. "I should have made her come with me today. She'd be safe now. Damn it, if he hurts her, I'll make him wish he'd never been born!"

Ida sank to the front steps as she remembered the ridiculous claims Baxter Hawthorne had made about Gabby's sanity. "He said she was suffering from paranoia. He was going to get her treatment." She lifted stricken eyes to Austin. "What if he and that doctor decide to put her in a private sanitarium some-where?''

He would never see her again. His gut clenched. "The hell they will! I'm going after her—" He swore, suddenly remembering that he didn't have nearly enough cash for an airplane ticket to Kentucky, and all his credit cards had been left behind back in his apartment for safekeeping. "I'll bet you that Hawthorne's taking her to Louisville. Can you loan me the money to go after them, Ida? I can't explain now, but I've got the money to pay you back. I just don't have time to get to it—"

She was already pushing herself to her feet. "I don't need any explanations. I trust you, and I know there's nothing wrong with Gabby's mind, regardless of what her stepfather says. Let me get my purse, and I'll drive you into Memphis to the airport."

She turned to hurry into the house, but she hadn't even taken a step when a car turned into the yard. It was the same white Ford that had been there earlier. Surprised, she stiffened as the driver got out and she saw it was the same man who had stood silently by while Gabby was drugged and spirited off. "He's one of the men who was with Gabby's father," she told Austin when he looked at her inquiringly.

Austin's narrowed eyes snapped back to the other man, recognition pulling at him as he noted the rugged, cynical face, the shrewd brown eyes. He'd seen him somewhere.... The clouds fogging his memory parted, and suddenly he was seeing Gabby as she had been last night, dressed in the skirt and sweater he'd bought her, her face flushed with excitement after learning she and Ida had won the cooking contest.

They'd stepped outside and Gabby had plowed right into the arms of a stranger.

At the time, they'd all thought it was nothing more than a harmless accident. But now, looking back on it, it didn't seem like an accident, but a setup. Austin could still see the way the man had stared at Gabby, as if he were stripping away the makeup and the dyed hair, searching for the woman underneath. As if he knew who she was and only needed a close look to confirm it. Then this morning he'd led Baxter Hawthorne right to her.

Enraged, Austin crossed the yard to him, not even stopping when he saw the man was about to speak. Pulling back his clenched fist, he hit him in the jaw with all the strength of his pent-up fury. "That's for Gabby," he snarled as the stranger went down with one punch. "I don't know who you are or what your connection to Hawthorne is. But you're going to tell me where Gabby is, or I'm going to beat the hell out of you!"

As Nick Bonadero picked himself up off the ground, he gingerly felt his jaw, wincing at the blood that trickled from a cut at the corner of his mouth. "If you'll just calm down a minute, I'll tell you everything you want to know," he retorted as he wiped away the blood with the back of his hand in disgust. "My name is Nick Bonadero. I'm a private investigator. If you want to get the girl back, I can help."

So he was playing both ends against the middle. What little control Austin had left snapped. "You son of a bitch!" he growled, and planted his fist in the other man's hard stomach. "Do you think I'm going to *pay* you to tell me where she is when you're the one who led her old man to her? Think again, you bastard!'' he grunted, hitting him again. "You'll rot in hell before I'll give you one thin dime."

"Did I ask you for money?'' Nick demanded harshly, shoving Austin back before he could hit him again. "Damn it, I don't know what you had going with the girl, but you're not going to use me for a punching bag when I came back here to help you!'' Slowly straightening, he ignored the pain screaming through his body and faced Austin with eyes that were as hard as flint. "You want to fight, we'll fight. But we're only wasting time we could be using to get Gabriella back."

Austin's mouth curled contemptuously. "I don't want any help from the likes of you."

"Fine," Nick spat. "Then you can find her on your own." Reaching inside his jacket for the envelope of money Baxter Hawthorne had given him, he threw it at Austin. "There! That's every dime the old man gave me to find her. You can burn it, for all I care. I don't want anything to do with it or Baxter Hawthorne. When he hired me, he didn't tell me the job included terrifying women. That's not my scene."

Austin stared down at the money he'd automatically caught, sudden doubts cooling his anger. Even at a glance, he could see that the envelope held a tidy sum of one-hundred-dollar bills. His gaze snapped back up to Nick's. "Why are you doing this?'' he asked suspiciously.

"I told you. I don't want anything to do with terrifying women. Hawthorne told me Gabriella was sick, that she was confused and her thinking had been all screwed up lately. But she didn't look confused to me when she saw Hawthorne. She looked scared out of her mind."

Austin's fingers clenched around the money, crumbling it. "I think we need to talk."

"That's a good idea," Ida said from the porch. "Why don't you both come into the kitchen and cool off with something to drink. Mr. Bonadero, you look like you could use some ice on that cut lip."

He grimaced and tenderly felt his already swelling lip. "I think you're right, ma'am. And the name's Nick."

She nodded. "I'm Ida, and this is Austin, though I imagine you already know that," she said as she hustled them into the kitchen.

She quickly put together an ice pack, then began to make iced tea. Austin motioned for Nick to take a chair at the kitchen table, then took the one across from him. "So Hawthorne told you Gabby had run away because she was sick. Was it your idea to offer a reward for her return?"

The other man lifted a brow in surprise. "You knew about that?"

He nodded. "I saw it on the front page of the paper. Gabby must have, too. She did everything she could think of not to be recognized. How'd you find her?

"Luck," Nick retorted as he took a long drink of the tea Ida sat before him. "We got a lot of calls about her, but most of them were from nuts. Then a man called from southern Kentucky who remembered seeing her walking on the side of the road and tried to give her a ride. I tracked her down to a farmer named Frank Jones, who told me about the two of you traveling together. But by the time I found him, you'd already hopped a train and were long gone."

But they hadn't gone far enough. Austin frowned. "How'd you find out we came here? When we left Promise, Gabby didn't look anything like that picture in the paper."

"I figured you'd take the first train out, no matter where it was going," he explained with a shrug. "I found out from the railroad that Weiner was the first stop, so I planned starting out here and working my way west until I found you. No one recognized the picture I flashed around town, but a doctor remembered treating a woman by the name of Gabby, who claimed to be Mrs. Beauchamp's niece. But he knows the family, and he was puzzled when her story didn't make sense. I still wasn't sure I was on the right track until I saw Gabriella for myself last night at the festival."

Austin swore at his own stupidity. If he hadn't been so wrapped up in Gabby and his plans for making love to her after they got home, he might have been suspicious of the hard, searching look Nick had given her when he'd bumped into her. "You took a good look at her," he said accusingly. "Couldn't you see that she wasn't sick? Did it even cross your mind that she might have a damn good reason for hiding from Hawthorne?"

An uncomfortable flush slid under the other man's bruised cheeks. "I wasn't hired to think, just to find her. It wasn't until I saw her with the old man that I knew something was wrong. He might be her stepfather, but she didn't even want him to touch her."

"Where are they now?"

"On their way back to Louisville in a private jet. Hawthorne told me she was no longer my concern. I don't agree." His brown eyes locked with Austin's. "I don't usually stick my nose into other people's problems unless I'm paid to do so, but I think I just landed that girl back in a hell of a mess. If you want my help getting her back, it's yours for the asking.''

Austin studied him for a long, thoughtful moment and saw an anger that almost matched his own. "Does Hawthorne know you came back here?''

"No.''

"Good.'' He tapped a finger on the envelope full of money he'd laid on the table, his mind making plans. If he was going to get Gabby back from a man as powerful as Baxter Hawthorne, he was going to need help and a hell of a lot of luck. "When can you leave for Kentucky?''

The tight, hard smile that spread across Nick Bonadero's face was that of a man who would dare just about anything. "There's a flight out of Memphis in an hour and a half. If we leave now, we can just about make it.''

Austin didn't even hesitate. Scooting back his chair, he snatched up the money. "Let's go. Baxter Hawthorne's going to pay for our trip.''

Something wasn't right. The thought slipped into the oblivion that shrouded Gabby's mind, nagging at her for only a second before it flitted away again. She stirred, a frown rippling across her brow. Had she overslept? she wondered drowsily. Austin should have woken her. Ida would need help with breakfast.

Guilt urged her toward consciousness, but her blood seemed to be thick and slow moving in her veins, her eyelids too heavy to lift. Her frown deepened, uneasiness suddenly sliding into her stomach. What was wrong with her? She couldn't move, couldn't hardly think without wanting to slip back into sleep. Her heart lurched in growing panic. She had to wake up. Now!

Fighting the pull of the black weight that tried to drag her back into a hazy world of forgetfulness, she forced her eyes to open to mere slits. In the late afternoon sunshine, the pale yellow walls of her own bedroom stared back at her like the bars of a jail.

"Oh, no!"

Her soft cry of horror was weak and slurred as memory swamped her, threatening to drown her in wave after wave of throat-clenching fear. Home. She was back home, drugged, at Baxter's mercy. And Austin didn't even know she was gone.

A sob shuddered through her. Why hadn't she told him who she was and what she was running from? He couldn't come for her now even if he wanted to. She'd never told him where she was from. Dear God, what was she going to do now?

Run! Run back to him! It was her only chance.

Panic gave her the strength to push the comforter off of her, but she almost cried aloud at the energy it took just to ease her legs over the side of the bed to the floor. Her head swimming, she stared down at the pink satin nightgown that covered her and had no memory of being undressed. That, more than anything else, terrified her. Baxter had taken control from her, control of her mind, control of her body, when she was too weak to stop him. Where would it all end?

Fear galvanized her, urging her from the bed. Struggling to her feet, she swayed, her eyes trained on her closet, all her concentration focused on the distance between the bed and her clothes. Five steps. She only had to take five steps to reach her clothes.

She'd only taken two when her bedroom door opened and a woman in a nurse's uniform walked in. Big-boned and as solid as a tank, she took one look at Gabby wobbling on unsteady legs in the middle of the room and quickly hustled to her side. "Honey, you shouldn't be up," she scolded as she slipped her arm around Gabby's waist to urge her back to bed. "Now you get right back in bed. I'll get whatever you need. My name's Elizabeth, and your daddy hired me to take good care of you."

"No, please...he's not my father—"

"Well, of course he is," she soothed placatingly, clicking her tongue. "And he's worried sick about you. Now come on and be a good girl and get back in bed."

The arm at her waist was insistent and as strong as tempered steel. Gabby knew she couldn't win, but she had to try. She pushed at the nurse, her eyes wide and desperate. "Let go of me!" she cried. "You don't understand. I have to get out of here. He's trying to drive me crazy!"

"Honey, that's just the medication talking," the nurse said as she determinedly helped her into bed. "You just lie down and close your eyes, and I'll give you something to make you feel better."

"*No!*"

She patted her hand, easily combating Gabby's feeble attempts to climb back out of the bed. "There's nothing to be afraid of. When you wake up, you'll be thinking a whole lot clearer."

Gabby watched in growing horror as the woman prepared another needle. "No! I don't want another shot!" she cried hysterically, but her strength was depleted. Helplessly, she watched the woman take her arm, tears spilling from her eyes as the drug was injected into her veins. Darkness descended before she was ready for it, pushing her down into the thick, black clouds. With a whimper, she gave herself up to it and lost herself in the inkiness.

Set in the middle of six hundred acres of Kentucky's finest bluegrass country, the Winters family home looked like something out of a movie. Stark white with green shutters and a wide portico that stretched the length of the house, it had an elegance about it that immediately reminded Austin of Gabby. At first glance, a man could be forgiven for seeing only the purity of line, the classiness that had nothing to do with an excess of money. But there were undercurrents in the air, shadows that seemed to speak out of the wide, paned windows, just as he'd often seen pain in the depths of Gabby's eyes. Was she in there somewhere waiting for him to come to her? Or had Baxter Hawthorne already hidden her away out of his reach?

He'd been asking himself the same questions for hours, ever since he and Nick had boarded the plane for Louisville. Nick had been almost positive Hawthorne intended to bring her home, but any man who would track down his stepdaughter and have her drugged couldn't be trusted to do the expected. Until they knew where she was for sure, they couldn't make any plans to rescue her. Since Hawthorne had already paid Nick for his services, he couldn't come snooping around the family estate without looking suspicious. That suited Austin just fine. He wanted to see for himself that Gabby was all right, and then he wanted just five minutes alone with Hawthorne.

Parking in front of the columned, white porch, Austin strode up to the front door, his face grim as he hammered on it with his fist. The angry pounding echoed through the house, but he only knocked louder, the fury that had been raging in him ever since he'd come back to Ida's to find Gabby gone suddenly straining his control, demanding release. If a hair on her head had been harmed, he promised himself, there was going to be hell to pay!

"All right, *all right!*" a feminine voice shouted from inside the house. "Hold your horses!"

The door was abruptly jerked open by a woman who could only be Gabby's younger sister. Tall and model thin in jeans and a red turtleneck sweater, her dark brown hair tumbling around her shoulders, her features were almost identical to Gabby's but for her expressive blue eyes and wide, unsmiling mouth. Standing in the doorway, she took a quick inventory of Austin's worn jeans and cotton shirt and lifted a brow. "Yes?"

"My name's Austin LePort," he said coolly. "I'm here to see Gabby."

"Gabby?" Sarah frowned. "I don't know how you know my sister, but Gabriella can't have visitors. She's sick."

She started to shut the door in his face, but with an angry growl, Austin put his shoulder to the thick wood portal and sent it flying back on its hinges. Stepping inside, his gray eyes dared her to get in his way again. "Lady, I'm not asking for your permission to see her. Now which room is Gabby's?"

Gasping in outrage, Sarah stepped back. "Now just a damn minute! You can't come barging in here—"

Austin only pushed past her to the wide stairs that spiraled up to the second floor. Taking the steps two at a time, he yelled Gabby's name. Throwing open the first door he came to, he found nothing but an empty bedroom. Muttering a curse, he moved down the long hall to the next door and then the next.

Sarah ran after him, swearing at him all the way. "If you don't leave right this minute, I'm going to call the sheriff! Daddy! Craig!" she called in growing panic as he drew closer to Gabriella's room. "Help!"

Austin ignored her and was reaching for the next door when a voice bellowed behind him, "What the hell's going on here?"

Sarah whirled and sighed in relief at the sight of her father striding down the hall with her husband, Craig, right at his heels. "Thank God! This . . . man is demanding to see Gabriella. I told him she was sick—"

"If she is, it's because she was forced to come back here against her will," Austin cut in coldly. Turning to face Baxter Hawthorne, he saw in an instant that he was a man who was used to being in charge, a man who didn't like to be crossed. Tall and solidly built despite his thick white hair, he radiated a power that Austin wasn't surprised Gabby had run from. He would make a dangerous enemy. "I'm not leaving till I see for myself that she's all right."

Hawthorne didn't bat an eyelash at the threat. "Who are you?"

"Austin LePort. Gabby and I were traveling together."

"As husband and wife," the older man added, his eyes hard. "Isn't that right, Mr. LePort?"

Austin's lips thinned. "Yes."

Craig James stepped from behind his father-in-law, his classically handsome face tight with disdain as he looked Austin over as if he were something the cat had dragged in. "You want me to call the sheriff, Baxter?" he asked the older man without taking his eyes from Austin. "He can be here in ten minutes."

For a long, tense moment, Baxter, too, stared at Austin, weighing his options, before he finally shook his head. "No, I don't think so. Mr. LePort obviously believes Gabriella is in some type of danger. I think he should see for himself that she no longer needs him to watch over her."

"But, Daddy—"

"Damn it, Baxter, you don't owe this man any explanations!"

His daughter and son-in-law might as well have saved their breath for all the attention he paid their protests. Motioning to Austin to follow him, he strode down the hall to Gabriella's room and quietly pushed the door open. "As you can see, Mr. LePort," he said quietly from the threshold, "Gabriella is perfectly fine. She's exhausted from the trip, but she'll be back to normal as soon as she catches up on her sleep."

She had a room fit for a princess, decorated in yellow and white and filled with the late afternoon sunshine that streamed in through the western windows. Next to the bed, a nurse sat reading quietly, but it was the woman nearly lost in the folds of the satin comforter who drew Austin's eye. She looked so small, her lashes dark fans against her pale cheeks, her palm turned up on top of the comforter as if she were reaching for him even in her sleep. Austin felt his heart twist, his arms ache with the need to hold her. Without stopping to think, he stepped toward her.

The arm that came up to block his path was as strong as steel. Shooting him a look that dared him to trespass farther, Baxter said, "You won't wake her, Mr. LePort. You wanted to see her. That's all. Now I suggest you come down to the library with me. I'd like to talk to you if you have a few minutes before you leave."

It wasn't a request, but an order. For a fleeting moment, Austin thought of the satisfaction it would give him to ignore it, but that wouldn't help him get Gabby back. To do that, he would have to make Hawthorne think he was playing by his rules. The old man would learn soon enough he took orders from no man where Gabby was concerned.

The fury seething in him carefully controlled, he stepped back, dragging his eyes from the slender figure on the bed. "I have a few minutes," he said curtly, and followed Hawthorne back downstairs.

Once they were in the library, the older man motioned for Austin to take a seat in the leather chair across from his Queen Anne desk, but he declined. This wasn't a man it would be wise to drop his guard with. "What did you want to talk about?"

Baxter leaned back in his chair and steepled his fingers, Austin's hostile tone sliding right off him. "I just wanted to know how you met Gabriella and where. I've only been able to glean bits and pieces of what happened after she left here."

Austin stuck his fists into his jacket pockets. "I ran into her in a boxcar not too far from here. If you want to know anything else, you'll have to ask Gabby."

Baxter lifted a brow in surprise. "So you were with my daughter the entire time. I hadn't realized." Suddenly making a decision, he reached into the desk drawer and pulled out a checkbook. "I don't imagine I have to tell you that the night you ran into Gabriella was the first time she was ever on her own. And I don't have to ask if you took care of her. I can see that you're a man who can take care of whatever problems come his way." Writing out a check with bold, sure strokes, he tore it off and held it out to Austin, silently daring him to take it. "It seems I am in your debt, Mr. LePort. This should compensate you for all your trouble."

A muscle ticked along Austin's jaw, the only sign of his fury as he stared stonily at the check before lifting his gaze back to Gabby's stepfather. "I don't think you want me to tell you where you can put that check," he said silkily. "I didn't come here for your money."

"No, you're after much more than that, aren't you?" the older man countered as he laid the check on his desk, then rose to his feet. "You want my daughter. I imagine you fancy yourself in love with her." His smile was understanding, cool, deadly. "Gabriella is a beautiful girl, but let's face it, Mr. LePort. You don't fit into her world any better than she fits into yours. So I suggest you go back to wherever you came from and forget you ever met her."

Without a word, Austin picked up the check, studied the very generous sum of ten thousand dollars, then calmly ripped it in two and let the pieces fall to the desk. When his eyes lifted to Hawthorne's, his smile was just as understanding, cool and deadly as the older man's. "First of all, Mr. Hawthorne, Gabby is not a girl, but a woman. As for forgetting I ever met her, I'll do that when she tells me she never wants to see me again," Austin agreed. "But not until then.

When she wakes up, tell her I was here. You can also tell her I'll be back,'' he said softly, then headed for the door. It was a threat and a promise he intended to keep.

It was almost three a.m. when he returned, the plan he and Nick had concocted a simple one. While the family slept, Austin would slip into the house and make his way to Gabby's room. He'd wake her, and together they would sneak out of the house as quietly as he sneaked in. Nick would be waiting for them at the airport with tickets for the flight to Miami.

Dressed all in black, Austin parked at the entrance of the long drive to the house and approached it on foot. Moving from shadow to shadow, he darted to the porch and flattened himself against a column. A minute passed, then two, while his heart pounded loudly in his ears. So far, so good, he told himself. Now all he had to do was find an unlocked basement window.

Five minutes later, he stood under Gabby's window, cursing silently. Every downstairs window was locked, and his only hope of getting inside was the oak tree that hovered protectively over Gabby's end of the house. Staring up at the thick limb that almost brushed the balcony outside her window, he swore again and reached for the nearest branch. Seconds later, he dropped soundlessly onto the small platform.

The french door was, thankfully, unlocked. His mind already jumping ahead to the climb with her back down the tree, he eased the window open and slipped inside. Through a connecting door that led to the adjacent room, a night-light softly cut through the darkness. On silent feet, Austin moved to the door and looked into the room beyond. The nurse he had seen

earlier slept in what had probably once been a nurs-
ery. Without a sound, Austin carefully pulled the door
shut before turning his attention to Gabby.

She lay unmoving on the bed, her breathing hardly
disturbing the dark silence of the night. Suddenly impatient to hold her, Austin quickly moved to her side
and leaned over her. "Gabby? Wake up, sweetheart," he whispered in her ear as he gave her a gentle
shake. "I'm going to get you out of here."

She never moved.

Frowning, Austin tried again, this time his hands
more insistent, though he was careful not to raise his
voice above a whisper. But her head only lolled on the
pillow, and her eyes remained stubbornly closed. With
a muttered curse, Austin lifted her hand and watched
it drop like a stone to the bed. Drugged, he realized.
Dear God, she was still drugged!

He sank to the side of the bed, fury battling with
concern. One day, he promised himself, Hawthorne
was going to pay for what he'd done to her! But right
now he had to get her out of the house, and the only
way he was going to do that was by carrying her
downstairs and out the front door. Without making a
sound.

He almost groaned at the thought before he caught
himself. Dragging back the comforter that covered
her, he scowled at the pink satin gown she wore. It was
gorgeous, but she could hardly wear it onto an airplane. And he couldn't take a chance on changing her
into something else when they could be discovered any
second. He'd have to take her as she was.

Hurrying to her closet, he blindly grabbed a pair of
pants, a blouse and a pair of tennis shoes and brought
them back to the bed. Moving to her bedroom door,

he slowly pulled it open, the tension knotting the back of his neck not easing in the slightest at the sight of the dark, empty hall. He glided back to her bed and was reaching for her when he saw the prescription bottle on the nightstand. He shoved it into his pocket, determined that Hawthorne wouldn't have a way to trace her this time, then scooped her up, clothes, comforter and all.

The trip through the sleeping house was nothing short of hell. Afraid of tripping on the trailing quilt, he moved with agonizing slowness, desperately trying to recall the placement of the furniture when he'd been there earlier. With every step, he half expected a board to creak and a suspicious Hawthorne to come blazing out into the hall to confront him. But the snores from the old man's room followed him all the way downstairs, never once abating.

Even then, he wouldn't let himself believe that he'd actually succeeded in rescuing her until after he'd wrestled one-handed with the locked front door and managed to open it. The coolness of the night rushed up to greet them, almost drawing a laugh of triumph from him. Under the triumph, however, was an anger that burned like an inferno in the depths of his eyes. Clutching Gabby close to his heart, he slipped back through the shadows to his rental car. By the time the sound of the engine being started drifted back to the house, he was already driving away.

Chapter 11

Resisting the urge to flatten the accelerator all the way to the floorboard, Austin headed for the airport at a sedate speed that soon had him grinding his teeth in frustration. A quick glance in the mirror assured him they weren't being followed, but that did nothing to alleviate the tension knotting his nerves. They still had a hell of a way to go before they were free of Baxter Hawthorne's powerful reach.

With one eye on the road, he glanced down at Gabby. She'd whimpered once when he'd put her in the car, but other than that, she hadn't moved. Covered from her chin to her toes in the comforter, she lay across the front seat with her cheek pillowed on his leg, sound asleep. With a will of their own, his fingers moved to the bright curls that caressed his thigh, his gut clenching with the need to hold her and finally reassure himself that she was there with him, where she belonged. But there wasn't time. They had a plane to catch in twenty minutes. How was he going to get her on board in her condition without raising someone's suspicions?

The question worried him all the way to the airport. Ten minutes later when he drove up to the main terminal and saw Nick pacing out front, he still didn't have any answers. He pulled up beside him to tell him they had a problem, but he never got the chance. "Where the hell have you been?" Nick demanded as he jerked open the passenger door and leaned down into the car. "I was beginning to think you were going to miss your plane." Suddenly noticing the comforter surrounding the sleeping Gabby, he looked at Austin as if he had lost his mind. "What'd you do? Grab her right out of her bed without even waking her?"

"I didn't have much choice," Austin retorted. "They must have sedated her again. She's dead to the world."

Nick swore softly. "Now what? You sure as hell can't carry her onto the plane. And in a nightgown, no less," he added, frowning down at the bit of pink satin that peeked out from under the comforter. "You'll get arrested for sure."

"The gown's not a problem. I brought her clothes. I've just got to find a place to change her into them." His mind working furiously, Austin stared unseeingly at the short-term parking across from the terminal entrance and found himself gazing at a darkened corner that wasn't nearly as well lighted as the rest of the lot. "There!" he said suddenly, pointing to the empty space. "I'll park in the shadows and change her in the car. While I'm doing that, you go get some coffee from the coffee shop. As much as you can carry. I've got a feeling we're going to need it."

"We've got ten minutes," Nick warned him as he slammed the passenger door. "Hurry!"

The minute he stepped back out of the way, Austin whipped the car into the parking lot and shot into the dark space, cutting the engine an instant later. Easing his leg out from under Gabby's cheek, he let himself out of the car and quickly came around to her side.

"Come on, Gabby, you've got to wake up," he urged as he pulled back the comforter and reached for the clothes he'd brought her. "Can you hear me? Wake up, sweetheart! Open those big brown eyes and look at me."

She didn't, but her murmur of protest was all the encouragement he needed. Talking to her as if she heard every word, he pulled her gown up to her thighs and closed his mind to everything but getting her dressed. "That's right. Wake up," he coaxed as he pulled the jeans up her legs. "Much as I like this gown, I'd just as soon no one saw you in it but me. We'll get you changed into your jeans and shirt, and then you're going to have to wake up. You hear me, honey?"

Tugging the jeans up to her slim waist, he quickly zipped and snapped them, then pulled her limp body up until she was leaning against him, her face buried against his neck. "Now for the blouse," he said gruffly. Glancing quickly around to make sure there was no one in the parking lot to witness him stripping an unconscious woman, he whisked the gown up over her head.

Whatever emotional distance he'd been able to achieve vanished at the sight of her. God, how could he have forgotten how beautiful she was? How soft? Cursing the sudden clumsiness of his fingers, he drew the blouse on with jerky movements, unable to drag his eyes from the paleness of her skin next to his rough, tanned hands. With slow, agonizing movements, he buttoned the buttons one by one, the muscles along his jaw clenching every time the backs of his fingers brushed her breasts.

"I'm getting too old for this," he muttered to himself when he finally finished. Propping her against the back of the seat, he bent down to slip her tennis shoes on her.

"How's it going?" Nick called softly as he crossed the parking lot balancing three Styrofoam cups of coffee. "Has she come around yet?"

"She murmured something, then went right back to sleep," Austin replied as he straightened and took one of the cups. "How much time we got?"

"Six minutes."

Austin swore and leaned over her to give her a rough shake. "Wake up, Gabby. I've got some coffee for you. Come on, babe, snap out of it."

Somewhere in the back of her mind, Gabby heard him calling to her, pleading with her through a dark fog. She never knew if she murmured his name or just hugged it to her heart, but it was suddenly imperative that she find him in the shadows that surrounded her. Struggling up from the deepest chasms of sleep, she turned toward his voice, a frown wrinkling her brow. "Austin?"

"Yes!" He sighed in relief as he slipped his arm around her shoulders and brought her against him. "Open your mouth and drink the coffee, sweetheart. It'll wake you up."

He held the cup to her mouth, urging swallow after swallow down her. Warmth cascaded through her in waves, bringing her, for the moment, to full consciousness. But her eyes were still too heavy to stay open for more than a second, and sleep beckoned temptingly. With a groan, she turned away from the cup. "Please . . . take it away. I'm tired."

"One more cup," he insisted, turning her face back to his and pressing the cup to her lips. "You've got to wake up long enough to walk onto the plane. After that, you can sleep as long as you like. I promise."

She was too exhausted to question where they were going, her mind too muddled with drugs to wonder how he had found her when he didn't even know her last name. But she would have done anything to get the sleep he promised her. Gulping down the last of the coffee, she leaned her head against his shoulder with a sigh. "No more. I can't drink any more."

His arm tightened around her. "All right, sweetheart, no more." Glancing up at Nick, he said, "Help me get her to her feet. She should be able to walk now with some help."

Between the two of them, they quickly got her across the parking lot and into the terminal just as the flight to Miami was called. Nick already had their tickets for them; all they had to do was get to the boarding gate. It wasn't easy. Her legs leaden, Gabby leaned heavily against Austin, using all her strength just to put one foot in front of the other.

When they finally reached their gate, the boarding area was deserted but for the airline personnel. Nick checked them in just as the last call echoed from the loudspeaker. "Okay, you're all ready to go," he said as he handed Austin their boarding passes. "I finally contacted your friend, Sam Bradford, while you were getting Gabby. He'll meet you at the airport."

Austin held Gabby against him with one hand and offered the other to Nick. "Thanks, Nick. I don't know what I would have done without your help."

The private investigator's mouth twisted wryly as he returned his handshake. "You wouldn't be in this predicament if I hadn't led Hawthorne to you. You know he'll come after you, don't you? He's not going to take this kind of slap in the face sitting down."

Images of the swamp flashed before Austin's eyes, drawing a mocking grin from him as he urged Gabby toward the boarding ramp. "Where we're going, he'll need a pack of bloodhounds to find us. If anything comes up that I should know about, contact Sam at the *Tribune*. He'll know how to get in touch with me."

The stewardess waited impatiently by the entrance to the plane, and with one last wave of thanks to Nick, Austin handed her their passes and maneuvered Gabby down the aisle of the half-empty jet. Any fears he'd had that someone might notice Gabby's grogginess vanished as he helped her to their seats at the rear of the plane. What few passengers there were, were already half-asleep and paid little attention to their awkward progress, and the stewardesses were too busy preparing for takeoff. Easing Gabby into her seat, he took the one next to her and immediately reached for her seat belt.

Gabby felt herself losing the battle to stay awake and fumbled blindly for Austin's hand. She wouldn't lose him again! "Austin?"

"I'm here, sweetheart," he assured her huskily, closing his fingers around hers. "You're safe now. Go back to sleep."

Questions hovered in the dark clouds that loomed over her consciousness, but she couldn't find the words to ask them. The answers didn't matter, anyway. Nothing mattered now that Austin was close. Holding tightly to his hand, she finally gave in to the sleep that pulled at her.

Austin felt the moment she gave up the battle to stay awake, though her fingers never relaxed their grip on him. Buckling his own seat belt one-handed, he waited only until the plane was in the air before he, too, closed his eyes.

Dawn was just breaking over the Atlantic when they landed in Miami. Instantly awake, Austin tried to rouse Gabby as the plane taxied to the terminal, but she only groaned and buried her face against his shoulder. Three more attempts didn't even draw a groan from her, and he had no choice but to give up in defeat. After everything she'd been through and the drugs that had been pumped into her system, nothing short of a nuclear explosion was going to wake her.

One of the stewardesses, noticing his difficulty, hurried to his side as the rest of the passengers tiredly began filing off the plane. "Is something wrong, sir? Can't you wake her?"

Austin swore under his breath and forced a grimace he hoped would pass as a chagrined smile. "No.... I was afraid this would happen. You see, my wife is terrified of flying, and she took a sleeping pill right before we left Louisville. It knocked her out cold."

Eager to help, the woman didn't bat an eye at his lie. "Would you like me to call for a wheelchair? I can have one just outside the gate in a matter of minutes."

"No...really, that's not necessary," he said quickly as he rose to his feet and lifted Gabby into his arms. "We have friends waiting, and I'll just carry her to their car. Thanks, anyway."

He hurried down the aisle before she could argue further and sighed in relief at the sight of the man impatiently pacing at the end of the boarding ramp. Sam Bradford was a Pulitzer Prize winning reporter with a reputation for doing just about anything for a story, but he would never betray a friend just to make a headline. Gabby's identity and whereabouts would be safe with him. Austin shifted Gabby more comfortably in his arms, then strode toward him with a grin. "This is an ungodly time of the morning to meet a plane. Thanks for coming."

Sam stopped abruptly at the sight of him, the smile that started to spread across his roughly sculptured face taking a quick downturn when his gaze dropped to Gabby. "My God, what happened? Is she all right? Damn it, Austin, what the hell's going on?"

"It's a long story, and yes, Gabby's fine. Now that I've got her away from her father," he added. "He had her sedated, and it's going to take a while for her to sleep it off. Where's Katie? I thought she'd be with you."

"When you didn't deplane with the rest of the passengers, we were afraid you'd missed your flight. Katie went to check with the ticket office to see if you were booked on the next one." He glanced back over his shoulder to see his wife hurrying toward them. His face softened. "Here she comes now."

Four months pregnant and glowing, Katie Bradford rushed up with a smile that was belied by the concern in her blue eyes as they ran over Gabby. "If you wanted to draw attention to your arrival, Austin, you certainly picked a fine way to do it," she teased. "What have you done to that poor girl?"

"Saved her from her wicked stepfather," he retorted. "Come on. I'll tell you all about it on the way to the swamp."

Within moments, they were in the car and Sam was heading out of town for Austin's cabin hidden away in the Big Cypress National Preserve while Austin gave the other couple a quick, concise rundown on everything that happened from the moment he'd come to Gabby's rescue the night they met. "I don't know what she's running from, what Hawthorne could have done to her to terrorize her so," he concluded, "but I mean to find out."

From her position in the front seat, Katie turned to stare at the woman who still slept in Austin's arms. "I can't believe it. Gabriella Winters riding the train like a hobo! She must have been desperate to do something like that."

"If you ever meet Baxter Hawthorne, you'd know why she felt like she had no choice but to run from whatever was scaring her," he replied tightly. "He wears power like he invented it. A woman would have to be as tough as nails to stand up to him, and that's just not Gabby."

"Well, she's going to have to do something," Sam said as he turned from the highway onto a narrow dirt road that wound into the dark, shadowed recesses of the swamp. "She's worth a fortune. She can't just disappear like a bag lady. She's going to have to take a stand and face Hawthorne, or she's going to be running for the rest of her life."

"Oh, she'll face him, all right," Austin promised. "But next time she won't be at the mercy of a needle-wielding doctor who drugs her into submission. *I'll* be with her, and anyone who tries to hurt her is going to answer to me."

Sam's and Katie's eyes met in a silent communication of surprise at his fierce, protective tone, but before either could find a way to ask him about his feelings for Gabby, the road ended at the boat dock where Austin kept his airboat tied up and his battered green pickup parked. Pulling to a stop next to the truck, Sam and Katie helped him get Gabby onto the boat, then stood on the dock as he untied the mooring lines that held the craft steady and prepared to start the motor.

"So what now?" Sam asked. "How long are you going to hide out here?"

Austin looked down to where he'd laid Gabby on the boat's padded bench seat and frowned. "I don't know. After everything she's been through, she's not going to want to go back any time soon. I've still got a book to write. We may just stay here until I finish that. Everything depends on Gabby." He reached for the starter. "I'll keep in touch. Thanks for the ride."

"Be careful," Katie called, but her words were already drowned out by the roar of the motor.

With a final wave, Austin carefully steered the boat away from the dock and headed up the dark, slow-moving river that led to his cabin. He didn't have to look behind him to know that Sam and Katie were already lost to view by the thick foliage that clung to the edges of the almost-bankless river.

Within seconds, civilization was but a memory, and the swamp in all its glory surrounded them. Overhead, the bald cypress trees towered like giants, only their highest branches touched by the morning sunlight. Before him lay nothing but the river and a wilderness that stubbornly resisted the intrusion of man. The wind whispered through the trees, a redheaded woodpecker knocked on a hollow branch somewhere in the distance, an alligator moved through the dark water with only his eyes showing, leaving a trail of silent ripples in his wake.

Taking it all in with eyes that missed little, Austin saw his cabin come into view. Located on a spit of land that was nothing more than a sandbar in the middle of the river, its paned windows caught the morning sun and glistened a welcome. For the first time since he'd returned to Ida's farm and found Gabby gone, Austin felt himself relax. He was home, and Gabby was safe. Baxter Hawthorne would never reach her here.

Gabby came awake abruptly, the fear that had been her constant companion while she slept clutching at her throat and setting her heart pounding. Expecting to find herself surrounded by the yellow walls of her bedroom, she found herself instead lying on her side in a strange bed, staring at bare, rough-hewn log walls. A weak, dusky sunlight streamed in through the open window as shadows lingered in corners. Was it late afternoon or early morning? Her eyes wide, she searched her memory for some clue as to where she was, but all she came up with were blurred, dull images that faded into nothingness before she could make sense of them. Dear God, where was she? And how had she gotten here?

Panic chilling her blood, she started to throw off the sheet that covered her when she suddenly realized she wasn't alone in the bed. She froze, her heart thundering wildly as a bare male leg brushed against her own. Hardly daring to breathe, she glanced cautiously over her shoulder.

Her heart constricted at the sight of Austin lying next to her, hot tears welling in her eyes and spilling over her lashes to her cheeks. How had he found her? How had he even known where to look? Lost in the enveloping darkness Baxter had forced on her, he had been the only reassuring force in the nightmares that stalked her. How many times had she tried to call to him, knowing that even if she could manage the words, he couldn't possibly reach her?

She'd been so afraid she had lost him forever, but somehow he was here, wherever they were, so close she only had to reach out to touch him. His tousled head just inches from hers on the pillow, his hard, dearly loved face was relaxed in sleep, his jaw darkened with stubble. Unable to stop herself, she turned to face him, her fingers outstretched, trembling.

Austin came awake instantly to find her leaning over him, her hand cupping his cheek, her brown eyes drenched in tears. Alarm stopped his heart before it jerked into an uneven rhythm. "What?" he demanded in a voice that was low and scratchy from sleep as his hand lifted to cover hers. "What is it? What's wrong?"

How could she tell him everything that was in her heart? He had come for her and somehow managed to steal her away from Baxter, but even now, she didn't know why. He was a man without ties who lived for today. She couldn't tell him of her love without asking for tomorrow. Forcing a smile, her fingers moved under his, caressing his rough cheek. "Nothing," she said thickly. "It's nothing."

She was holding something back, he could see it in her eyes. A frown slid across his brow. "Gabby, we have to talk—"

"Not now," she whispered, leaning down to press a kiss to the corner of his mouth. "I just want to kiss you . . . love you."

She'd been through hell during the past twenty-four hours, and he'd had no plans to touch her until he was sure she had completely recovered from the ordeal. Before he could stop himself, his arms slipped around her even as he said, "You need to rest—"

She brought her mouth to his again before he could finish the protest, needing to show him the love she couldn't put into words. "No, I need you," she murmured. "Only you."

Her words alone were enough to stop him in his tracks; her kiss destroyed him. Images of the slow, lazy, good-morning kisses they'd shared in the past went up in flames as her tongue boldly slipped into his mouth to seduce him, to tease him, to slowly drive him out of his mind. He'd thought he'd known what it was like to want her, to love her, to lose himself in her. With nothing more than a kiss, she showed him that he'd known nothing about desire until now. Groaning, he reached to pull her hard against him.

But she only laughed, her breath a dark, suggestive caress against his hot skin, and pushed him onto his back, her fingers linking with his to trap them against the mattress. "My treat," she whispered, her eyes now free of tears, smiling down into his. "Just lie there and enjoy."

He would have told her that he had no patience for a slow loving. She already had him hot and hard and desperate for her. But her lips moved from his mouth to his cheek to his ear, her breath and lips a lethal combination, and suddenly the words were lost, along with his will. Her fingers released his to slide to his shoulders and then down his chest to his waist and beyond, tentatively discovering, enticing, and he couldn't move, couldn't do anything but sink deeper into the pleasure.

He was naked... and hers, she thought as her hand closed around him, drawing a groan from him. The thought went to her head like wine, intoxicating her. How could she have known she could have him like this, his skin heating under her hands, his bones melting at her touch? He was the one who always kept such a tight rein on his desires, the one who always led, who turned her to Silly Putty with nothing more than a hot kiss. How far could she push him before she shattered his control?

Seduced by the idea, she straddled his lean hips, her smile flirting with him as she brought his hand to the top button of her blouse, which was all she wore. "Later, I'm going to find out how you got me out of my gown into this," she said huskily, "but right now I just want you to take it off. I need you to touch me."

Her eyes dared him, bewitched him, making his fingers clumsy. Cursing, suddenly impatient, he grabbed her blouse with both hands and sent buttons flying with one sharp yank. At her gasp, he grinned wickedly and filled his hands with her. "That's better."

Gabby sucked in her breath as his skillful fingers gently tugged a moan from her. Her heart racing wildly, she had to fight the need to sink back to his chest and let him take control. Not yet, she thought dizzily. There was so much more she had to show him, to give him.

Taking his hands from her breasts, she pressed a kiss to one palm and then the other and watched his eyes darken. Trailing her mouth over the pulse pounding at the inside of his wrist, she touched the inside of his elbow with her tongue and felt him shudder. With a touch as light as the fading sunlight that spilled onto the bed, she moved over him, tasting the moisture on his skin, seducing them both. Blindly, with infinite care, she discovered how to make him tremble and ache and curse with frustration.

And with every new discovery, she found a corresponding weakness in herself. She trembled and ached and let the frustration grow until hunger destroyed thought and defied reason. She felt herself losing control, and for once in her life, gloried in it. This was what she wanted. *He* was what she needed.

Her hair teased him; the scent that belonged uniquely to her filled his senses; her touch drove him mad. No woman had ever pushed him to this, no woman had ever made him so desperate that he became rough and thought of only ending the ache that was turning him inside out. But no other woman was Gabby. Her hands, untutored and endearingly hesitant, shattered what was left of his control.

Pushed beyond reason, his body screaming for release, his hands clamped onto her hips and guided her to him, teaching her the rhythm, letting her race with it. Exhilaration poured from her to him and back again. A laugh, a moan, a whispered endearment floated on the sultry air. The gathering night closed in upon them, but then he was sweeping her under him, driving into her, and even that ceased to be.

Minutes, hours, an eternity later, Gabby floated back to earth to find herself still locked in his arms, his face buried against her neck. Sated, replete, her body singing with happiness, she pulled him closer. During all the lonely years, whenever she'd allowed herself to think of love, she'd never dreamed it could be like this. If she could hold him just like this for the rest of the night, she wouldn't want for another thing.

Austin pressed a lingering kiss to her collarbone, more content than he had ever been in his life. "How are you feeling?" he murmured against her skin.

"Wonderful," she purred as her fingers lazily traced the strong line of his shoulders. "How about you?"

He chuckled. "Wonderful," he echoed, lifting his head so he could see her face. "But I'm not the one who's been through hell the past twenty-four hours."

She could have argued with him about that—even in the growing darkness, she could see there were lines etching his face that hadn't been there the last time she'd seen him—but she didn't want the world to intrude on the peace they had found. Not yet. Pulling him back down to her, she clung tightly. "I'm fine," she whispered huskily. "Really. Just hold me, Austin. Please."

Her simple plea undid him. Rolling onto his back, he took her with him and wrapped his arms around her, wanting to draw her inside of him. She asked for so little, yet at that moment he would have given her everything. Even himself. He could think of no other woman he'd wanted to give so much to. He knew he was going to have to deal with his feelings for her somewhere in the very near future. But not now. Now, he just wanted to hold her. Running his hand possessively over her back, he pressed her head to his chest, letting the silence, the minutes, lengthen.

It was she, not he, who finally broke the hush that had fallen over them. The steady, reassuring cadence of his heartbeat in her ear, she watched the room grow darker and darker, until all she could make out was the rough walls and a dark strand of trees outside the window. "Where are we?"

"In my cabin in a Florida swamp."

Surprised, she pushed herself off his chest, her eyes finding his in the shadows. "Your cabin? But I thought—"

"That I was a hobo," he finished for her, grinning. "That was only temporary. I've been researching a book on hoboes, but the only way I could get them to talk to me was to pretend to be one myself."

"'A book,'" she echoed, stunned. "You're a writer?"

"Mmm-hmm." Intrigued by the way her breasts teased his chest, he pulled her back down to him. "You may have heard of me. I write under the name of A. E. Tanner."

"The anthropologist?" She knew she was beginning to sound like a parrot, but she couldn't help herself. A. E. Tanner was only one of the hottest lecturers in the country on the college circuit! He'd first come into prominence when he pretended to be a convict and did a book on life in San Quentin. His books had been on the bestseller list ever since. "Why didn't you tell me?"

"Because I never tell anyone who I am when I'm working on a book. It's the only way to get at the truth.'' Wrapping his arms more securely around her, he held her close. "I was also waiting for you to trust me enough to tell me who you were, Ms. Winters.''

Was that hurt she heard in his voice? She winced, wanting to explain but unable to find the words. "I couldn't," she rasped. "I couldn't take the chance—''

"That I would turn you in for the reward?" He felt her stiffen as if she would bolt from his arms, but he only tightened his hold, determined to have the truth from her once and for all. "I knew from the day we arrived in Arkansas who you were. I saw your picture in the paper and read the lies Hawthorne was spreading about you.'' His fingers worked through her hair to frame her face and drag her eyes up to his. "I know there's nothing wrong with your mind, sweetheart. The private investigator Hawthorne hired to find you knew it, too, after he saw you two together at Ida's.'' He told her how, with Nick's help, he'd spirited her out from under her stepfather's nose and got her on a plane while the old man snored in his bed. "What did Hawthorne do to you to make you run away the night we met? Talk to me. How can I help you fight your demons if I don't know what they are?''

All this time, while she'd ached to confide in him, he had known! Tears flowed unchecked down her cheeks. "He's trying to drive me crazy so he can get control of my money.''

Once the admission was spoken aloud, all her pain and fear came pouring out, along with the tears she couldn't seem to stop. She told him everything, even her own doubts about her sanity after she'd been nearly smothered in her bed. And through it all, he just held her and let her talk and cry until it was all out of her system.

When she was spent, her face and his chest wet with her tears, it took all Austin's self-control to clamp a lid on the rage boiling inside him. Hawthorne would pay for what he'd done to her, he silently promised himself as he struggled to keep his hands gentle. He knew she wasn't ready to hear what he had to say, but she'd been running long enough. "You're going to have to go back and face him, honey," he said quietly. "There's no other way to stop him."

"No!"

"He'll win if you don't. Is that what you want?"

"I don't care!" she cried desperately. "Don't you understand? I'm not very good at confrontations. I never have been. I can't go back! I can't take a chance that the next time he might succeed."

He could almost feel the panic racing through her, tightening her muscles, chilling her. "All right," he soothed, pressing a kiss to her teary eyes, the curve of her cheek. "I wasn't talking about tonight or tomorrow, but we'll forget about it for now."

She frowned at his placating tone, while the gentle, lingering kisses he trailed across her face slowly stole her breath. Heat stirred in her as she struggled to hang on to reason. "Austin, you're changing the subject—"

"I know. If you're going to get all hot and bothered, I'd just as soon it be about me." And before she could even begin to think of a reply, he took her mouth in a hot, erotic kiss. The world shifted beneath them and slipped away, and they never even noticed.

Baxter Hawthorne's name wasn't brought up again that night or well into the next morning. As effectively secluded as if they were on a deserted island in the middle of the Pacific, they laughed and loved and pretended, if only for a little while, that they were the only two people in the universe. There were no phones to disturb them, no newspapers to remind them that they were once again on the run, no visitors to drop in unexpectedly and disturb their lovemaking.

Lying on the dock the following afternoon with Austin within touching distance, Gabby thought she could have asked no more of heaven than what she had at her fingertips. An instant later, the silence of the swamp was suddenly set humming by the buzz of an outboard motor somewhere in the distance. Her heart jerked in alarm as her eyes flew to Austin's.

"It's not Hawthorne," he said flatly. "Even if he knows by now that we went to Miami, he couldn't possibly know where we disappeared to. It must be Sam."

It was. Ten minutes later, Sam Bradford came into sight up the river in a flat-bottomed fishing boat and spied them standing on the dock, waiting for him. Pulling up next to the airboat, he killed the engine, his face grim as his eyes locked with Austin's. "I got a call from Nick Bonadero," he said into the tense silence. "You're going to have to go back to Louisville. Baxter Hawthorne is pressing charges against you for kidnapping."

Chapter 12

Stay calm. You're not going to be able to do anything if you're too upset to even think straight.

How many times had that same litany hammered at her during the past few hours? Gabby wondered. Keeping time with the beat of her heart, the words had echoed in her head when she'd called Baxter to tell him they were coming home, just before she and Austin had boarded the first available flight to Louisville. Whenever she'd found herself sitting on the edge of her seat, the silent voice in her head had grown stronger, easing her knotted nerves, soothing her, preparing her for what was to come.

She'd thought she had herself well in hand, until the taxi she and Austin had taken from the airport pulled up in front of her home. Memories assailed her, childhood images of laughter and love combating with the dark, sinister clouds that had threatened her sanity for so many months. A sense of betrayal nearly choked her, bringing a hot flood of tears to her eyes and throat.

"He's not going to get away with it," she muttered, her eyes suddenly blazing. "Not this time. I've had enough!"

She pushed out of the taxi and stormed up to the house before Austin had even finished paying the fare. Swearing under his breath, he told the driver to keep the change and quickly hurried after her. He caught up with her just as she reached for the handle to the front door. "Whoa, honey, not so fast!" he said, grabbing her arm. "You go barging in there madder than hell, and you're going to play right into Hawthorne's hands."

They both knew he was right, but the steadying breath she dragged in only seemed to fuel the fires of anger burning in her. Her mouth thinned into a flat line, she struggled to regain control, wishing just this once she could allow her temper free rein. Hurting her was one thing, but threatening Austin was something she wouldn't tolerate. Especially when it was her money that gave Baxter his power!

"I'm all right," she finally said with a calmness that was only skin-deep. "I'm not going to strangle him. At least not until I have a chance to tell him what I think of him and this horrible game he's been playing."

She swept into the house before he could offer another word of caution, none of the nerves dancing in her stomach visible in the determined line of her jaw. Marching down the hall, she headed straight for the library, where she knew her family would be waiting for her, no doubt quietly gloating over the success of their plan.

As she'd guessed, they were in the library, but they weren't gloating. Sarah and Craig sat on the couch before the fireplace, their faces drawn with worry, while Baxter paced like a caged tiger. At the sight of her, the tension that crackled in the air seemed to snap, and they rushed toward her.

"Gabriella! Thank God!"

"Are you all right? It's so late, we were afraid—"

She knew what they were afraid of. That she had changed her mind and they would have to come up with some other plan to get her back under their control. Dressed in Austin's shirt and her jeans, she suddenly felt like a stranger in her own house. Stopping three steps inside the door, the look in her eyes dared them to touch her. Behind her, she felt the reassurance of Austin's strength.

"I want the charges against Austin dropped immediately." Ignoring her sister and brother-in-law, she spoke directly to her stepfather in a voice that was as cold as ice.

Respecting the distance she silently demanded, Baxter stood halfway across the room from her, with a look on his face Gabby was all too familiar with. *Trust me. I know what's best for you.*

"He stole you out of this house like a thief in the night, Gabriella," he stated coolly. "You were under a doctor's care and in no shape to go anywhere. If something had happened to you . . ." His voice thickened and dwindled into a choked silence before he forced himself to go on in a cold, hard voice. "I'm sorry, sweetheart, but I won't change my mind on this. He took a risk with you he had no right to take."

Gabby paled, a sick feeling of dread seeping into her stomach. He wasn't going to budge. She could see it in his eyes. She had to do something! Suddenly frantic, hardly realizing what she said, she blurted out, "Yes, he did! He had every right. We're engaged, and he was only trying to protect me!"

It was only when a shocked silence dropped into the room like a bomb that Gabby realized what she had done. The blood drained from her face, only to rush back in on a wave of heat. Oh, God! she thought wildly, desperately wishing the floor would open up and swallow her. What must Austin be thinking? She wanted to turn to him, to explain, but her nerve had deserted her, and she could only stand there miserably and wait for him to deny it.

Baxter's narrowed eyes shot past her to Austin. "You've asked my daughter to marry you?"

Asked? If he hadn't been so shocked, he would have laughed at the suggestion. No, he hadn't asked, but when had free choice ever had anything to do with their relationship? From the very beginning, she'd pushed her way into his life, into his heart, until his only option had been to drag her into his arms. He hadn't wanted to want her, and he sure as hell hadn't wanted to need her, but somehow she'd managed to make him do both. And even though he knew her announcement was nothing more than her misguided way of protecting him, he wanted it to be real.

Slipping his arm around her waist, he pulled her protectively close. He felt her start of surprise, saw the embarrassment flooding her cheeks and promptly forgot everyone else in the room, knowing only his need to reassure her. Lifting her chin, he leaned down and gave her a tender kiss that was, by necessity, all too brief and chaste. When he lifted his head, he smiled right into her stunned eyes. "Yes," he murmured. "Gabby has agreed to become my wife."

If his arm hadn't been around her waist, anchoring her to his side, Gabby was sure she would have melted to the floor at his feet. Her eyes searched his, looking for the truth, but all she saw was the love and tenderness that a man would show his fiancée. Was it real or feigned? What he truly felt or what he knew Baxter expected the man she was engaged to to feel?

Cursing the doubts that bombarded her, she dragged her gaze back to her stepfather and continued the charade. "You will drop the charges."

It wasn't a question, but a statement. Baxter hesitated. "Do you really love him?"

"With all my heart." It was the only answer she could give and no less than the truth.

Baxter Hawthorne had never been a man to fight a losing battle. Admitting defeat, he forced a smile that didn't quite reach his eyes. "Then I suppose congratulations are in order. I hope you'll be very happy, sweetheart."

He opened his arms for an embrace that Gabby couldn't refuse him, but his congratulations and the hugs she received from Sarah and Craig were bittersweet. She could see the wariness in their eyes, the disappointment they couldn't conceal, the questions they were dying to ask as they each somewhat gingerly welcomed Austin into the family.

Curiosity, however, finally got the better of Craig. As Baxter passed glasses of champagne around and handed Gabriella ginger ale, the younger man looked Austin over casually. "So what do you do, Austin? We don't know anything about you except that you met Gabriella on the train. You do work, don't you?"

Austin's lips twitched, amusement glinting like ice in his eyes. They were all horrified that Gabby was marrying a hobo, but they didn't quite know how to express their disapproval. "Actually, I do a number of things," he replied easily. "For the past few months, I've been hoboing. Several years ago, I spent three months in San Quentin."

Sarah gasped. "You're an ex-con? Oh, God, I knew it! Daddy, do something!"

For the first time since they'd left the swamps, Gabby smiled. "He's not a criminal, Sarah. He was doing research for a book. Austin is a writer. A. E. Tanner."

Her sister dropped back onto the couch as if her knees would no longer support her. "A. E. Tanner!" She ran her eyes over him, looking for the signs of the scholar and award-winning writer she knew Tanner to be, but all she saw was a hard man with worn clothes and a ragged haircut, his mouth curled in mocking amusement. "But you can't be!"

Always one to do the proper thing, Baxter had the grace to look uncomfortable. "Sarah, you're forgetting your manners!" he said sternly. "It seems we misjudged you, Mr. LePort. We won't do it again, I assure you."

Austin nodded, his hand tightening around Gabby's waist. "I'd appreciate it if you didn't. I was only doing what I had to to protect Gabby. As long as you all realize that I'm not going to stand by and let her be mistreated, we'll get along fine. And make it Austin, please."

As far as threats went, it wasn't very subtle. But he didn't intend it to be. He wanted it well understood that where Gabby was concerned, they would have to go through him to get to her.

Baxter stiffened. "If you're suggesting that we would try to hurt Gabriella—"

"That's exactly what I'm suggesting," he retorted.

"Austin," Gabby began, alarmed by the sudden turn in the conversation, "I don't think we need to go into this now—"

"It does put a damper on an engagement announcement," Craig agreed when no one else in the room quite knew what to say. "So when are you two getting married? Or have you even had time to discuss it?"

"No—"

"As soon as possible," Austin said at the same time. "Before the end of the week."

Startled, Gabby's eyes flew to his. "The end of the week!" Dear God, he was serious! Did he actually think she meant to hold him to this farce of an engagement when she was the one who had announced it? "We have to talk."

"Obviously," Sarah said dryly, watching them carefully. "Someone seems to have gotten their story twisted."

"It's not a story," Gabby said, then caught the glint of suspicion in her sister's gaze. Shutting her mouth with a snap, she knew that further protests would only create more doubts. "Let's go for a walk, Austin. I'll give you a tour of the farm."

She rushed him out of the house without another word, silently heading for one of the horse barns in the distance. Shoving her hands into the back pockets of her jeans, her head downcast, she felt the heat once again climb in her cheeks as the silence between them grew awkwardly. Dear God, how could she have made that stupid announcement? She'd only wanted to save him from Baxter's wrath, and had, instead, landed him in a phony engagement that was quickly getting out of hand.

Why did he want to marry her before the end of the week? Was it only to protect her?

Mortified at the thought, she kept her eyes stubbornly fixed on the worn path before them and said huskily, "I don't expect you to marry me, Austin. I don't know what I was thinking of. I guess an engagement was the only way I could think of to get Daddy to back off."

Now was not the time to admit to loving her and wanting to go through with the marriage. She'd never believe that he was doing it for any other reason than to save her from making a fool of herself in front of her family. He pulled her to a stop beside him. "You don't want to marry me?"

Her heart tripped over itself at the quiet question. How was she supposed to answer that? She swallowed, looking anywhere but at him. "It isn't a question of wanting or not wanting. I appreciate your backing me up in front of my family, but I can't let you marry me just so they won't find out I was lying."

"I'm afraid you're going to have to."

She blinked, convinced she had heard wrong. "What?"

His hands reached for her, turning her to face him. "Gabby, honey, I don't think you realize what you did back there just now. When you announced our engagement, you also put your head in a noose."

"Austin, you're not making any sense."

"Think about it," he said softly. "Who has the most to lose if you get married. Who are your heirs?"

She frowned. "Sarah and Daddy, of course. You know I don't have any other family."

"Yes, but you would if you married. Your family would no longer have any control over your health or finances. Your husband would. He would also be your principle heir."

Her cheeks turned ashen. "What are you saying?"

The fear was already there in her eyes, stirring up all his protective instincts. Did she know how much he ached to hold her, to shield her from everything that could hurt her, when she looked at him like that? But she needed logical reasons for the engagement, and logic always deserted him when he touched her.

He released her. "Whoever's trying to drive you crazy knows the minute you're married your money's lost to him—or her—forever. He's not going to stand by and let that happen without trying to stop it. That's why we have to go through with this wedding. To force him out into the open. It's the only way you're going to know for sure who's doing this to you."

But at what price? How could she let him sacrifice his freedom for hers when she didn't know why he was doing it? She searched his face for some sign of the love that was burning so brightly inside her, but all she saw was a determination and ruthlessness that didn't tell her anything about his real feelings for her. It wasn't enough. "I can't let you do this," she whispered. "What if nothing happens and we really end up married? I'd feel like I coerced you into it—"

"No one coerced me into anything," he cut in, with a lightness that was belied by the sharp intensity of his eyes as he watched the ever-changing emotions flicker across her face. "And nothing's carved in stone, Gabby. We can get an annulment if things don't work out the way we planned."

She paled. He spoke of beginning and ending a marriage in the same breath. Nothing could have told her more clearly how he felt about her. Sick at heart, she wondered why she was trying to protect him when he so obviously didn't need it. "Then I suppose we should set the date as quickly as possible," she said stiffly. "How does Friday sound?"

If she hadn't been so miserable, she might have seen the flash of triumph in his eyes before he quickly concealed it and slipped his arm around her waist. "Great! Let's go back to the house and tell your family."

The three days that followed were, by turns, the best and worst of Gabby's life. Arranging a last-minute wedding took up every minute of the day and half the night, and there hardly seemed time to catch her breath. There was a dress to be found, guests to be called and invited, the church to be reserved and flowers to be decided on, a reception to plan. With Austin constantly at her side, never letting her out of his sight, even for the choosing of a gown, she could almost believe he was the anxious bridegroom impatient to finally make her his. But then she would see the wariness in his eyes as he watched Baxter and Sarah and Craig, and the fantasy would turn into a waking nightmare. She, too, found herself watching them, waiting for something to happen. Nothing did.

By the day of the wedding, she was a nervous wreck. They all arrived at the church, Austin reluctantly left her at the small dressing room where she and Sarah would dress, and suddenly time was running out. The trap they had laid had backfired. No one had tried to stop the wedding, and in less than an hour, they would be husband and wife. Dear God, what was she supposed to do now? She loved him. If she hadn't, going through with the ceremony would have been much easier. They could part company next week, next month, and never feel the loss. But loving him made that impossible.

Pacing restlessly after Sarah helped her dress, she couldn't look in the mirror without wanting to cry. The dress was too real, the lie they were on the verge of acting out too sacrilegious to be perpetrated in a church. She should have insisted on a garden wedding at the farm. Maybe then she wouldn't feel as though she and Austin were pulling a hoax on God.

Sarah watched her move around the dressing room like a death row inmate, dragging the satin train of her gown absently behind her, and finally said, "I've seen nervous brides before, Gabriella, but you look like you're almost in a panic. Are you sure you want to go through with this? It's not too late to back out, you know."

Gabby stopped in her tracks and stared at her sister with wide, tortured eyes. Was Sarah the one who was trying to drive her crazy? During the past three days, she hadn't once tried to talk her out of marrying Austin after she had discovered his true identity. Why did she wait until now, when her nerves were stretched to the breaking point, to encourage her fears?

Sick with doubts she didn't want but couldn't ignore, she turned away. "Of course I want to go through with it. I'm just a little nervous. I'll be fine once the ceremony starts."

Sarah still looked doubtful, but she only shrugged. "Well, if you're sure. I'll go tell the minister we're ready. You stay here till Daddy comes for you."

She had hardly gone before there was a soft knock at the door. Her heart jerking in her breast, Gabby hurried to open it and found Baxter standing before her in a black tux holding a tea tray complete with a steaming pot and two cups. His smile was hesitant, as if he weren't quite sure of his welcome. "How about a cup of tea with your old man before I have to walk you down the aisle? If you're as nervous as I am, I figured you could use it."

"Oh, Daddy!" She smiled tremulously, wanting to hug him, needing to cry. The hostility and confusion that had been between them for months was gone, and she found herself facing the man from her childhood who had always been there for her, the only father she remembered. Just for this moment, she desperately needed to pretend that she'd never doubted him, never feared him and that any moment he would, with loving reluctance, hand her over to the man she loved. She opened the door wider. "Come in."

He set the tray on a table across the room, then poured them both a cup. Handing Gabby one, his eyes swept over her before lifting once again to meet her gaze. "You make a beautiful bride, honey, but I always knew you would. You look just like your mother."

"I wish she were here," she said wistfully, taking a sip of the tea. But if Margaret Hawthorne had still been alive, Gabby knew she wouldn't be standing there, preparing to marry Austin under false pretenses. Her mother would have believed her from the minute she suspected someone was playing tricks with her mind.

Her stomach clenching at the thought, she hastily set her cup down, resuming her pacing. "I guess it's almost time to start."

"We have a moment or two," he replied. Letting her walk off her nervousness, he watched her for a few long moments before setting his half-empty cup next to hers. "If you're having second thoughts, honey, we can stop this right now. And you don't have to worry about me dragging up kidnapping charges against Austin," he said quickly when she started to protest. "I realize he thought you were in danger—"

"No!"

"I only want what's best for you."

She lifted her chin, her heart breaking. First Sarah and now him. When would the lies end? "Then you'll stop trying to talk me out of marrying Austin. He's what's best for me."

From the hallowed halls of the church, organ music suddenly floated on the air. The time for talking, for persuading, was over. Baxter held out his arm to her. "Shall we go?"

Seconds later, they were walking down the center aisle to the strains of the wedding march. Her heart in her throat, Gabby looked down the length of the church to where Austin stood waiting for her, watching her, devouring her with his eyes. Suddenly the circumstances that had pushed them into marriage didn't matter. Nothing mattered but that it felt right.

Lost in Austin's eyes, Gabby never saw the sudden paleness that drained the color from Baxter's face or the pain that twisted his mouth. Halfway down the aisle, he clutched at his chest. Startled, Gabby glanced at him, but it was too late. With a muffled cry, he collapsed at her feet.

"Daddy!"

Horrified, Gabby dropped her bouquet, then reached for him as chaos erupted all around them. The guests spilled from the pews, straining to get closer, while Sarah frantically fought her way toward them, yelling for someone to call for an ambulance. Gabby never took her eyes from her stepfather's face. Already unconscious, he was as pale as death, his breathing ragged. Sick with fear, Gabby quickly leaned over him to loosen his tie, when her sister, Austin and Edison Hill pushed through the crowd to her side.

She reached for Austin as she lifted stricken eyes to the family doctor. "Oh, Dr. Ed, thank God! Help him, please! I don't know what happened—"

"Easy, Gabriella," the doctor said quietly as he quickly dropped down on the other side of Baxter and jerked open his medical bag to pull out his stethoscope. "Get his shirt open. And get these people out of here," he said irritably. "I want this aisle clear when that ambulance gets here."

Austin quickly moved to do as he asked, urging the guests outside as Sarah came down on her knees next to the doctor, her tear-filled eyes trained in horror on her father's pale, still face. "What's wrong with him? Is he going to die?"

"No!" the older man muttered, working over his friend feverishly. "Not if I can help it." Ignoring everything but his patient, he checked Baxter's pupils and found them constricted, his pulse accelerated, his breathing strained, his blood pressure dropping fast. Edison's face, already grim, became positively dour at his findings. "It looks like his heart. Damn it, where is that ambulance? If it doesn't get here soon, I'll take him myself!"

Gabby opened her mouth to protest but could only manage a silent cry of denial. No! She'd already lost both her parents to heart attacks at an early age. She wouldn't lose Baxter, too!

Suddenly, from the back of the church, a sudden commotion cut through the anxious silence that had descended over the small group waiting for the ambulance. Startled, they all turned to see Nick Bonadero holding a gun on Craig with one hand while he held a teapot in the other.

Sarah jumped to her feet, her blue eyes wide in her ashen face. "What's going on here?"

"Sorry to interrupt," Nick said quietly, "but I think the doctor better look at the contents of this teapot before he makes his final diagnosis. I was watching from the back when Mr. Hawthorne collapsed, and his son-in-law here was the only one who didn't seem the least bit surprised. In fact, just as soon as he could get through the crowd, he made a beeline for the dressing room where Gabby changed. By the time I caught up with him, he was just about to pour out this tea. Unless I miss my guess, it's been tampered with. Probably poisoned."

The group before him couldn't have been more surprised if he'd just announced that Craig was a serial murderer. He watched shock, disbelief and sudden wariness flicker across their faces before Sarah finally snapped, "That's ridiculous! That tea was for Gabby. I made it myself. If it had been poisoned, she'd hardly be standing here perfectly healthy."

Gabby had risen to stand beside her sister, but at her words, her knees almost buckled. "I only took a sip," she whispered hoarsely, staring in growing horror at her brother-in-law. "Daddy drank almost half a cup."

"You bastard!" Austin hissed, advancing toward Craig with murder in his eyes. "It was you, wasn't it? You're the one who's been playing with Gabby's mind, trying to make her think she was going crazy. She thought it was her father, but it was you, wasn't it?"

"No!" Sarah cried, stepping in front of him before he could reach her husband. "That's ridiculous! Craig would never—"

"No?" Austin taunted, knowing there was no time to soften the blow. "Look at his face, and then tell me that he's innocent."

Pale, furious, she turned to her husband, ready to protect him, but then she saw his eyes. Hostility warred with a fear and guilt he couldn't disguise. She swayed, her face bloodless. "Oh, God, no!"

Gabby slipped her arm around her sister's waist and felt as if her heart were being squeezed by a tight fist. "How could you?" she stormed, glaring at Craig. "You . . . monster! All this time I was blaming Daddy and Sarah, it was you! And I thought you were the only one who believed me. Why, damn it? What have I ever done to you to make you hate me?"

His handsome, boyish face twisted with resentment. "You had all the money, and Sarah had none," he said accusingly. "Just because an accident of birth gave you the rich father. It wasn't fair! I wanted to give her the world, and you already had it."

"So you were going to kill her and my father to get it?" Sarah demanded, her voice rising on a note of hysteria. "Do you think money means that much to me?"

"I wasn't going to kill anyone. Not at first," he amended with a guilelessness that was horrifying to watch. "Gabby was never interested in the money anyway, so why shouldn't we have control of it? I wasn't going to hurt her, just get her mixed-up. But then she ran away and came back engaged." Fury rippled over his face, turning him into a stranger. "I couldn't let her get married, Sarah. You would've been cut out of everything. So I thought if I just put some of Baxter's sleeping pills in her tea, I could stop her. I never meant it for Baxter. Hell, he doesn't even like hot tea."

"Are you saying it's his own fault he's lying there possibly dying?" she asked softly. "God, you make me sick!"

He winced as if she had slapped him, then tried again to make her understand, but the doctor cut him off before he could even begin. "Sleeping pills?" he said sharply, looking up from his patient. "What sleeping pills?"

"The ones you gave him for insomnia after Gabriella ran away."

"You gave him Nembutal?" he asked. "My God, how many?"

"Five or six. I don't remember."

"You'll remember, young man, if he dies!" Edison thundered in outrage as the ambulance came screeching into the church parking lot with sirens blaring. "Get that stretcher in here," he called to the paramedics. "We've got a drug overdose."

Within seconds, Baxter was strapped onto a stretcher and quickly rolled out to the waiting ambulance. Unable to bear the sight of her husband, Sarah turned away and hurried outside with Gabby and Austin flanking her.

"Sarah, wait, please!"

Craig's hoarse cry followed them out the church, but they never checked their stride. Sarah stiffened when the wail of another siren signaled the arrival of the police, but she didn't look back. Seconds later, the church and her husband were left behind as Austin drove her and Gabby to the hospital.

What followed was nothing short of a nightmare. Still dressed in their wedding finery, Austin, Gabby and Sarah prowled the hospital hallways, waiting for news. A police detective tracked them down in the waiting area outside the emergency room for a statement, then informed them that Craig had given a full confession. The final charges against him, however, would rest on Baxter's recovery.

Murder. The word was never spoken but hung in the air like a guillotine blade waiting to drop. Ignoring it, Gabby and Sarah refused to admit that there was even a possibility that Baxter would die. After four hours of waiting, they learned just how close he had come. If he'd had one more gram of the sedative, if Dr. Ed hadn't been on the scene immediately, if Craig hadn't confessed to the drug he'd slipped into the tea, Baxter would have never made it to the hospital alive.

It wasn't until they were actually allowed in to see him, however, that Gabby was able to accept that it was over. Finally. The betrayal, the lies, the doubts. With Austin at her side, she took up a position next to Baxter's bed and reached for his hand, tears stinging her eyes at the sight of his pale, drawn face. "Daddy...."

He squeezed her fingers, then held out his other hand for Sarah's as she moved around to the opposite side of the bed. "I let you both down when you needed me most," he said huskily. "I don't know if I'll ever be able to forgive myself for that."

"There's nothing to forgive," Gabby said firmly. "We all made some mistakes and trusted and distrusted the wrong people. But it's over. We have each other again, and that's all that matters. We're going to put this behind us."

"How can we?" Sarah asked, her eyes tortured as they lifted to Gabby's. "You have every right to hate us both. We didn't believe you, Gabby. Even after you were terrified enough to run away, we didn't believe you. If Craig had succeeded—"

"He didn't. And I didn't trust you enough to know that you couldn't possibly be the one trying to hurt me," she countered. "Let it go, Sarah. We have to if we're going to be a family again."

"Gabriella's right," Baxter said quietly. "We can't live with 'what ifs.' And speaking of family, it looks like we have a wedding to reschedule."

Gabby's fingers jerked in his and were quickly withdrawn. The wedding! How was she going to tell her family that Austin had only been marrying her to keep her safe, and now that Craig was in custody, their marriage was no longer necessary? "Dad...about the wedding..."

Austin had been waiting for her to confess, anticipating it. "Gabby and I have to talk about it," Austin cut in smoothly as he slipped his arm around her waist to give her a warning squeeze. "If you two don't mind, we'll go do that right now. Sarah, can you get a ride home with Dr. Ed?'' At her nod, he grinned. ''Good. Good night. Baxter, we'll see you tomorrow.''

He pulled her out into the hall before she could do anything but wish her father a good-night. Giving her no time to protest, hardly giving her time to think, he hustled her out of the hospital and into his rental car. Seconds later, they were heading for the farm.

Gabby sat stiffly at Austin's side, her palms damp, her heart suddenly pounding. For the first time since they met, there were no secrets between them, no threat of danger throwing them together. They were free to part company without any pangs of consciousness. Her heart breaking, Gabby decided to make it easy for him to leave. ''We really don't need to discuss the wedding, you know. There's nothing to talk about, anyway. Craig's in custody and—''

''Our marriage has nothing to do with Craig.''

Her eyes flew to his, but the lights of the city were already behind them, leaving his face a dark silhouette, his thoughts hidden by the night. Her hands tensed in her lap. ''What do you mean? Of course it does.''

A rueful smile pulled at his mouth, but his gaze stayed stubbornly on the road. ''Gabby, sweetheart, I really don't think you want to have this discussion in the car. Can't this wait until we get home?''

It would have been the wise thing to do, but suddenly she didn't want to be wise, she didn't want to be patient. She wanted the truth, and she wasn't going to wait for it. ''No. I want to talk about it now.''

Without a word, he pulled onto the side of the road and cut the engine. Time was suddenly measured in

the tick of the engine as it began to cool. Sliding his
arm across the back of the seat behind her, Austin
turned to face her. "Okay, you want to talk, we'll
talk," he said softly, his fingers reaching for her hair.
"Baxter should be released from the hospital tomorrow afternoon. We can reschedule the wedding for
tomorrow night."

Gabby's heart skidded at his words, at the feel of his
caressing, possessive fingers on the back of her neck.
"No...." Wincing at the hoarseness of her voice, she
swallowed, willing herself to ignore his touch. Her
sudden breathlessness, the need to melt into his arms,
told her she failed miserably. "We can't get married," she tried again, and couldn't know that her eyes
were pleading with him to persuade her otherwise.

Austin smiled, his hand at her neck moving to slip
around her shoulders and draw her closer. Did she
really think that he had only been hanging around to
protect her? "Why not?" he murmured. "What's
stopping us?"

He was so close she could see his eyes growing
smoky with desire, feel the warm moistness of his
breath against her cheek. Somehow she found her
head resting against his shoulder and couldn't stop to
think how it had gotten there. "I...I can't let you
marry me now. There's no reason."

"How about this one?" he suggested, and covered
her mouth with his. He gave her no time to think,
dragging her into a need that was immediate, intense,
scorching. His hands roamed over her, claiming,
heating, sliding over the satin of her wedding dress
with a knowledge that had her trembling and aching

for him between one heartbeat and the next. But it wasn't enough. He wanted all of her, heart and soul.

Capturing her face in his hands, he wrenched his mouth from hers, his breathing harsh in the dark silence as his eyes locked with hers. "Do you think I would marry you just because of some crazy sense of obligation? Damn it, Gabby, I love you! I don't want just a few weeks of hoboing with you. I want forever!"

His words went through her like a caress, warming her heart and flooding her eyes with tears. "Oh, Austin—"

At the sight of her tears, his fingers tightened in her hair. "Don't you dare try to tell me you don't love me back. Damn it, we belong together! I never thought I'd find a woman who could fit in all my worlds like she was born to them. I can't lose you now, not when I've just found you. Damn it, say something! And it better be yes."

Joy bubbled up in her, dragging a laugh from her at his demand. "Shouldn't I know the question first before I answer it?"

He would have kissed her again, but he needed to hear the words. "Do you love me?"

"Yes."

"Say it."

The smile on her lips vanished, the amusement in her eyes stripped away to reveal a love she couldn't deny. "I love you." Something in her heart soared free at the sound of the words at long last spoken. Tears tumbling down her cheeks, she threw herself against him. "I love you! Hold me, please. I thought I was going to lose you."

His arms wrapped around her, crushing her to him. "Never," he promised with a low groan and sealed it with a kiss that cherished and wooed and seduced. When he finally lifted his head, his voice was thick with need and love. "There was never any chance of me walking away from you, sweetheart. Not from the minute I laid eyes on you. You are going to marry me tomorrow night, aren't you?"

Gabby scattered kisses over his face, unable to stop smiling. "Yes. Unless you're planning on waiting till after we're married to start the honeymoon."

He grinned, rubbing his thumb across her bottom lip. "And if I am?"

"Then we'll find a justice of the peace and get married tonight," she replied promptly. "I've waited my whole life for you, Austin LePort. I'm not waiting one more night."

Laughing, he dragged her close for a long, lingering kiss. "No, you don't have to wait," he said when he finally lifted his head. "But we've got one more thing to clear up before we go home. When I make love to you, I want you wearing my ring."

Gabby looked down at the fake wedding ring she hadn't taken off her finger since the day he'd put it there. "I already am."

"No, this time I mean a real one." Reaching into the pocket of his tux, he pulled out a ring box and snapped it open. Inside, a wedding band exactly like the one she wore glimmered in the darkness, its golden glow too rich to be anything but genuine. Next to it was nestled a stunning diamond and ruby engagement ring.

She gasped. "Oh, Austin!"

"The ruby reminded me of your hair," he teased as he drew off the fake band and replaced it with the new set of rings. Pressing a kiss to her finger, his eyes lifted to hers. "Now you're mine."

Pulling his mouth down to hers, she kissed him and gave him a promise straight from the heart. "Always."

* * * * *

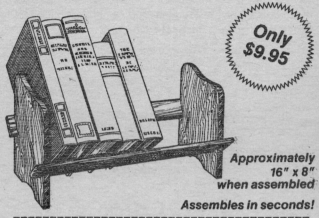

Silhouette Intimate Moments®

It's time...for Nora Roberts

There's no time like the present to have an experience that's out of this world. When Caleb Hornblower "drops in" on Liberty Stone there's nothing casual about the results!

This month, look for Silhouette Intimate Moments #313

TIME WAS

And there's something in the future for you, too! Coming next month, Jacob Hornblower is determined to stop his brother from making the mistake of his life—but his timing's off, and he encounters Sunny Stone instead. Can this mismatched couple learn to share their tomorrows? You won't want to miss Silhouette Intimate Moments #317

TIMES CHANGE

Hurry and get your copy...while there's still time!

Wonderful, luxurious gifts can be yours with proofs-of-purchase from any specially marked "Indulge A Little" Harlequin or Silhouette book with the Offer Certificate properly completed, plus a check or money order (do not send cash) to cover postage and handling payable to Harlequin/Silhouette "Indulge A Little, Give A Lot" Offer. We will send you the specified gift.

Mail-in-Offer

	OFFER CERTIFICATE			
Item:	A. Collector's Doll	B. Soaps in a Basket	C. Potpourri Sachet	D. Scented Hangers
# of Proofs-of -Purchase	18	12	6	4
Postage & Handling	$3.25	$2.75	$2.25	$2.00
Check One				

Name _____

Address _____ Apt. # _____

City _____ State _____ Zip _____

ONE PROOF OF PURCHASE

To collect your free gift by mail you must include the necessary number of proofs-of-purchase plus postage and handling with offer certificate.

SIM-3

Harlequin®/Silhouette®

Mail this certificate, designated number of proofs-of-purchase and check or money order for postage and handling to:

INDULGE A LITTLE
P.O. Box 9055
Buffalo, N.Y. 14269-9055